BIOWATCH

BIOWATCH

LARRY ENMON

For Presley

This book is dedicated to the men and women who work in the BioWatch program. While not known to the people they server, they labor 24/7 to keep America safe from biological attacks. My decade-long involvement in the program remains one of my most exciting assignments.

BioWatch is a Department of Homeland Security early warning system designed to detect the presence of dangerous biological pathogens into the air. The program can detect select biological agents in time by monitoring strategic locations to provide prompt life-saving treatment. Should a bioterrorism attack occur, local, state, and federal partners coordinate a rapid response to reduce illness and death.

ONE

US COAST GUARD CUTTER SANTA BARBARA
US/CANADIAN WATERS NEAR VICTORIA, BC
0422 HRS.

Chris Hardesty thought he was the luckiest man in the world. Four years out of the Coast Guard Academy and a new promotion to Lieutenant. If that wasn't enough, his transfer request back to Washington came through, and he'd been given command of one of the last, sleek Island-Class Cutters. This had long been a dream for Hardesty—he loved this ship.

The 110-foot boat was equipped with twin V-16 Paxman Valenta diesel engines and had a maximum speed of 30 knots. Some of the enlisted crew were very young, but with his new executive officer, LTJG Adams, they could whip them into the best crew on the West Coast. Hardesty had grown up in Seattle, and coming back home had been his career goal. Now he had a chance to show what he could do, and he intended to do it.

The bridge was dark, and only the lights from the instruments illuminated the area, so everyone marveled at the first orange sliver of rising sun appearing over the eastern horizon. But the ocean around them remained black. They'd sailed from Port Angeles almost six hours ago. Their patrol took them north to the Strait of Juan de Fuca at the Canadian border. By the time they arrived at Point Roberts and set a return course, the excitement of the night cruise had worn off. Hardesty didn't care. Just sailing these waters was enough for him.

Hardesty checked his watch and shifted in the bridge chair, fighting to stay awake and focused on the mission. He took a sip of stale coffee and made a face—*nasty*.

"Fresh coffee, skipper?"

He turned and Adams handed him a new cup. "We just officially entered the Haro Strait, sir." Adams pointed left and waved his hand back and forth. "That's the lights from San Juan Island." He leaned forward and pointed right. "That's Victoria, up ahead."

Hardesty appreciated his XO's efforts—being the newest member of the crew, Hardesty still had a lot to learn about the patrol area—especially at night. As a kid he'd done a lot of day sailing in these waters, but at night the local landmarks weren't there to guide him. He needed this instruction to get up to speed. He suppressed a yawn. "We still on schedule?"

Adams nodded, checking his watch. "Yes, sir. Should make base in a little less than two hours. After 0400 we usually don't encounter much in this part of the operational area."

From the other side of the bridge, Seaman Quinn called, "Radar contact, sir."

Hardesty swung the chair around. "Location and speed?"

"Bearing one-eight-one degrees, about five thousand yards—looks like it's dead in the water, sir."

Hardesty glanced at his XO. "Mr. Adams, let's check it out. Might be the most excitement of the night." He was ready for any distraction that might help keep the crew on their toes. He'd had little opportunity to evaluate them in action. This might be instructive.

"Aye aye, sir." Adams turned to Seaman Quinn. "Radar, what size is it?"

"Small—very small, sir."

Adams strolled to the helmsman and put a hand on his shoulder. In his command voice Adams said, "Make turns for ten knots—come right heading one-eight-one."

"Come right heading one-eight-one. Aye, sir," the helmsman repeated.

Hardesty lifted his binoculars and scanned the night—nothing. Whatever was out there showed no running lights. That alone made it highly suspicious unless it was in distress and had lost power. Smugglers often ran with no lights, but it was unusual for a ship to be dead in the water without first putting out a distress call.

"Mr. Adams, get the lights up," Hardesty said, keeping the binoculars to his eyes.

"Aye aye, sir." Adams flicked a switch on the console, and two bright spotlights on each side of the bridge cut through the veil of darkness. A low mist moved over the water, giving it a dangerous, threatening appearance.

"Range two thousand yards, sir," Quinn reported.

Hardesty searched the clear night—nothing except the spotlight reflecting off the small ripple of ocean.

"Reduce speed to five knots," Adams ordered.

"Reduce speed to five knots, aye, sir," the helmsman repeated.

Hardesty spotted the contact first. It looked like a sixteen-foot daysailer, the kind he had as a kid. The sail wasn't set, and the small white boat bobbed in the water, powered only by the current and wind. The craft showed no lights or movement on deck—a ghost ship. The Santa Barbara was closing too fast. Hardesty glanced over his shoulder. "Target dead ahead—all engines stop." He continued studying the small boat through the binoculars.

"All stop, aye, sir," the helmsman repeated.

Hardesty checked his watch and made note of the time for the ship's log. "Mr. Adams, let's maneuver alongside and get some lines on that craft—make it secure."

"Aye aye, sir."

Hardesty stood, stretched, and made his way across the bridge. He unclipped the mic from its holder on the console as the distance closed between the two boats. He keyed the button, and his voice boomed over the outside speakers into the featureless, cold night. He chuckled to himself. This should wake them up.

"This is the United States Coast Guard. Do you require assistance?" He gazed outside at Adams and three seamen on the starboard side of the cutter as the spotlights zoomed tighter onto the craft. When the cutter pulled alongside the small boat, Adams looked back at Hardesty and shook his head. Hardesty tried again. "This is the United States Coast Guard. Prepare to be boarded for inspection." If this was just an orphan boat that had come loose from its mooring, Hardesty would be pissed. He mentally crossed his fingers, hoping to recover a hole filled with drugs or other contraband.

Hardesty hiked across the bridge, out on the deck, and down the side ladder as Seamen Cass and Phillips slid into the tiny craft below. The sudden bite of cold ocean air made Hardesty shiver—he should have slipped on his jacket.

After securing lines, seaman Phillips shrieked, "God, something stinks." He shined the battle lantern around the deck. The beam outlined nothing out of the ordinary. Seaman Cass stood from securing the final line and sniffed the air. He made a face and shook his head.

Hardesty gritted his teeth—this didn't bode well. It wouldn't be the first ripe body he'd found on a boat. He shot a look at Adams, whose frown and grim expression matched his.

Both seamen swung their lights to the area below deck. They took two steps forward before jumping back. In his retreat, Cass stumbled and crashed to the deck. His eyes were wild, and he shook his head, pushing hard with his legs, putting more distance between him and the dark hole below. Phillips rushed to the side of the boat and vomited.

"What is it?" Adams yelled.

Cass didn't speak but looked straight ahead—shaking.

Breaking established protocol, Hardesty slid off the side of the cutter and into the sailboat. He rushed to Phillips and grabbed his shoulders. Phillips wiped his mouth with his sleeve.

"You okay?" Hardesty put a hand on his back, giving him a gentle pat.

Phillips swallowed hard and took a sharp breath between his teeth. "Yes, sir."

The odor from below turned Hardesty's stomach: whatever it was had putrefied. He grabbed Phillips' light and swung it into the dark hole. Old childhood fears of vampires and zombies rushed through his mind—an uncomfortable tingle ran up his spine, and he took several steps back. The small, dark-haired Asian man below deck lay on his back with his head and shoulders resting on the folded sail. His bare chest hardly moved as he gasped to take in air. His shirt was wadded up and bloody in his hand, and bloody tears streaked his cheeks. The dead-looking eyes stared into space as the bloody lips slowly moved. Streams of fresh blood drained from the man's nostrils, left ear, and nipples. The fellow's pants were soaked red, and the hole of the small craft resembled a slaughterhouse floor.

———

The report scared J. Thomas Fuller as he sipped his third cup of coffee this morning and studied the last page of the email.

He disliked the way the CIA did their briefing sheets—they confused him. If they'd been in his International Studies class at Princeton, he'd have flunked the lot. His mind drifted back to his years at the university. They were some of his happiest, but when your good friend and former roommate requests that you serve in his administration, you can't say no. His friend now kept residence at the White House, and Fuller, as national security advisor, struggled with this ridiculous report. He reread it a second time before being satisfied.

Last months' *TIME* magazine article said Fuller had grown into the national security advisor's job and praised the way he interacted with other members of the intelligence community. Fuller grinned remembering the article. He'd made a lot of good decisions; one of the best, keeping General Harry Cook in command of the Proactive Preemptive Operations Group at the Pentagon.

If the deputy CIA director hadn't personally passed this report to Fuller, he would have blown anyone else off. Since he owed the Agency a couple of favors, he should at least feign interest. Actually, it was quite interesting. A man, near death, found adrift in a small sail-boat, and contaminated with some kind of biological pathogen—it demanded immediate action.

Fuller picked up his encrypted phone and dialed General Cook's number. He answered on the second ring.

"Good morning, General."

"Morning, Mr. Fuller." The voice had the short, clipped diction Cook was famous for. He never wasted time on unnecessary words. "To what do I owe the pleasure?"

Fuller sat back in his chair, balancing the coffee cup on his knee. He needed to frame this question just right. "I was trying to remember something from a few years back, but my memory's a bit fuzzy. Perhaps you'd be kind enough to refresh it."

"I'll do what I can," Cook replied.

Fuller sat the cup on the desk and began doodling a biohazard symbol on a pad as he spoke. "I recall that business in North Korea. You know, they were producing the plague bacteria and planning to provide it to that extremist bunch in—"

"Iraq, sir?"

"Exactly, that's the one. I remember we had a successful resolution to the affair, but go over the details again." Fuller took a slow sip of coffee and settled back in the chair.

Cook cleared his throat. "The president wanted to send a subtle reminder to the North Koreans to stay out of our Middle Eastern oper-ational area."

"Yes, yes, I remember that, but how did we handle it?"

"We sent in an agent/operator who destroyed the facility. By coin-cidence, the lead researcher in charge of production was inside the plant at the time of its destruction."

Coincidence—Fuller grinned as his memory was restored. "Right, I remember now." Where Cook found men who could penetrate a top-secret bioweapons lab in the heart of North Korea, kill their head scien-tist, blow the place up, and get out alive boggled Fuller's mind. No doubt one of the ex-special forces types he employed. Cook's ability to procure personnel and equipment was envied and legendary in intelli-gence circles.

"Anything else, sir?" Cook asked.

Fuller lowered his voice. *Don't want this to come across as crass.* "Did our man happen to get out alive?" He held his breath, waiting for the answer.

A low chuckle drifted over the line. "Yes, sir. Lieutenant Colonel Bishop is still among the living."

Fuller scratched through the doodle and printed "Bishop" below it, then pushed it aside. *Yes, he remembered Bishop.* "Excellent. I'm sending over a top priority assignment that needs immediate attention. Might be right up Bishop's alley."

"He's currently out of the country. Should be back any day."

Fuller didn't like this—it couldn't wait. "General, you decide how to handle it. The president was informed this morning at his CIA daily brief. I'm sure he'll expect an update."

TWO

"It'll kill hundreds and contaminate a wide area," Troy Bishop said while balancing the black leather briefcase on his lap. "And the best part, no one will know they're infected until the incubation period is over and disease takes hold. By then, it'll be too late. Once they become symptomatic, it's all over." He lifted the hermetically sealed, quart-size glass bottle containing a tan powder from the cushioned case interior and set it on the table in front of the skinny Filipino man. Bishop didn't like his looks—had crazy eyes. People with crazy eyes were capable of anything. The fellow stared at it and said nothing. Only the squeaking of the lazy ceiling fan broke the silence. Bishop wanted out of this place. Let the government special forces team move in and take these guys down.

Finally, the Asian man spoke. "Will this be enough?"

"That depends on how large your target area is." Bishop reached for the bottle. He tilted the half-full container back and forth, and the tan powder slid like water from top to bottom. "You wanted the good stuff—that's what you got. This is weapons-grade." Bishop pointed at the bottle. "See that little cloud it forms when I tilt it? When released, the powder will dissipate into an invisible plume and be picked up by the wind. It'll move downrange and infect people for miles."

The man held out his hand, and Bishop acted like he was about to toss the bottle to him. The guy flinched and his eyes widened.

Bishop chuckled. "Just kidding. This isn't the kind of stuff you want to play around with."

Sneering, the Filipino held out his hand again, and Bishop gave him the bottle. He twisted the container, watching the silky powder flow from side to side. A grin cracked his lips. He set the bottle back on the table and nodded toward it. "The release area is quite large. It's a military base."

Bishop already knew this from the intelligence report. The target was the US air base, Mactan-Benito Ebuen. Bishop shrugged before lounging back in the chair and showed his most confident air. "Then do a line release, not a point release. You'll need a five- to ten-mile-an-hour wind behind you. Have as much elevation as possible. And make sure your people are in hazmat gear and you do a proper decon afterwards. Anything less and you end up killing yourself."

A smirk washed over the man's lips. "I have people who know how to do that." He lovingly caressed the bottle on the table with one hand while reaching behind his back with the other. Drawing the pistol, he leveled it at Bishop. "I believe our business is concluded."

Bishop hadn't expected this. He wasn't surprised by it but hadn't expected it. The intelligence reports on this ISIS terrorist group indicated they were a notorious bunch with a tendency toward larceny. He frowned and motioned at the pistol. "What's all this? Thought we had a deal. Where's my two hundred and fifty thousand dollars?"

The Filipino didn't answer but lifted the pistol in an up and down motion for Bishop to stand. *This had not been in the ops plan.* The plan called for Bishop to exchange the bottle for the cash. When the suspects left, the drone circling above would follow them back to their headquarters. A SEAL team was on standby for a decisive *direct action* that would eliminate the threat from this terrorist cell permanently. Bishop's closest help was at least an hour away. Did this guy just want to rip him off or was this a *don't leave any witnesses* type of move? Bishop didn't like the odds, but right now would be his best chance, so he made his move. As he slid the chair to stand, he snatched the bottle of powder off the table and held it at his side by the short bottle neck using just his thumb and index finger. He allowed a trace of a smile to show. "Your move. If this thing breaks, we're both in trouble."

From the sour expression on the guy's face, he hadn't expected his fortunes to turn so soon. He steadied the pistol and cocked the hammer while holding his aim on Bishop. "Put it back."

Bishop shook his head. "Uh-uh. You put the gun on the table first." But something about the crazy-eyed look of the Filipino convinced Bishop the man wasn't buying his bluff. "If I drop this, we're both infected," Bishop warned. "No one needs that kind of problem."

The guy pointed the cocked weapon closer to him. "I might be infected, but you'll be dead. As long as I receive the vaccine within four hours, I'll be fine. We have it loaded in a syringe out in the car." His eyes narrowed and again showed the crazy stare. "Your move."

Bishop's plan had collapsed. Only one thing left to do. He shrugged. "Well played—you win." He moved the bottle back over the table, lowering it to within a couple of inches from the surface before flicking his wrist, tossing it into the air at the Filipino.

The man sucked in a frightened breath and reached to catch it, directing the pistol away from Bishop. Bishop lunged over the table, both hands locking onto the pistol as the bottle smashed onto the tile floor. When it shattered, the powder spilled into a glass-filled heap. An almost invisible cloud, like a little puff of smoke, rose from the floor and was picked up by the ceiling fan. The man fought for control of the weapon, dragging Bishop across the table.

Bishop wedged his index finger inside the pistol's trigger guard. His finger behind the trigger prevented the gun from firing. But the large, black semi-automatic was slowly slipping from his grip as the man pulled and twisted it. Bishop swung his legs to the left, off the table, and his feet made solid contact with the floor. Now he had leverage. He trapped the man's right hand with his left, pivoted his weight, and swung to the right. A sickening crack echoed when the Filipino's wrist and arm snapped. He screamed and released his grip on the weapon just as the front door burst open. Bishop finished pulling the weapon from the man's hand and shot him twice in the head as he fell. He landed on his back on top of the brown powder on the floor.

One of the two guards who had charged in from outside already had his pistol in the firing position when he rushed into the room. Bishop swung around, dropped to one knee, and his first shot caught the guard in the sternum. His second, in the mouth. The guard fell in such a way that he deflected his partner's first shot. Wood paneling a foot above Bishop's head exploded and splintered. The guard got off two more wild shots before Bishop hit him in the upper chest. He stopped in mid-stride and looked down at his bloody shirt, like he was surprised. Bishop's second shot took off the top of his head.

Bishop released a long-held breath and stood. He raked a lock of hair off his forehead and kept the pistol in the combat shooter position while approaching the open door. The two dead men sprawled across the room like broken and discarded dolls. The familiar smells of blood and gun smoke hung heavy in the air. Bishop did a quick glance outside—all clear. The jungle remained quiet except for the hoot of a mawmag somewhere in the distance.

Bishop searched the bodies, taking the men's identification, phones, jewelry, car keys, and wallets. He scanned the dingy room and imagined what a police investigator would see. A violent robbery with three victims—possibly drug-related. Some kind of fine powder scattered beside one body, and broken glass. The harmless, simulated pathogen had served Bishop well. The specially designed jar shattered into a thousand pieces, destroying any trace of fingerprints. He grabbed the briefcase, dumped all the guys' possessions inside, and eased back to the threshold, wiping the doorknob clean.

Backing up, his heel bumped a small table to the right of the entrance. It wobbled twice and a pitcher of ice water tipped over, spilling down his leg and soaking his shoe. "Damn." He hated cold water.

Bishop stepped outside into the clearing of the front yard and looked up into the cloudless sky. Bright sunshine blinded him, and he squinted as he slowly brought his right hand to the top of his head. He then took his left hand and also placed it on top of his head. The drone operator would read the signal as, *I'm safe/threat neutralized/no further assistance required* and report it up the chain back to General Cook.

Bishop searched the dead guy's truck for intelligence—it was clean. He slid into the seat of his open-top Jeep and scanned the area one last time before heading down the mountain toward Manila. He kept a close watch during the drive, fearing the trio might have a backup team waiting. But after a couple of miles without meeting or even seeing another vehicle, he understood he was safe.

Bishop wasn't prone to looking back on his life or career often. There was too much ahead of him for that. But sometimes, after a close call like he'd just experienced, his mind reflected on his past decisions and how they'd brought him to this place. His first big decision had been to attend West Point. Since his dad was a career military man in naval intelligence, the decision hadn't been a hard one. Bishop had grown up all over the world. A military brat who had lucked out and had been able to attend all four years of high school at the US Naval Air Station on Bermuda. But Bishop hadn't seen the Navy in his future —he'd wanted the Army. During his years at West Point, they'd stressed leadership and career advancement. Several of his classmates were already generals now, but another decision Bishop had made early in his military career nixed that. He'd wanted Special Operations —not much career advancement in small, elite units.

After graduation, he had been assigned as a second lieutenant with 505 Infantry Regiment of the 82nd Airborne. He hadn't been surprised how much he enjoyed being in a special ops unit. The grueling training suited him, and he'd excelled. After two years, he'd received a promotion and transferred to the 75th Ranger Regiment at Fort Benning— more grueling training.

A lot of top-level missions were being assigned to special operations units like the 75th Rangers as the war on terror heated up. Bishop's last major career decision in the army had come a year later when he'd applied to the Delta Selection Course in 1999. Ninety-three percent of the applicants flunked or dropped out—Bishop had passed.

That seemed like a lifetime ago. Bishop understood he had an expiration date in this line of work. It was a young man's game. But his experience had allowed him to keep his edge, at least for now. Besides, Special Operators always went out in one of three ways—transitioned to another assignment, retired, or killed.

THREE

US ARMY MEDICAL RESEARCH INSTITUTE
OF INFECTIOUS DISEASES (USAMRIID)
FORT DETRICK, MARYLAND
18:36 HRS

An uncomfortable tingle raced up Bishop's back as he thumbed through the CIA report while occasionally glancing at the three closed-circuit monitors on the wall. Tom Lynch, with CIA's Science and Technology Branch, sat in the other chair and sipped his coffee, waiting for the autopsy to begin. Bishop hadn't spent much time at Fort Detrick. He'd been here once a couple of years ago for a bio-terrorism briefing—that was it. The old Cold-War bioweapons facility gave him the creeps.

Bishop finished reading the report and stared at the three wall monitors again. The heavy-duty gray plastic body bag, bathed in powerful overhead lights, resting on the stainless-steel autopsy table had a disturbing effect—especially after reading the report. Bishop had been on edge since he'd arrived, and it wasn't getting any better. He slid the paper back across the table to Lynch and kept eying the monitors. "So, the guy was picked up two days ago, drifting in a boat?"

Lynch finished his coffee and tossed the Styrofoam cup into a trash can under the table. "Yeah, it was barely in US waters. We're waiting on autopsy confirmation, but it looks like some kind of viral hemorrhagic fever. The Coast Guard crew who found him was quarantined."

"Hemorrhagic fever—like Ebola or something?" Bishop asked.

Lynch stretched his legs and assumed a more comfortable position in the straight back chair. "Yup, that's how it came over to CIA. The CDC's freaking out. This stuff makes the worst cases of COVID-19 look like the common cold."

The viewing room, as it was known, wasn't built for comfort. The white tile floor and light blue tile walls didn't exactly give it a cozy, living room feel. Bright fluorescent lights revealed every crack and crease in the old outdated 1980s decor.

Movement on the monitors caught Bishop's attention. Three people stepped into the chamber through the air lock and waddled into full camera view. They all looked the same. Each wore a powder blue biocontainment space suit, yellow plastic boots, and white latex gloves taped securely over the sleeves. The faceplates of their flexible, bubble-like helmets were fogged, hiding their facial features. They looked like a team of blue gummy bears.

"How can they see out of those things?" Bishop asked.

Lynch kept his attention on the monitors. "The suits are airtight. Positive air pressure protects them against a pathogen entering if there is a tear or leak. They'll unfog in a second."

Bishop studied the three figures working themselves to different sides of the autopsy table. "They call this chamber the Submarine?"

Lynch looked his way. "It's a hot zone morgue for doing autopsies on biosafety level four cadavers—maintains a negative air flow. Thing's completely sealed from the outside. Has a lever on its stainless steel door that looks like a pressure door on a submarine."

They both faced the monitors and waited. Two of the gummy-bear figures drifted to each end of the autopsy table, while the third one, the shortest, remained facing the main video camera. Each reached up and tugged at the nearest coiled yellow hose dangling from the ceiling, plugging it into the manifold of their blue suit. Moments later, the fresh air cleared the faceplates, and the features of each person came into focus. The one facing the main camera was a middle-aged female. Dark blue, piercing eyes gazed from behind the faceplate at the lifeless, triple-bagged figure on the table before her. Her palms rested on the side of the table. Bishop wasn't certain, but he thought he detected a trembling in her hands.

Her lips moved from behind the face plate, and the assistant to her right reached over and unzipped the body bag with the red biohazard trefoil stamped across the middle. She took a step back to give him room. Bishop leaned closer, hoping to hear what she was saying.

"There's no sound?" Bishop asked.

Lynch removed a small notebook from inside his coat and set it on the table with a pen. "There's no audio in the morgue, no need—high resolution cameras and recorders pick up everything. All the verbal findings are explained later in front of cameras outside the submarine." He pointed at the female on screen. "That's Doctor Irene Fletcher, or Colonel Fletcher as she's known around here. She's head of pathology at USAMRIID."

After fully unzipping it, the assistants tucked the thick, gray bag underneath the corpse. This revealed another creamy white Tyvek bag. The outline of a face showed through it. The brow, nose, and chin were distinguishable. Dr. Fletcher nodded, and an assistant unzipped this bag as well. The last bag was coal black. A nylon zipper ran around three sides.

Bishop studied Colonel Fletcher's eyes. He wasn't sure what he saw—dread, fear, or just sadness. She took a deep breath and motioned to the assistant. The man unzipped the third bag from right to left, pulling back the plastic flap. Bishop involuntarily jerked his head back as a queasy sensation rumbled in his stomach.

The corpse was in a terrible condition. The small, dark-haired man hardly looked human. His skin had a charred-black appearance, and dark, dried blood remained around the nose and eyes. The mouth gaped open, revealing a set of black blood-stained teeth. Dr. Fletcher took a piece of gauze, dipped it into some clear liquid in a red plastic tray, and used it to clean the middle of the chest down to the pubic area. She then began the primary incision with a scalpel down the center of the chest. Finishing, she dropped the scalpel into the same liquid-filled plastic tray she'd dipped the gauze in. All her motions were exaggeratedly slow, like she didn't want to knock over or spill anything. The hairs on Bishop's arms rose, watching this macabre show.

"What's in the tray?" Bishop asked.

The CIA man never took his eyes off the monitors. "The strongest solution available for medical device sterilization."

One of the assistants opened up the chest cavity with rib cutters, and they finished the autopsy using only surgical scissors. Bishop had seen autopsies before, but this one was different. All the blood was black and thick. After taking fluid and tissue samples of the enlarged liver, spleen, and kidneys, Colonel Fletcher rinsed her gloved hands in the red tray with the sanitizing solution. She turned to an assistant and her lips moved. He nodded, and she headed to the airlock. Thirty minutes later, wearing fresh scrubs after a decon shower, she sat behind her office desk. The CIA man and Bishop waited for her diagnoses.

She leaned both arms on the desk, clasped her fingers tight, and her brow wrinkled before saying, "Well, it's definitely some kind of filovirus. Congealed blood on body orifices, petechial and maculopapular rash, massive hemorrhaging in the body cavity, spleen turned into an ugly blood sausage. But..."

Lynch shifted forward in his chair. "But what?"

She folded one hand on top of the other, and Bishop caught sight of the tremble again before she could hold it down. The blue eyes fixed on the two men. "*But* there's something else." She frowned. "We'll know more after the test results, but I also observed hemorrhagic spots on all the internal organs, as well as subcutaneous bleeding. While I'm not discounting Ebola, the appearance of these hemorrhagic spots is concerning."

Bishop's briefings on biological pathogens had included hemorrhagic viruses. Cases were so rare that, when a patient exhibited symptoms anywhere in the world, doctors and researchers were dispatched to the scene to study and quarantine the patient. Finding it in US territorial waters was the reason he'd been rushed to view the autopsy after stepping off the plane from Manila. A disease like this had a high burn rate. That is, it could race through a population so fast that victims—patients—might die before infecting others. The problem is, thousands could die before any effective measures could be employed.

The next afternoon, Bishop hit the print button on his laptop and closed the folder. He saved the document and uploaded it onto the mainframe. "Done at last," he sighed before draining the water from the plastic bottle. While the report printed, he ambled across his office to the full picture window. The dark woods of the Virginia countryside had a cool and inviting appearance. The shaded glade surrounded by tall trees and ferns outside his office window contained a clear water creek meandering down the hill with dark green ivy covering the ground on each side. Three cameras kept watch on everything on this side of the building. It was a nice view and made him feel cooler just staring at it. But it was deceiving. The outside temperature climbed above a hundred each day, and with the humidity, the heat index held at close to 105—dog days of summer. With arms extended, he stretched his 6'2" frame and yawned. Maintaining the six-day-a-week runs meant getting up well before dawn to beat the heat. Easier twenty years ago when he was a Delta officer.

He checked his Rolex Submariner—almost three o'clock. He slipped the top secret–SCI folder back into his safe and locked it. Nothing bored him more than paperwork. For a second, Bishop wondered where his top secret reports ended up. They were classified at a level that only about a dozen people could access. Must be a super-secret mainframe somewhere where items like this are stored. Then again, it could be that huge warehouse depicted in the movie *Raiders of the Lost Ark*.

Bishop's years with Delta taught him patience. Sitting around waiting for the big op took up most of the time back then. Training helped with the monotony, but even that got routine after a while. He grabbed the report from the printer and flopped back into the chair. He propped his feet on the desk and reviewed it one last time.

After signing and dating it, he dropped it in the dispatch case. He wanted another assignment. Something to get out of this sweat box—anywhere cooler. The chime from his computer signaled a new email. General Cook. *My office at 4 o'clock, if you please.*

Bishop hit the reply button. *With pleasure.*

Bishop called the duty desk and told them he'd transport the dispatch case downtown today. The Proactive Preemptive Operations Group (P2OG) only had two facilities. The main contingent of the organization worked out of this covert off-site location in Virginia. The two-story, nondescript office building with basement parking was well hidden among other commercial businesses nestled at the bottom of a long hill west of DC. The sign out front read Virginia Consulting, but the reception area had bulletproof glass surrounding it. Only an identity badge with built-in microchip and a six-digit code allowed entry. It was no coincidence it was close to CIA headquarters and Dulles Airport.

The headquarters component was at the Pentagon. General Cook and his deputy commander, Colonel Gary Maxwell, worked there with one administrative assistant, Mary Sweeney. P2OG employed as many civilians as military. If you had a specialty they wanted, General Cook wouldn't stop until you were the newest member of his team. That's how he rolled.

Bishop gathered up his gear and headed for the duty agent room. Because the facility remained covert, no mail correspondence between it and the Pentagon was allowed. A courier made two runs a day and transported inter-office mail between the two locations. Bishop grabbed the briefcase, waved at the duty agent, and stepped outside into the oppressive heat. He drove to the metro station in McLean and caught the train into the city. Just like the mail, no vehicle could travel from the off-site location to the Pentagon or vice versa. They could only utilize the metro, and only after the courier confirmed he wasn't being tailed. Thirty minutes later, the train pulled into the Pentagon station and Bishop meandered toward the "A" ring—mezzanine level.

Before he could enter his code on the door scanner, Mary buzzed him in.

"Afternoon, Bishop," she muttered, before going back to her typing. The reception office was small, but well furnished. Besides Mary's desk, it had a brown leather sofa and two comfortable leather chairs surrounding a coffee table. Above the sofa was an oil on canvas of the Siege of Carthage. Mary looked tired today, probably in one of her moods. Her close-cropped light brown hair showed signs of the roots needing another retouch, but Bishop tried not to stare—it would only invoke her wrath.

"The general called me over. Here's the mail," he said, setting the briefcase on the edge of her desk.

"Don't put it there—it'll fall. Set it on the floor. I'll go through it in a minute."

Her usual bossy tone was on full display. He knew how to put her back in place. Bishop carefully picked up the case and set it beside her desk, then made a show of gradually backing away toward the couch. He lifted his hands in the air showing he had surrendered.

She glanced his way before saying, "Everybody's a smart ass today," and then went back to her keyboard.

Bishop grunted—if he ever found her in a good mood, he'd be alarmed. He picked up a magazine off the coffee table and fell onto the comfortable leather couch. Before he found anything worth reading, the phone buzzed. Mary answered it.

"Yes, sir, he's here," she said, glancing at Bishop. "Right away, sir." She hung up. "Okay, sport, you're in." Only Mary could get away with calling a lieutenant colonel *sport* in the Pentagon. Bishop couldn't care less. His rank wasn't a big deal; his work was.

Bishop knocked three times before entering Cook's office—that's what Cook expected. The thing Bishop liked about Cook's office was it was solid. Being on the Pentagon's basement level gave you the feeling you were in a fortified bunker. The solid walls supported the maps and charts that covered them. A solid oak desk faced the door, adorned with framed VIP photos from a distinguished military career.

The solid man behind the desk welcomed him with the usual smile. The major general always kept his gray hair short. That, with his stocky frame, made it hard to guess his true age—probably early to late 50s. He'd stopped wearing his uniform years ago, and now preferred a business suit.

Dr. Fletcher sat in front of the desk, looking up as Bishop strolled in. Today she was in uniform. She sat erect, a colonel's eagle resting on each epaulet. The lapel insignia indicated Medical Corps.

"Bishop, I believe you already know Dr. Irene Fletcher." Cook nodded at the colonel.

"Yes, good afternoon." Bishop shook the warm hand.

She forced a smile. "Mr. Bishop."

He took a seat and directed his attention to the general.

Cook leaned back and studied a folder. "What do you know about synthetic biology?"

Bishop glanced at the colonel, whose lips stretched into thin white lines. "I read a briefing paper on it awhile back. I believe it's DNA sequencing and genetic engineering, something like that."

"Quite right," Cook said. "We're sending you to Canada—Victoria —for a few days. Have a little problem up there that needs sorting out."

Cook retold the story about the man in the boat. This wasn't necessary as Bishop had already read the CIA report, but Cook always started at the baseline and worked up—stickler for details.

Cook tilted his head toward the guest. "Dr. Fletcher has some additional information which may be useful." Cook eyed the woman. "Colonel Fletcher."

She wrung her hands in her lap, leaned forward, and hesitated before speaking. "Mr. Bishop, we've conducted tests on the pathogen which infected the man. Our findings have badly shaken us. The best we can determine, it's a recombinant virus—one that's engineered in a laboratory."

Bishop squirmed, and the queasiness he'd felt at seeing the corpse returned to his gut. He feared no man, but his training made him wary of ugly viruses and germs. The thought of using disease as a weapon was distasteful. "What does the virus do?"

Dr. Fletcher's brow folded, and her expression darkened. "It's a pathogen which causes smallpox and Ebola."

Bishop slowly released a breath and said, "It causes both?"

"Yes."

Bishop had had a lot of training in virus, bacteria, and toxins. What she described sounded like something from a horror film—a Frankenvirus. "Any idea where he picked it up?"

"That's the most disturbing part. You see, we've recovered pathogenic material from his clothes."

Her answer confused Bishop. He held up a hand to interrupt her before saying, "Wouldn't you expect pathogenic material on an infected man's clothing?"

Colonel Fletcher flashed an embarrassed half grin. "I'm sorry, I didn't make myself clear. We not only found evidence of the infection in him, but also of the exposure. Microscopic particles of a viral material embedded in his hair and clothes which tested positive for the pathogen."

Bishop glanced at Cook.

Cook sat silent, twisting the Masonic ring as he pursed his lips. Bishop knew that look—this worried him.

"Mr. Bishop, the biological agent was weaponized," she said. "We're sure of that much."

Bishop turned back to the colonel. "Weaponized—how?"

"Dry particles between two and five microns, with the electrostatic charge removed."

Cook added, "Most likely a foreign-sponsored program."

Bishop hung his head. Something he'd read kept coming back. "Aren't all the stocks of smallpox kept at the CDC in Atlanta and a similar facility in Russia?"

"All the *declared* stocks," Colonel Fletcher corrected. "After the eradication program in '77, all countries sent their reference samples to the World Health Organization for cataloging and permanent storage. The declared stocks and different strains were split between the CDC and the Vector Laboratories in Russia. But it's widely believed there were many undeclared stocks that remain in the countries of origin."

"Any friendly to the US?" Cook mused.

"No," she said. "North Korea, China, Cuba."

"The usual suspects." Bishop sighed.

"Afraid so," Cook agreed.

"There's one additional piece of information you should be aware of, Mr. Bishop."

Colonel Fletcher drew in a breath. "As you're probably aware, there are few effective cures for Ebola. This is an exceptionally hot strain with a ninety-five percent mortality rate. And this smallpox pathogen is the strain most likely to go hemorrhagic—it's vaccine resistant. Hemorrhagic smallpox is usually fatal. The only thing we can do is offer supportive care."

"Supportive care?"

Dr. Fletcher wrung her hands tighter. "Yes, we put the victims into a medically induced coma and wait for them to die in quarantine. We ran the virus stats through our computers. If our calculations are valid, about sixteen ounces of this weaponized pathogen, properly aerosolized, could infect everyone in DC."

An uncomfortable tingle crawled up Bishop's back just before Cook spoke. "We're calling this op *Biowatch*. Mrs. Sweeney can provide more briefing material and your itinerary. You'll fly to Tacoma tomorrow and meet with a Navy intelligence officer for an additional update." Cook shoved several stacks of papers aside until finding the right one. Reading from it, he said, "His name is Gregory... Lieutenant Gregory. He'll bring you up-to-speed on what they've found." Cook leaned his arms on the desk, the firm stare cutting deep into Bishop, and in a slow even voice said, "Find the source. That's the mission."

"Yes, sir," Bishop said and stood.

"Oh, by the way," Cook added, "good work in the Philippines. Sorry we couldn't have bagged the whole bunch, but you did more than your part. Another close call, huh?"

Bishop cut a glance at Colonel Fletcher's confused expression before saying, "Yes, sir. Another close call."

Bishop walked back into the reception office with this new information rattling around in his head. A weaponized virus with no cure. While it was probably a Canadian problem because of where the boat originated, the national security implications for the US were huge.

Sweeney stopped typing and showed a smirk he didn't like. "Do you want to sleep in your bed tonight, or one in Tacoma?"

She sat back and crossed her arms, waiting for an answer. Bishop understood this was a trick question with no winning answer, but he'd play along.

"Mine," he said. He'd not expected to go out on such short notice and still had a few things to do, plus packing for a week or more.

When her lips formed a devilish smile, he suspected he'd lost the bet, again. She reached across her desk and picked up a manila envelope. "I thought as much. Here."

He accepted it with a degree of caution. "Did you reserve me an aisle seat?"

Sweeney began her typing once more. "I did better than that. You've got the whole plane to yourself. You leave out of Andrews tomorrow morning on a C-17 Globemaster delivering a load of machine parts. Flying time four hours and forty-one minutes to McChord Field in Tacoma."

Bishop thumbed through the itinerary and briefing papers. So much for first class travel. "No commercial flights available?"

She shook her head. "Nothing that would get you to Port Angeles in time for the ferry to Victoria before five o'clock tomorrow. Cook wanted you there by then, and that's what I scheduled."

He shrugged. The C-17 was the newest air force cargo plane with few amenities, but since it wasn't a trans-Atlantic flight, it wouldn't be too bad. Bishop strolled toward the door and focused on the departure time. "Three-dark-thirty?! That's cruel and unusual."

Another brief smirk from her, "Comes from being married to a retired Sergeant Major."

Just before he walked out, she called, "Hey, Bishop."

His jaw tightened and he turned, ready for another round of banter. A sweet, concerned, motherly face greeted him. He knew it was genuine—he'd seen it before.

"Be careful. And don't forget your jacket."

He winked. "Thanks."

Striding down the hall, he pulled up the weather report for Victoria, British Columbia. His iPhone showed the expected high for today, and he did a double take. 18 degrees Celsius? After a quick calculation, he worked it out—64 degrees—*yes!*

FOUR

The next morning, Bishop arrived at the Andrews VIP reception desk at 2:27. He got an ugly glare from the sergeant working check-in. They liked their passengers there at least an hour and a half before flight time. After less than five hours sleep and waking up in what most people would consider the middle of the night, Bishop didn't really care what they liked. A car and driver arrived, and a few minutes later he stood on the flight line, eyeing the C-17 crew finishing their pre-flight checks. Bishop wasn't in uniform, so no salutes were rendered.

He introduced himself to the pilot and co-pilot, and the flight engineer escorted him to a green nylon strap seat on the port side near the front of the plane. The engineer handed him a pair of earplugs. "Sorry, sir—we didn't get the word you'd be joining us until just this morning, or we would have installed some better seating."

Bishop waved off the apology. "I'll be fine, thanks."

Twenty minutes later, they were buttoned up and taxiing for take-off. After the giant plane roared into the dark sky, Bishop switched on an overhead reading light and sorted through the briefing material Sweeney gave him. He found a Department of Justice report. The FBI had done interviews and found nothing of interest. They'd partnered with the Royal Canadian Mounted Police in Victoria. The best they came up with was it appeared the sailboat and dying passenger originated from off the Canadian coast, but no exact location could be identified. Canadian public health officials and an army of epidemiologists from the CDC and WHO had spent the last few days searching for an index case, but none was located—only the lone man dying in the boat. That alone made the case unusual. An index case always leads to additional cases somewhere.

This was good and bad news. Good that no others were exposed or infected, but bad because it still led to a dead end. The boat apparently had little history. Registration, sales, and ownership of the ghost craft were sketchy. A police report indicated it had been stolen years ago—that was it.

In the briefing packet, he discovered a copy of an official message from the US State Department to Canadian authorities, announcing his arrival and giving his hotel name and address. He also found a return message from the Canadian State Department informing him that an RCMP inspector would meet him and provide escort through customs.

A separate notification indicated a member of the Canadian Security Intelligence Service would be made available to assist during his inquiry. This was the result of him being declared a foreign intelligence officer. Bishop always preferred to be undeclared when working in another country. It gave him more freedom of movement without the prying eyes of handlers dogging his every move. The downside, of course: he couldn't enjoy any official standing. If he were caught as an undeclared, the US would disavow any knowledge of him or his employment with the government. As crazy as it sounded, he would trade his security for freedom of movement—especially in Canada.

The flight engineer turned the corner and handed him a steaming black coffee in a Styrofoam cup. "Compliments of the flight commander, sir."

Bishop studied the kid. He looked maybe twenty-four at best, but they were all kids. He recalled his last visit back to his old Delta unit. All the veterans had long since departed. The original group he'd served with after 9/11 had faded away a little more with each visit.

Fresh faces replaced them—stronger, and with more stamina. Yeah, Special Ops remained a young man's game.

"Thank him for me." Bishop accepted the hot brew. The engineer nodded and turned toward the crew compartment. Bishop went back to his homework. A CDC document described how a naval reservist—a doctor—met the doomed Coast Guard cutter when they docked with the daysailer in tow. One look at the dead man on board and he immediately quarantined the entire crew. That saved the base, and perhaps the town, from a devastating outbreak.

Bishop dug deeper inside the envelope and found a report from the 20th CBRN Command. Members of this group were dispatched to the Port Angeles Coast Guard Station to recover the body of the man in the boat and relocate the Coast Guard crew to a special hospital in Seattle for treatment and quarantine.

Lastly, Bishop located the reports from USAMRIID regarding the pathogen. Colonel Fletcher's name appeared on most of the documents, and he recalled her disturbed countenance yesterday—this thing scared her.

He tucked the papers back into the envelope, switched off the overhead light, and rested his head against the small cushion as he sipped the coffee. So much raced through his mind—so many questions. He wished he could catch a nap before landing, but with an active brain, the roar of the engines, and vibrations of the huge air truck, he didn't count on it.

He still enjoyed the ride. It wasn't especially comfortable, but it brought back fond memories. The smell of a big plane and military hardware, the bucking of the aircraft, and old friends' nervous laughter before going into the thick of an operation. The sounds of weapons being checked, straps being pulled tighter, and equipment dragging across the metal floor.

Like most Special Operations types, Bishop didn't have much time for those who ran down the military or country. Yeah, things weren't perfect, but where else could so many enjoy the security and freedoms Americans have. And he had less time for the bleeding-heart critics, the ones who found fault with everything done on their behalf but were unwilling to lift a finger or get their hands dirty to change it.

Teddy Roosevelt had been right: *The credit belongs to the man who is in the arena. The man whose face is marred by dust and sweat and blood. And not those cold and timid souls who neither know victory nor defeat...*

Someone shook his shoulder and he jumped awake. The flight engineer stepped back with a surprised look. "Sorry if I startled you, sir, but the skipper wanted to make sure you were buckled in for landing. We're on final—wheels down in about fifteen minutes."

Bishop focused on the man and yawned. "Guess I slipped away for a little while."

The engineer glanced at his wrist and grinned. "More like three hours, sir. Check your seatbelt—we'll land at McChord Field in a few minutes."

FIVE

Colonel Ye Hong squirmed in front of Claudine Mercier's desk. He felt like a schoolboy who had been sent to the principal's office. He hated this assignment and longed for it to be over.

"Well, what did you find out?" she asked.

Hong also hated when she did not apply makeup to cover her disfigurement. The slender, middle-aged brunette was once beautiful—he had seen photos. She chose to look her worst today—probably to intimidate him. He stammered for an answer. "The man believed he had been infected and thought we planned to do away with him—so he fled." He hung his head, not meeting her stare. "The sailboat was apparently the best option at the time."

Her suspicious glare locked on him. "Was there a leak in one of the canisters? How did the exposure happen?"

"We have checked them all and did another decon. Nothing appears abnormal. He might have picked something up during the process of transferring the pathogen—probably did not follow SOP."

She turned the ugly side of her face toward him. The deep, purple scarring could not be concealed by any amount of plastic surgery or makeup. The skin appeared to have melted. Hong's fist knotted behind his back. He hated this woman. He hated her security chief, Stewart Anderson, and he hated this house. But if he pulled this off, his promotion to general was assured. *Only a few more days,* he told himself, *and it would be over.* She stared at him in that condescending way he hated.

"Very well. Get out and send in Stewart."

He released a breath and turned for the door.

Outside, Stewart waited in the hall, smoking as usual. He blew a smoke ring toward the ceiling and raised his eyebrows. "She can be a real bitch when she wants to be, huh?"

Hong turned and marched down the hall. "She wants to see you."

————

Anderson snuffed out the cigarette in the ashtray on the table and strolled inside Mercier's office.

She turned her attention to him. "Stewart, can we be connected with this man in the boat?"

He shook his head. "The boat wasn't registered to us. If anyone checks sales records, they'll come up with a blank. It'll show the thing was stolen years ago and never recovered."

"We owned a stolen boat?"

"No ma'am, but my government contact altered the official computer record. That's what'll be found."

She smirked. "You're clever. I'll give you that."

"If you told me what all this cloak and dagger between you and Hong was about, I might offer a few ideas along those lines—I *am* your director of security." This might convince her to spill the beans on what she and Hong were up to. He'd tried before, but she'd always avoided the subject. She and Hong had a deal working—a big deal, probably big money, and he wanted in.

She turned her back, crossed her arms and ambled toward the panoramic window. "We've talked about this. You're only my director of security, not my business partner, and I pay you well." She abruptly swung around and faced him. "And Colonel Hong represents an international interest in my business. Your background is not business." Her eyebrows knitted together. "A deal with Hong's country is worth millions. They demand secrecy as a condition of their partnership. Understand?"

Anderson understood perfectly. He would remain on the outside. "Yes, ma'am."

"What do your sources say about this dead man?"

Anderson shifted. "The police aren't any closer to figuring it out than the first day. The visiting FBI agents didn't come up with any new ideas—they left day before yesterday."

She turned her back and gazed out the large window, staring at the ocean below. Anderson shifted to see what she was looking at. Only a whale-watching boat from Victoria, chugging its way back to port— she was a strange woman with strange ways. She didn't utter a word for some time. Finally, she marched back to the desk and claimed her chair.

"Make sure they keep their ears open. This couldn't happened at a worse time. At this stage, we have little choice but to go ahead. If there are any additional inquiries, let me know. We'll deal with problems when they arise. Hopefully, because of the cross-jurisdictional issues, the bureaucracy will screw it up as usual."

SIX

When Bishop stepped off the plane, it was still early morning, West Coast time, but he felt invigorated. The hot, humid days of summer were over—at least for the next week or so. A shuttle took him to the reception area, and a young airman paged him to the desk.

"You Troy Bishop?" he asked.

"That's right."

The airman handed over the keys. "It's the black Toyota SUV out front. Tank's full, unlimited mileage, bring it back in one piece."

"Thanks." Bishop headed for the door.

Sweeney did him right. She'd reserved his favorite. A black Highlander sat out front, looking like it just drove off a showroom floor. He tossed his bag in the back, and his cell rang when he opened the driver's door.

"Is this Troy Bishop?" the voice asked.

"Depends on who's calling."

The man cleared his throat. "Mr. Bishop, I'm Lieutenant Gregory. I'm here at the reception area—supposed to brief you."

Bishop glanced around. At the far corner of the building, leaning against a sedan, stood a young lieutenant talking on a cell. "Eyes right," Bishop said.

The man turned, spotted him, and hung up. After introductions, Bishop invited him to have a seat in his SUV. This Highlander still had that *new car* smell. Gregory looked in his mid-20s, with short red hair and wire-rimmed glasses. He extracted an iPad from its soft leather case and powered it up. The image showed the Canadian coastline around Victoria in detail.

Gregory tilted the iPad so Bishop could see. "I've spoken to our oceanographic section and they're about ninety-five percent certain the boat originated from Canadian waters."

Bishop examined the image, picking out familiar locations. San Juan, Shaw, Lopez, and Orcas Islands all east of the Haro Strait. "How did they conclude it came from Canada?"

Gregory had a nervous energy as he dug through his briefcase and found a folder. He pulled out a stack of papers and handed them to Bishop. They were all colored maps showing the same image as the iPad. A dozen different colored lines streaked across the maps with numbers printed below each. Looked like a hurricane prediction map.

"And so you see, they've run numerous computer models charting the possible origin of the boat according to current and wind patterns." Gregory leaned over and ran his finger down several colored lines from the Canadian coast to an X just inside US waters. "This area is where the Coast Guard intercepted the boat."

Bishop examined each map page and handed them back to Gregory, one at a time. It didn't take a mathematician or an oceanographer to see the pattern. Almost all the colored lines ending in US waters began life in Canadian waters, in the southern part of the Saanich Peninsula—just east of Victoria, BC.

Gregory neatly assembled the papers and slid them back into his folder. He showed a curious grin before saying, "This information is classified the same as everything else related to the inquiry. Don't share it with the Canadians."

Bishop did a doubletake. "Why?"

Gregory's eyes shifted back and forth a couple of times. A confused look followed. "Why what?"

Bishop leaned closer. "Why not share it with them? Don't you think they already have it, for god's sake? Aren't we on the same side?"

This bit of logic appeared to confound Lt. Gregory. He was only following orders. He'd not classified the thing in the first place. Some nameless bureaucrat in the Pentagon, CIA, or who-knew-where decided that the whole file should be classified. In all probability, the Canadians already had a copy—leaked to them by another nameless bureaucrat in one of the aforementioned agencies.

"Never mind, Lieutenant. Sorry to complicate matters."

If Gregory was put off by Bishop's outburst, he didn't show it. He ran his finger along the iPad screen, tapping the area around Victoria. "And so you see, that narrow strip of Canadian coast should be your starting point when you begin your investigation."

Gregory, like many in intelligence work, had developed annoying habits. His was, he prefaced almost each sentence with the words, "And so you see." Bishop had had enough.

"Thanks again, Lieutenant. I'd better be off—I've got a ferry to catch."

Gregory gave him directions off base, and Bishop soon found the road to Port Angeles. The two and a half hour drive up the Olympic Peninsula relaxed him. He drove with the windows down and the radio up. Cool, clean air filled the SUV's cabin—felt great.

Looking for a better radio station, he came across a talk show discussing post-traumatic stress disorder. He immediately changed the channel. He'd known men who'd become disabled from it—some had taken their own lives. Ironic how the war continued to kill even after the battles. He thanked god he'd never fallen into that trench. Emotional numbness, strong guilt, and frightening thoughts never affected him. He'd been responsible for so many deaths during his days with Delta, and seen so many horrible things in Afghanistan, that it sometimes caused him to wonder if he'd lost part of his humanity. Had he become so hardened to killing and death that it no longer affected him? No, he hadn't—because of the dream.

In the spring of 2001, Bishop had been promoted to captain. For six months, he and his Delta team conducted covert missions all over the Middle East. In early September, he and several other Delta Operators were sent to Pakistan to assist in the training of their elite anti-terrorist unit. A week after arriving, the terrorists attacked his own country— 9/11. Bishop and his team were rushed to Tora Bora in hopes of trapping and eliminating them. After the completion of that mission, he and his men worked to pick off the stragglers left behind. On a cloudy day, high up in the cold mountains, they breached the door of an Al-Qaeda safe house said to have several high-level targets inside. Capturing them for interrogation and sweeping the area for intel was Delta's primary assignment.

But that wasn't how things worked out. They weren't able to take anyone alive, and Bishop and a sergeant were wounded by a grenade blast. The sergeant died and Bishop lived, but his tour of Afghanistan was over. He spent weeks in a hospital and more in physical therapy.

Bishop shook himself out of the memory and thought again about the dream. It came so infrequently that he couldn't recall the last time he'd had it. The dream never changed, almost like an obnoxious relative dropping by from time to time just to irritate you. Lots of lights and sounds, explosions, people screaming, guns being fired, and then total silence and the smell of gun smoke and explosives lingering in the thick air. Silence until he heard the low whisper of the sergeant: "Bishop, help me. I've been hit." The voice repeated the words over and over until finally it screamed, "Bishop, help me! I've been hit!" But he couldn't help because he'd been hit, too. The grenade got them both.

All those years ago, when Bishop received treatment at Walter Reed Army Hospital for his wounds in Afghanistan, he'd wondered what would happen to him—where would he go after being released? Going back to Delta was iffy. Sooner or later, he'd have to take a physical assessment test to show he was still up to standards. For the first time in his life, he'd had doubts. The way the system worked was if you couldn't measure up, they quietly eased you out and back to the unit you'd transferred from. Bishop had been certain he could pass any test the 75th Rangers administered, but being sent back seemed like failure. There was no shame in being wounded in combat and returning to a lesser tier unit, but Bishop thought there was. Sure, it was a stupid way of looking at it, but he couldn't help it. Going back would have affected his mind and confidence.

By the time Bishop crossed the Hood Canal Bridge, the rolling mountains and ridges crowded with 300-foot Douglas firs, red cedars, and mountain hemlock blocked out all light in the vast forest. The cool air had a sweet scent. He shivered before rolling up the car windows halfway. Bishop arrived at Port Angeles with time to spare, but he was starving. He bought the Black Ball ferry ticket for Victoria, parked his SUV at the head of the line, and walked to the Downriggers Restaurant. They seated him at a table with a nice view of the water and ferry dock. A seafood platter and beer later, he strolled back to the SUV while more vehicles filed in behind him.

He relaxed in the car, enjoying the clean, salty air and listening to seagulls squawk overhead. He could have easily forgotten about the mission and just enjoyed the moment except for the encrypted phone ringing.

"Bishop here," he answered.

"How's it going?" It was Colonel Maxwell—Cook's deputy commander.

"Good. Waiting for the ferry at Port Angeles." To confirm his last statement, the blast from an approaching ship's horn drove away the seagulls. Several hundred yards away, the behemoth ferry crawled toward him across the deep blue waters. The name on the bow came into focus—*Coho*.

"Cook wanted me to give you a call," Maxwell said. "Several members of the Coast Guard crew who intercepted the boat have become symptomatic."

Bishop winced: exactly five days since the exposure. *They were all going to die.* They'd seen what the disease could do, and now waited their turn. "Anything else, sir?"

"That's it," Maxwell concluded.

"Thanks." He ended the call when the *Coho* eased up to the dock. The sea breeze and gulls didn't have such a nice quality anymore. A ship's crew waited for death to catch up to them.

Bishop followed the signals from the ferryman and parked on an upper deck. Once all the vehicles were loaded, the giant ship began the ninety-minute crossing to Victoria. He got a cup of coffee from the onboard concession and found a table with a good window view. His mind drifted back to the day he'd met Cook at Walter Reed.

Cook had gazed at Bishop across the table that day and made him an offer he couldn't refuse. Cook wanted him to serve as an agent/operator in a new outfit. Bishop was flattered Cook had remembered him, but to be honest, Bishop had doubts. Was he ready to hang up his military career for a covert intel assignment? What Cook said next cinched the deal.

————

"You know, Captain Bishop, you wouldn't be leaving the military, or for that matter Delta."

"Huh?"

Cook leaned closer and lowered his voice. "You're still officially a Delta man. Just detailed to my new unit for the duration. I'm positive I could swing a promotion as well."

Bishop was always suspicious of people overpromising and underdelivering.

Cook stood, ready to depart the room. "Take some time to think it over, Captain. If you want to give it a go, sign up for a one-year, no-obligation tour. After that, you're free to return to your old unit." Cook rested both palms on the table before saying, "And I'll put that in writing, Major Bishop!"

————

General Cook was a persuasive man. Bishop thanked god he'd taken him up on the offer.

About a half hour into the ferry crossing, a man stopped beside him. Bishop had been watching the guy walking around since they'd departed. He looked lost or was trying to find someone, perhaps.

"Excuse me, but are you Troy Bishop?" the fellow asked, trying to mask an embarrassed grin.

Bishop eyed the stranger. "Yes."

"How do you do. I'm Inspector Edward Koner—RCMP." He flashed his identification.

Bishop had never met a member of the Royal Canadian Mounted Police, but from movies and travel videos, he'd almost expected a tall, broad-shouldered, dark-haired man in a red uniform with black riding boots. Inspector Koner didn't exactly fit the profile. Wispy, short, middle aged, with thinning hair, he wore small, wire-rimmed glasses that gave him a Heinrich Himmler look.

Bishop stood and shook the limp hand. "Nice to meet you—have a seat."

Inspector Koner sat and fidgeted with his jacket a moment. He extracted a customs declaration form from a small black notebook. "May I see your passport, please?"

"Sure."

The inspector examined Bishop's Diplomatic Passport and copied the name and number on the form. "Do you have anything to declare?"

"Excuse me?"

"For your visit." Koner tapped the form with his pen.

"Oh, no, nothing."

Koner passed the form to Bishop. "Sign and date at the bottom, please."

Bishop signed and handed the form back to the inspector.

Koner's face took on a very serious expression. "Mr. Bishop, we're aware it's highly irregular for intelligence officers to travel armed but forgive me for asking. Do you have a weapon?"

Bishop's head snapped up, "Me—armed?" He made a snorting sound while shaking his head. "No way. This is Canada." Bishop hoped Koner didn't insist on checking his bag.

Inspector Koner released a curious half smile, placed Bishop's passport and custom's form back into his notebook, and sat back. "So, who do you work for?"

Bishop studied the man—it was none of the RCMP's business. The Diplomatic Passport answered all the questions they needed. He started to give his usual cover story of being assigned to the 902nd Military Intelligence Group but decided against it. Instead, he leaned forward on the table separating the two, scanned both ways, and whispered, "I'm with the Defense Department."

Koner's dissatisfied countenance at his answer was laughable. He adjusted his glasses and cleared his throat. "That doesn't tell me much."

Bishop met his stare without blinking. "No, it doesn't."

Koner shifted in the seat. "Perhaps I could be of more help if I knew a little more about you, was my meaning."

This guy must be the densest RCMP on the force, or he didn't understand basic intelligence protocols. The one thing a friendly law enforcement official never asked a declared intelligence officer was whom he worked for or what his mission was. If he needed to know, he would have been told by his agency. No, this was just stupid, dangerous curiosity. *Never divulge unnecessary information.* Bishop decided not to satisfy his curiosity. "Inspector, were you instructed to inquire about me and my agency?"

Koner blushed. "No, I just thought—"

"Then I wouldn't be concerned if I were you."

Koner showed an embarrassed expression. "Yes, I see… I do see."

No, he didn't see—he was a jerk. Something about this guy's manner or demeanor turned Bishop off. He needed to get away from him for a while. "I think I'll hit the head before we dock." Bishop slid out of the seat.

Just before rounding the corner of the Purser's office, Bishop glanced back. Koner had his eyes trained in his direction. Leaving the restroom, Bishop strolled toward the open bow of the ship and stood beside the rail. Several other passengers milled around enjoying the sunshine and cool air. The views of the out-islands were spectacular. Rich, blue water, splashing on rocky shorelines, covered with dark green trees. A few minutes later the announcement came over the PA.

"All drivers report back to your vehicles. We'll be docking in ten minutes."

Bishop craned his neck to the right as the entrance to Victoria Harbor came into view. He made his way back to the table and found Koner working a newspaper crossword puzzle. Bishop had noticed it as he sat down earlier, no doubt left behind from a previous passenger. "Ready to go?" Bishop asked.

Koner looked up, neatly folded the paper, and laid it back on the seat, presumably for someone else to finish the puzzle later.

"Thought I'd lost you for a minute," Koner said.

"Needed some fresh air—the rocking of the boat, you know," Bishop lied, making a wave sign with his hand and holding his stomach.

"Of course, I understand," Koner answered in a way that meant he definitely didn't.

They sat in the SUV and waited for the ship to dock. Koner remained quiet, hands in lap, patiently watching the ferry pull into the Red Ball Terminal dock. They were one of the first to drive up to the customs checkpoint booth. The young woman manning it had dark features and wore a long-sleeved navy blue sweater with the Canadian Customs insignia on the left shoulder. Koner reached across Bishop and handed her his RCMP identification along with Bishop's passport and customs declaration.

"Inspector Koner—RCMP. I'm escorting this fellow."

She examined Koner's credentials, opened Bishop's passport, and extracted the form. She took a quick second look at him, stamped the passport, and returned it with Koner's identification. "Welcome to Canada," she mumbled, before waving at the next car in line.

Bishop felt sorry for the girl. In the military, people who worked fixed sentry posts in small buildings were known as "box creatures." The work was usually mind-numbing but required attention to detail and keen observation skills. From her dull eyes and lethargic manner, she needed a transfer.

"You can just drop me here at my car." Koner pointed to Bishop's left. There, under a sign that read *Police Vehicles Only*, sat an old silver Volvo.

Opening the passenger's door, Koner turned to Bishop and handed him back his passport and a business card. "If I or the RCMP can be of further assistance during your visit, please contact me directly."

Koner didn't offer his hand for a farewell shake. That suited Bishop just fine. The man gave him the creeps. "Thanks for your help, Inspector."

As Bishop drove up the short hill toward the main street, he glanced in his rear-view mirror. Koner had not gotten into his car. He stood looking toward Bishop's vehicle, writing in the black notebook.

Bishop sighed. "Well, that didn't go well." He dreaded his meeting with the Canadian Intelligence rep. If the RCMP were being jerks about his visit, there was no telling what the intelligence service guy would do. *Welcome to Canada—our neighbors to the north.*

He checked into the Coast Victoria Harbourside Hotel and Marina on Kingston Street. It had a small, well-appointed lobby, a quiet ambiance, and friendly staff. His room was on the fourth floor. Walking off the elevator, he counted the number of doors to each exit from his room. Good information to have in case he had to maneuver through a blacked-out hallway later. He tossed his bag on the king-size bed and threw the curtains back on the sliding glass door that led to the private balcony. Opening it, the sound of an engine revving greeted him, and he witnessed a seaplane taking off from the harbor below. His room overlooked the forty-two-boat slip marina. Water sloshed on the shoreline and several geese picked at something near the edge.

It was only two-thirty—he needed a workout. After stretching, fifty push-ups, and a hundred sit-ups, he looked forward to a long run. On the way out, he stopped at the desk, and they directed him to the walking path behind the hotel. It led downtown to the heart of Victoria. Bishop asked for a restaurant recommendation, and an assistant manager suggested Spinnaker's, across the harbor. They made him a reservation for seven.

He stood on the trail, adjusting the timer on his running watch, when a cold gust of wind hit his back. He turned, and a dark, rolling wall of clouds moved steadily southward. The smell of rain hung heavy in the cool air.

Something felt wrong. Bishop considered his surroundings, looking in all directions as an unsettling thought raced through his mind. *He was being watched.* On the battlefield, his sixth sense had saved him more than once—his men came to depend on it. That damn encounter with Inspector Koner must have rattled him.

Another gust of wind signaled time to get going or risk being rained out. He pushed the chronometer button and set off at a slow ten-minute warm-up pace. The flower gardens along the path and tranquil harbor waters relaxed him, and he extended his stride to his usual eight-minute mile. Sucking in cool air in Canada was ten times better than the hot humid air in DC.

———

The woman stood behind the drapes and focused the binoculars. From her perch on the seventh floor of Bishop's hotel, she watched him. He looked fit, and a determined resolve lined his face. So, he was the American intelligence officer sent to solve this. He must have been especially chosen for such a sensitive assignment. She wanted to know why and intended to find out.

<h1 style="text-align:center">SEVEN</h1>

Bishop ran till the trail ended in a maze of shops, restaurants, and other businesses surrounding the city harbor. The architecture of Victoria was more European than he'd remembered: a beautiful city with a mild summer climate, filled with tourists. He turned back toward his hotel, and a light mist brushed his face. The ominous clouds still marched toward the city from the north. By the time he made the cover of the hotel entrance, the mist had turned into a light, cold rain. The pleasant afternoon lost its appeal, and a steady northern wind chilled him.

He showered and let the hot water warm him up. Toweling dry, his phone rang. Maxwell again, and this time his voice sounded edgy.

"Are you in place?"

Bishop wrapped the towel around him and held the encrypted phone between his cheek and shoulder. "I'm in Victoria. When will the SIS make contact?"

"No idea. They know where you are—probably sometime tomorrow."

Bishop used his index finger and wiggled loose some water trapped in his ear. "Okay, guess I'll just wait."

"Keep us in the loop about any developments. It goes without saying the White House has requested daily briefings. If this virus ever gets loose on the mainland, we might not be able to contain it."

"Yes, sir—I'll keep you up to date."

"Take care, Bishop." The line went dead.

Bishop flopped into a comfortable chair and watched the local and international news before making any attempt at dressing. Rain dripped onto his balcony, and the sliding glass door fogged. It wasn't a good night to go out. He'd picked up the room phone with the intent of canceling his dinner reservations. He thought about it a second before setting the phone back into its cradle. His standing rule when traveling was never the hotel restaurant. There were always superior ones close if you took the time and trouble to look. He stared out the sliding glass door at the cold rain. *Sometimes it was more trouble than other times.*

He dressed in a warm black turtleneck sweater, British khaki dress pants, and a brown leather bomber jacket. He pulled the small, black case from his bag and laid it on the table. Sliding the clasps back, he opened it to reveal the .357 Sig Sauer pistol. He smiled, recalling Koner questioning him about being armed—he seldom traveled or worked without a weapon. All P2OG agent/operators carried their firearm of choice, and his was the Sig P229 Elite Dark. He tucked it snugly into the inside waistband holster and slid it to the small of his back. Few in the organization carried the title agent/operator. Those who did had the power of *ultimate discretion.*

Bishop never liked the word *assassin.* It had such a negative connotation. He instead preferred the term *enforcement officer.* Like in his Delta days, he was still a soldier against terrorism. When soldiers charged a bunker complex, they didn't stop to sort out who might or might not be trying to kill them inside the bunker. *Everyone in the bunker was trying to kill them.* Otherwise, they wouldn't be inside a bunker, pointing guns in their direction. Journalists, military scholars, and commentators could play around with semantics all day—they had that luxury. But when *you* were the *guy in the arena,* there was no time to think—thinking too much got you killed. You acted on instinct, muscle memory, and training. Yeah, he was vested with the power to kill if he deemed it necessary for national security. The fact he didn't have to clear it with headquarters was where the term *ulti-mate discretion* came in. He took the responsibility seriously. But in his mind, he was just a DoD investigator looking into national security matters.

When he walked into the bar off the lobby, he peered out the large window—a low fog had rolled in. He deliberated again about eating in the hotel restaurant and not going out in the lousy weather but decided against it. He drank a Glenlivet and watched the Blue Jays beat the Oakland A's on the TV over the bar.

"What's the best way to get across the harbor to Spinnaker's? Cab?" he asked the bartender.

The man turned his attention away from the closing seconds of the game. "Water taxi—leaves the back dock on the half hour." He motioned with head toward the marina.

Bishop checked his watch—6:25. He could just make it. He rushed out the rear of the building, blocking the wind and rain with an umbrella. As he walked down the hill, three passengers huddled under the dock light, also waiting for the taxi. A short older man, a taller middle-aged fellow, and a gorgeous young woman. The middle-aged man and woman shared a large umbrella, and even in the dim light of the dock, Bishop was smitten. He'd traveled the world and seen his share of beautiful women. Italy and Norway were tied as the best place to find beautiful women—but this one…

Through the foggy haze, the outline of a yellow and black-checkered water taxi approached the dock. The young woman laughed at something her escort said. A deep throated, sexy laugh, and she touched his shoulder in a way that indicated familiarity—lucky man. Bishop's timing was perfect. He reached the taxi just after the trio hopped aboard. They were the only passengers on this nasty evening. The rain peppered the boat's roof as they eased across the harbor.

Bishop sat at the back and kept watching the woman. She looked in her late twenties or early thirties—about fifteen years his junior. Her auburn hair was cut in a chin length bob, and her inquisitive eyes stayed fixed on her companion. She never gave Bishop a second look. The crossing was a little too short for him—he enjoyed watching her. A very pretty distraction on an otherwise ugly night.

Leaping onto the wooden dock after the trio offloaded, Bishop asked the water taxi operator, "Which way to Spinnaker's?"

The taxi man pointed toward his left. "About a hundred yards over there, along the water, and up the hill. You can't miss it."

Bishop kept the umbrella pointed in the direction of the blowing rain and turned left.

The two men shook hands with the woman before turning to the right along the wet path. She said, "A pleasure meeting you both," before also turning left.

Bishop had been wrong—she didn't know them. She used the hood on her dark gray, knee-length raincoat to cover her hair while struggling with an umbrella that refused to open. Well, of course, the gentlemanly thing would be to share his.

"Having trouble?"

He startled her, and she weaved off the concrete path onto the wet grass. She stared at him, still fighting the umbrella. "Just a little."

"You're welcome to share mine." He held it in her direction.

She considered the idea a second, then grinned. "Love to."

"We couldn't have picked a worse night," he said.

"Yes, it's a bad one. You a local?"

The smell of her perfume caused him to edge a little closer. "No, I'm from the States."

"Here on business or pleasure?" She picked up the pace a little.

"Business—and you?"

"I'm here on business, also."

The restaurant sat on the hill less than fifty yards away. Dare he ask her to dinner? Maybe she was dining alone—no harm in trying. "So, what do you do?"

She tilted her head in his direction. "I'm with the Canadian Security Intelligence Service, Mr. Bishop—sent here to work with you."

Bishop didn't get surprised often. Always applauded himself for being one or two steps ahead of the herd. But he'd just fallen for the oldest intelligence trick in the business. The CIA referred to it as the "Damsel in Distress Scenario." She kept walking in silence, a satisfied smirk crossing her lips. She could have led him on indefinitely. This little show of hers was just her way of introducing herself as a professional equal.

Bishop smiled and nodded. "Okay, you nailed me. Since I've already eaten out of your palm, perhaps you'd tell me your name."

She stopped, turned in his direction, and extended her hand. "I'm Gillian Hathaway."

Bishop shook the small hand. "I'm hungry. Will you join me for dinner?"

A sweet grin cracked her lips. "Thought you'd never ask." She grabbed his umbrella and led the way up the hill.

They were seated at a quiet table for two in a corner by a huge window overlooking the harbor. Because of the unpleasant night, the restaurant was only about half full. The quiet ambience and warmth of the place gave it a cozy, relaxed feel. The lights of Victoria sparkled across the water, and the soft sound of rain against the glass made for a romantic setting. They requested a bottle of Chardonnay, and both ordered fish.

"So, what's the SIS figured out?" Bishop asked.

She shrugged. "Not much. I requested a study of the possible areas the boat could have originated."

Bishop leaned forward. "And?"

"Potentially the search area could be huge, depending on probabilities. We've narrowed down a one-mile coastal area that looks most promising," she whispered. She reached in her purse and extracted a 5"x7" color copy of the coastline. "Based on wind and current conditions that night, our people give it an eighty-seven percent chance it originated from somewhere along here."

Her slender finger traced an area of coast between Gordon Head and Cordova Bay, highlighted by a yellow line transposed on the photo. Almost exactly the same area Lt. Gregory briefed him on earlier that day.

She looked up. "If we key on that first, then expand our search area out as needed, it'll give us our best chance."

Bishop studied the photo. He held it closer to the table candle and placed his index finger on the map. "What's this speck off the coast, here?"

Gillian pulled it closer, and her fingers brushed his. A wonderful sensation coursed through him.

"A private island," she said.

He tapped it. "It's within the target zone."

"Yeah, I haven't had a chance to check it out yet. Don't think we have to worry about it, though. Belongs to our resident billionaire. She lives there during the summer. Has a half dozen other homes around the world."

A dialog box under the island contained very small printing. Bishop squinted and leaned closer. *Picard Island*.

"Mind if I ask you a question?" she said.

He slid the photo back to her. "Go ahead."

Her eyes narrowed. "You work for the Department of Defense, right?"

"Correct."

"To be honest with you, we were a little surprised a DoD type showed up. We assumed CIA would run with this one."

Bishop took a sip of wine and leaned closer. He picked up another whiff of her perfume. He glanced around the area before whispering, "The division I work under maintains a close relationship with the Agency. Often, when an inquiry has a possible weapons of mass destruction component, they send it over to us."

"So, the virus being weaponized is what pulled you into this?"

"That and the terrorist threat."

Her lips pursed and she seemed to ponder the new information for a moment, then met his eyes. "Okay, I was instructed to ask."

He nodded. "It can be a little confusing with all the agencies having an intelligence arm." He'd told her more than he'd shared with Inspector Koner, but she had the need and deserved to know more. What he didn't tell her—what he could never tell anyone outside the organization—was that P2OG didn't officially exist. Even Congress didn't know that. She gazed out the window at the rain for a moment, apparently lost in thought, and then touched the cold glass. "Been working at DoD long?"

"Since I got out of the Army."

"Academy man, eh?" She motioned to the West Point ring on his finger.

He grinned. "Yeah, seems like a lifetime ago."

The waiter arrived with the fish and refilled the wine glasses.

"How long have you worked for the SIS?" he asked.

She scooped a piece of pasta and fish in her mouth, wiping her chin with the napkin, and held up a finger while she chewed and swallowed. "I spent four years in the Royal Canadian Navy – MARPAC, as an intelligence officer, before joining the SIS."

"MARPAC?"

A smile cracked the corners of her mouth. "We use almost as many acronyms as you do. It stands for Maritime Forces Pacific. It's located just to the west of Victoria, at the southern tip of Vancouver Island. I've worked at SIS for three years."

Bishop's stomach tightened. *My god, she's just a baby.* Only seven years of intelligence experience. He'd expected a seasoned agent, not a neophyte.

She set her fork down and took a sip of wine. "You make it to Iran or Afghanistan?"

"One of the first there."

"Which one?"

"Afghanistan, mid-September oh-one."

Her expression changed. "You kidding?"

"Nope, was already in Pakistan training with their military on 9/11. Got rushed straight to Afghanistan and wound up in the battle of Tora Bora. Did recon and targeted fire missions mostly."

"Which unit did you serve with?"

"Delta." He drained the last bit of wine from his glass. "Got wounded in early 2002 and transferred back stateside."

A sparkle in her eyes surprised him. She licked her lower lip and ran her finger around the top edge of her wine glass before looking into his eyes. "You a war hero, Bishop?"

He shook his head. "Not really—more like just a survivor."

She dropped her head a moment, then looked up. "I think we're going to get along fine." A sexy grin followed.

That look, plus the perfume, drove him crazy. Wasn't it enough she was one of the most beautiful women he'd ever seen? Now, her sexy, suggestive voice dripped of future pleasures.

The waiter returned and cleared the plates. Bishop helped her with her coat and felt the warmth of her body as he slipped it over her shoulders. The rain had slacked so they strolled back to the taxi dock. Heavy fog shrouded the nearby buildings and the hotel across the harbor.

"You want to walk part of that coastline tomorrow with me?" he asked.

She peered up into his eyes and a micro expression crossed her face, something not professional, but sensual. The face of a lover, filled with hunger and desire. "Most definitely—about eight for breakfast, and then off we go?"

"Sounds about right," he agreed.

When the sound of the water taxi broke through the heavy mist, she said, "I've set up an interview with someone tomorrow afternoon —I think you'll want to attend."

"What's it about?"

"Nothing much, except he knows how to weaponize smallpox and Ebola."

Bishop moved closer and whispered, "Sounds interesting. By the way, where are you staying?"

The taxi pulled alongside of the dock, and the man jumped out to assist her aboard. She stared back with that familiar girlish air. "I'm staying at your hotel—on the seventh floor."

EIGHT

Gillian slipped into her long Montreal Expos night shirt and stood in front of the bathroom mirror, taking off her makeup. She leaned closer and cleaned the last of the eyeliner before washing her face.

The night had gone better than she'd expected. Her plan to lure Bishop into asking her to dinner worked perfectly. Her mind drifted back to the last meeting she'd had with her section chief. He'd made it clear, since this was her biggest field assignment, that she'd be judged on her conduct in liaising with the Americans as well as her intelligence and operational skills. Since the FBI and RCMP had concluded their joint investigations and found nothing of interest, her primary assignment was to babysit the American from the Department of Defense. No one really expected much to come of it, but she saw it as a test of her operational skills. She'd show them she could handle the assignment. This was her first big chance to shine, and she wasn't going to screw it up.

Did Bishop have information the RCMP and FBI didn't? Something that might lead them to the source of the virus? If he did, he hadn't shared it tonight. He was much more experienced in intelligence operations than she. And serving in Afghanistan with Delta gave him credentials she couldn't question. She'd make note of everything he said and did. She could learn from someone like him.

She liked Bishop. His rugged good looks and square jaw was what she'd always looked for in a man. She might like him too much. Something about his quiet, unassuming nature and self-confidence excited her sexually. She wasn't prone to such things, but he flipped a switch she had forgotten she still had. She put it out of her mind. If she kept fantasizing about him, she would never get to sleep.

She finished washing her face and brushed her teeth. Bishop's image kept popping up in her mind. She slid into bed and turned off the lamp, but he was still there. Oh well—there were worse things she could think about before bedtime.

———

The next morning, Bishop strolled into the dining room and spied Gillian sitting by a window overlooking the marina, reading the morning paper. The sunshine outlined her profile.

"Morning." He slid into the chair across from her. "Sleep well?"

"Great." She handed him a map of the coastline they'd discussed the night before. "The area we'll search today is off Cordova Bay Road, along the Mt. Douglas Park beach."

The server arrived and filled Bishop's coffee cup while he looked over the map. "A park beach? Sounds an unlikely place a sick man would launch a boat from."

"I agree, but Picard Island is directly across from the park, about a half mile offshore. Since you inquired about it, we'll let you have a look before we expand our search area."

Bishop shrugged. "Okay."

After breakfast, they drove to the northern entrance of Douglas Park and hiked down to the beach. The tide was rolling out, and the trees seemed to back away from the water. Large boulders, pieces of driftwood, and tree trunks littered the shoreline. The dark blue water looked cold. Bishop had hated cold water since his special forces training days. It always seemed that, when they did water training, it was in the coldest water they could find.

But this was a nice morning for a walk. A cool wind still blew from the north, but brilliant sunshine flooded the pebbly beach, and the clean scent of rain lingered.

Gillian wore large sunglasses and a wide-brimmed straw hat, giving her a "Jackie O" look. The large green nylon bag she swung over her shoulder could have carried anything from a picnic lunch to a blanket for a lovers' tryst. They looked like any other couple out for a stroll.

After walking for ten minutes, Bishop cupped his hands and shaded his eyes. In the distance, the outline of a small island came into view. He pointed. "Is that it?"

"Uh-huh. Let's get a little closer so we can get a better look."

They walked a while longer, but Bishop realized this search of the beach was probably a waste of time. There wasn't a sign of anything out of the ordinary. He stopped and examined everything manmade along the shore, but nothing roused his suspicions. When the island was directly across from them, Gillian pointed to the wood line on the beach.

"Let's take a break over there."

They found an area with good views to the left and right. No one could surprise them without being observed well in advance. She straddled a log tucked into the edge of the woods. To Bishop's surprise, she pulled a mini telescope from the huge bag. She balanced it against the tree's trunk and focused it toward Picard Island while Bishop downed several swallows of water.

"Nothing much to look at, if you ask me." She handed him the scope.

He trained it toward the clump of dark green trees that seemed to grow out of the middle of the ocean. The island was small—about five acres. The shoreline had large rocks strewn about like obstacles set up to deny an amphibious assault. The land rose from the water's edge at a 45-degree angle through the thick woods. On top, the large two-story white house with open second-floor balconies and oversized windows enjoyed a commanding view of Victoria Bay.

"Looks quiet enough," he said.

"I contacted our intelligence analyst earlier this morning and requested they do a full workup on the place. Like I said, the woman who lives there is probably the least of our worries." Gillian uncapped a water bottle and sipped a few swallows before licking her lips. "Ready to go?"

Under ordinary circumstances, Bishop would have remarked how good she looked. The tight-fitting designer jeans and white body-hugging sweater gave her an appeal any man would notice. These weren't ordinary circumstances, but he still had a strong attraction to her. He handed her back the scope. "Yeah, let's go."

They strolled to the end of the search zone and found nothing. They did get a better look at the south side of Picard Island. Bishop hid behind a fir tree leaning out over the water and adjusted the scope. He could just make out a dock and a white yacht with powder blue trim. It stood three decks tall—looked like 200-footer. The walk back to their car gave him the chance to reexamine every yard of beach and tree line. He fully satisfied himself there wasn't anything there. Expanding the search area would take time and extra resources. They'd need boats and aircraft to fully cover it—Cook wouldn't be happy to hear that.

A nagging doubt hung back in his mind. The idea that Gillian might not know what she was doing worried him. She was a beauty and a nice enough girl, but with her lack of experience, maybe she wasn't right for this assignment. He put the notion aside for the moment. *Give her a chance*, he told himself.

She drove them to a sandwich shop, and they ate an early lunch of fish tacos. They lingered until noon before she made the call.

"Hello, Dr. Belousov—this is Gillian Hathaway. I called a couple of days ago, and you said you would see me." She paused a moment and listened. "Yes, I'm bringing an associate, if that's okay." She glanced at Bishop and winked. "Okay, we'll be there in less than an hour. What? Sure, what do you need?" She furrowed her brow, then looked at Bishop, shaking her head. "Fine, we'll see you in a bit. Thanks."

"Who's this Belousov guy?" he asked.

She headed for the door, searching in the bag for her sunglasses. "Dr. Viktor Belousov was a virologist in the old Soviet Union. When the wall fell and he discovered he had no job or retirement, he shopped the West to see if anyone wanted his talents. A Canadian company hired him to do pharmaceutical research before we realized his full involvement in the old Soviet bioweapons program. We've been picking his brain ever since. He's one of the last great bioweaponeers."

Bishop relaxed in the passenger seat while Gillian drove west on Highway 14 toward the small community of Sooke. In less than thirty minutes, they were enveloped in the dense evergreen forest with its moss and ferns. Heavy clouds rolled above, making it darker than usual for early afternoon. On the right a large, old-English home rested at the road's edge. A sign hung from the porch—*17 Mile House Pub*. Gillian swung off the road and stopped at a liquor store across the parking lot from the pub.

"Be right back," she grumbled, leaving Bishop wondering what she was up to.

A few minutes later she emerged, brown bag in hand, and hopped back into the car. Bishop slid the bottle of Canadian Mist whiskey out of the bag. "Plan on loosening his tongue, or is this for the party later?"

She pulled back onto the highway before answering. "He requested I pick it up—couldn't hurt if it loosens his tongue."

About two miles deeper into the darkening forest, she turned left down a loose gravel road and followed it to a clearing near the water. There stood a shabby log home with a circular drive and a great view of Sooke Basin in the rear. Overgrown shrubs surrounded the entrance, and the screens and shutters were in need of repair. Bishop got out and stretched, gazing at the vast blue water behind the cabin. "The view is worth more than the house." He followed Gillian to the front door.

"I've only met him once," she whispered, "two years ago for a debrief."

She shifted the bottle of whiskey to her left hand and knocked on the ancient wooden door. Moments later, the thing creaked open and the old man stood at the threshold.

She extended her hand. "Dr. Belousov, I'm Gillian Hathaway—we met a couple of years ago."

"Ah, yes, I recall the meeting."

"This is my associate, Troy Bishop."

The man stared deep into Bishop's eyes before extending his hand. "Happy to meet you. Please come in."

Bishop shook the hand—it was cold and dry. The man's voice had a deep, gravelly sound, like a sports announcer's, the Russian accent still strong. His thinning grey hair and ample gut put him in his seventies. He wasn't tall, and a slight stoop made him seem even shorter. They followed him while he shuffled down the dark, musty hallway. The smell of stale cigarette smoke hung heavy in the air. He led them to a rear living area where filtered light cracked through half-closed drapes. A table lamp lit the gloomy room.

"Please take a seat." He dropped into an ancient recliner near the back wall. Books and out-of-date magazines lay everywhere. The floor, sofa, and bookshelves were strewn with them.

"Just clear off a place," he ordered with a wave of his hand before running his fingers through his hair and exhaling.

She passed him the brown bag. "I hope this is okay."

He pulled the bottle out and his eyes widened. "Excellent, yes, most excellent."

Bishop pushed a stack of books out of the way, and Gillian joined him on the sofa.

Belousov grabbed a glass from a TV tray beside his recliner. He blew into it, but it didn't dislodge the dark residue inside. The old man greedily opened the bottle and filled the dirty glass. When it was halfway to his lips, he apparently remembered his manners. "Would you care for some?"

Bishop and Gillian shook their heads. "No thank you," she said.

A curious grin shadowed the old Russian's lips. "Cheers."

He downed half the whiskey in one gulp, took a deep breath, and relaxed back into the recliner. "So, how may I assist the Security Intelligence Service today?"

Gillian leaned forward, placing her elbows on her knees. "We issued you a clearance years ago—I ask that you recall the penalty if you violate it, because I'm sharing some information with you that's classified."

He raked a loose strand of hair back into place, and his bloodshot eyes focused on her. "I understand."

She briefed him on the dying man in the boat and USAMRIID's assessment of the synthetic biological pathogen. His expression darkened as he finished off the whiskey in the glass and poured another. When she finished, she clasped her hands together. "So, what do you think?"

He took a long, raspy breath and reached for a half-smoked cigarette lying on the TV tray. He lit it and stared straight ahead for a moment. "Someone finally did it." He ran his hand over his huge face.

"Did what?" she asked.

He pulled heavy on the cigarette, not answering. His mind seemed to be calculating a problem from the past. Only the sound of a clock ticking too loudly on the mantel broke the eerie silence.

Finally, he turned and spoke. "We always assumed it was possible to combine Ebola and hemorrhagic smallpox, but we could never figure it out. I mean, the problems were insurmountable." He pointed the cigarette at them. "Are either of you scientists?"

They shook their heads.

"Then you can't imagine the effort it took, combining these two pathogens into a weaponized form. Sit back and relax, and I'll tell you how the Soviet Union planned on killing everyone in the United States."

———

Bishop always had a personal prejudice against defectors, informants, and the like. Successful intelligence gathering counted heavily on them, but he kept his suspicions. Too many times they'd proved untrustworthy, or worse, downright wrong, or even double agents. Motivation was the factor that he looked for. Why did they suddenly decide to betray their country or way of life to help him and the United States? Few had altruistic motives. It usually came down to money.

What did this old man have to lose or gain by talking to them? His Canadian citizenship? Was SIS providing him a monthly stipend? Did they have the power to pull the money plug or deport him? Without knowing more about him, Bishop couldn't tell. He listened closely. Sometimes people gave things away without realizing it.

Belousov held his cigarette with thumb and index finger. The long ash dropped unnoticed onto his lap.

"I graduated from medical school in 1973. The government paid for my education, so I worked where they told me. I reported to a new agency—*Biopreparat*—under the Fifteenth Soviet Directorate. I worked with BSL-4 viruses in an effort to determine their usefulness as biological weapons." He paused and took a slow drink of whiskey. "In 1980, another scientist and I were sent to a secret city that appeared on no map. We traveled to Kazakhstan. We were to supervise construction of a giant bio-weapons facility—Stepnogorsk."

When Belousov spoke the name, he winced. The old Russian sipped the whiskey again and paused, apparently refocusing his thoughts. He noticed the ash on his pants and brushed it off. He dropped the smoldering filter into the ash tray and sighed.

"I assumed my assignment there would end after the construction phase had been completed." He took a ragged, deep breath. "But I never left." His voice contained a note of sadness. "That same year, the World Health Organization declared smallpox eradicated. Because of that declaration, the next year we targeted it for enhanced weaponization."

The mood in the small cabin became solemn. A coldness seeped in that Bishop hadn't noticed before. Only the sound of the ticking clock interrupted the long, loud silence. Bishop noticed Gillian edge closer; she hadn't taken her eyes off the old scientist.

She leaned forward. "Doctor, do you know why they chose it?"

He released a sheepish grin. "The perfect choice for the time. There is no doubt smallpox is the deadliest disease in human history. Over 500 million people died from it. Most of the US population born after 1972 has never been vaccinated. The rest were inoculated over sixty years ago. The vaccine loses its effectiveness after five to ten years." He covered his mouth, and a long coughing spell took hold. He wiped his lips with his shirt sleeve and turned back to her. "An unprotected population has no chance against such a virus."

Gillian jumped and grabbed Bishop's arm. He looked down in time to see something orange and furry running on the floor under her legs. Her startled movement scared the large cat and it jumped into Belousov's lap. He laughed and pulled the creature closer.

"Don't mind Avery—he's harmless. Now where was I? Oh, yes, we chose the India-1 strain of smallpox for development because it was especially lethal—the one most likely to go hemorrhagic. Exceedingly virulent—possibly vaccine resistant and the most contagious. We produced over 100 metric tons capable of being loaded into ICBMs in the event of war."

None of the history of the Soviet bioweapons program was news to Bishop. He'd received full briefings on it years earlier. They'd signed and ratified the 1972 Biological Convention Treaty to reject such weapons. Then they sped up research and production on the very things they'd promised to eliminate. It spoke volumes about the sinister nature of their government. The term "evil empire" popped into his head.

He spoke up. "It appears the India-1 strain is what we're dealing with in this new engineered virus."

Belousov gazed down at Avery and stroked the cat's head, his grim expression almost an apology for his part in researching such a horrible thing.

"Dr. Belousov, you mentioned you also worked on Ebola as a weapon," Gillian said, apparently trying to restart the conversation.

The Russian pulled himself out of his malaise and glanced her way. "Yes, that's correct. The Soviet secret code for smallpox was N1; Ebola was N2. We used them in all notes and correspondence in case our communications should be compromised."

She directed a confused gaze at him. "But if they already had a powerful smallpox weapon, why develop Ebola?"

He poured another half glass of whiskey but did not drink. He turned to her and shook his head. "They were mad. Hemorrhagic smallpox produces ninety percent mortality—they wanted a hundred percent. They selected Ebola Zaire for weaponization. In nature, it can't pass from person to person through the air, but only through direct contact with bodily fluids. But in 1990 we discovered a more effective way of reducing the particle size. We could then deliver it in an aerosolized powder that would disperse in the wind. We stabilized it so well we could infect people miles away after they breathed a few invisible particles."

As if he'd heard enough, Avery jumped off Belousov's lap and vanished behind a stack of books on the cluttered floor. The old man must have taken this as a signal and downed another long swallow of whiskey. He stared morosely at Bishop before continuing.

"Ebola's biological weapon effectiveness is diminished by its rapid lethality. Victims die before they can effectively spread the disease." He waved his hand in a matter-of-fact way. "We needed to improve it into a true weapons-grade virus."

"Have any success?" Bishop asked.

Belousov shook his head. "The problem was always the RNA and DNA. Ebola is an RNA virus, while smallpox is a DNA. Combining these two very different pathogens stumped us. We tried wrapping the most infectious DNA parts of smallpox around Ebola's RNA to make it more deadly but failed. They both serve as genetic blueprints but react with different chemical properties."

"Well, somebody did it," Bishop remarked.

Belousov downed the rest of the glass and reached for another cigarette, appeared to think better of it, and pushed it aside. "Yes, well, since my days at Stepnogorsk, much progress has been made. We broke the human genome, and that opened a whole new world for researchers. We know ten times more about DNA and RNA than we did in those dark days."

Gillian shivered and folded her arms across her chest, rubbing them. Bishop wasn't sure if it had been Belousov's revelations or the temperature, but the cabin was freezing.

"Do you know who might be behind the development of such a pathogen?" Bishop meant it as a question, but it came out more like an accusation.

"There were dozens of people on the research team. Any one of them, with today's technology, is capable of such a thing." The old man's accent became more pronounced with each drink, and his words slurred.

"Even you, Doctor?" Bishop asked, fixing his stare on Belousov.

Belousov's expression changed to one of confrontation as he eyed Bishop. "Yes, even me, Mr. Bishop."

Gillian placed her hand on Bishop's leg, signaling him to relax, while he returned Belousov's icy stare. Bishop believed his basic story, but Belousov knew something he wasn't telling.

"Doctor, when you moved to Canada, you worked for a pharmaceutical lab—refresh my memory," she said.

Belousov regarded her with hollow eyes. The stress of the interview showed in his crinkled brow, and a bead of sweat ran down his neck.

"I worked for Alo Vita Labs from 1992 until I retired early last year. They wanted to develop a vaccine for Ebola. My team and I worked the problem for over a decade before coming up with the best solution. It's been tied up in the FDA's red tape ever since. It could be deployed tomorrow for sale in Europe and the rest of the world, but the company wanted FDA approval before rolling it out. Something to do with marketing, I suppose." He shrugged.

He smirked, perhaps recalling something associated with the research, and then went into another uncontrolled coughing fit, and his face turned a deep red. He grabbed the empty glass—spitting into it.

"Is there anything else? I'm not feeling well these days," Belousov asked.

Gillian eyed Bishop and he shook his head. "That should do it for now, Doctor. Thank you for seeing us," she said. They stood, but Belousov remained seated, the cordial atmosphere gone.

Outside, the day had darkened with a thick cloud cover. The wind blew traces of light mist through the tall, swaying trees surrounding the cabin. It *was* much colder.

She opened the driver's door. "You were pretty rough on the old boy."

Bishop stared at the sky and trees a second. "Just wanted to see his reaction. He knows something he's not sharing. What's the name of that company he worked for, again?"

Bishop dropped into the passenger seat, and Gillian cranked the engine. She switched on the lights, and they illuminated the cloud of heavy mist surrounding them.

"It's called Alo Vita. Means *nourish life* in Latin."

"How do you know?"

She slammed the vehicle into drive. "Simple—I speak Latin. Oh, by the way, the person who owns Alo Vita Labs also owns Picard Island: Claudine Mercier."

He grinned. "Well, isn't that interesting."

Gillian turned right onto the main road heading back toward Victoria. "So where do we go from here?" She switched on the windshield wipers. The afternoon became darker, and more clouds enveloped them in the rainy gloom of the narrow, tree-lined road.

He studied the gathering storm. "Not much else we can do in this weather."

From the side mirror, a Land Rover pulling out from a hidden drive caught his attention. It didn't turn on its lights. They came to a hill and another car passed them going the opposite direction. It blinked its lights at the Land Rover to alert them theirs weren't on. It ignored the hint and moved closer behind Bishop and Gillian's car.

"What's that guy's problem?" Gillian mumbled, turning on the defogger. "Why's he blinking his lights at us?" She glanced into the rear mirror. "Or is it that guy behind us they were blinking at?"

Bishop kept his attention on the side mirror. He hadn't taken his eyes off the vehicle. Only one person, a driver, but he wasn't sure if it was male or female. Why weren't they turning on their lights? Gillian slowed down at a curve, and the Land Rover did the same—keeping the exact distance between the two cars. At some point it had to stop being a coincidence.

Light, cold rain splattered the windshield, and Gillian used a napkin to wipe the fog off before switching on the defroster. She must have noticed him entranced in the side mirror. "What on earth are you looking at?"

"That SUV behind us, what are the chances they don't realize their lights aren't on?"

She glanced at the rear mirror again. "How long have they been there?"

"Since we pulled out of Belousov's drive."

Her eyes widened. "Are they following us?"

He didn't answer—the vehicle held his full concentration.

"What do you think?" she whispered.

"Do you have a gun?"

"A gun? No!"

She must have seen his look of concern. "What do we do?"

He reached back and touched the Sig Sauer pistol in his waistband. He'd never mentioned he carried a weapon. "We'll keep driving for now."

Bishop's mind raced to come up with a plan. They were in the middle of nowhere, being followed by at least one person, and only had a single weapon. He needed an edge of some kind. Just then, the road curved and the edge he'd been hoping for came into focus. On the left appeared the 17 Mile House Pub and the liquor store they'd stopped at on the way to Belousov's. The parking lot between the two was well lit and half full of cars. If they kept driving, there wasn't anything else for miles except a dark forest and lonely country road.

He pointed toward the parking lot. "Turn in here at the first entrance, wheel around the cars in back, and park at the front of the pub near the road."

Gillian braked and made the left turn. The vehicle followed, closing the distance. She came to a stop, and the Land Rover parked directly behind them. At this point it turned on its headlights. They blinded any attempt to see what might be going on inside the vehicle.

Bishop immediately felt exposed—lit up like a Christmas tree. He grabbed the door handle. "Keep the motor running, don't put it in park, and get ready to hightail it at the first sign of trouble."

NINE

Stewart Anderson hated the thought of talking to her, so he put it off as long as he could before knocking on the study door. There was no answer, so he knocked louder.

"Come in," Mercier shouted.

He slipped just inside the door and heard her speaking in low tones but couldn't understand what she was saying. She sat behind the dark wooden desk with her back to him in the executive leather chair, a phone at her ear. She ended the conversation and turned.

"What is it?" she demanded.

Anderson stepped further inside and closed the door. He approached her desk and took a breath. "It's what I feared. Someone from US Intelligence is snooping around Victoria."

She glanced down, apparently in thought. "Which agency?"

"The Department of Defense." He waited for the follow-up question.

Her eyes narrowed. "That doesn't tell me a damn thing."

"I know, but that's all we have so far. Also, the Canadian Security Intelligence Service is involved."

Mercier's eyes showed a faraway gaze before asking, "What do you recommend?"

"Nothing at this point. We're not under any direct suspicion right now. We should wait and see what happens. Any preemptive strike could draw unwanted attention our way."

She seemed to consider the idea for a moment. "All right, but have a fallback plan if they get too close. Nothing must interfere with my timetable. If they even blink in our direction, get rid of them."

"Yes, ma'am."

"That's all." She again reached for the phone.

"Yes, ma'am," Stewart acknowledged, backing toward the door. It had gone easier than he'd expected—she must be having a good day. He still had to wonder about her timetable. Timetable for what?

———

Gillian's lips thinned and her expression said what Bishop thought—this might just end bad. When he slid from the passenger seat, the driver's door of the mysterious SUV behind them opened, and the interior lights revealed a tall man in his late 50s or early 60s. He turned off his headlights, giving both Gillian and Bishop a clearer picture of his features. A chilled, light rain still peppered down in the dark parking lot.

Bishop had good cover with the back of Gillian's car between him and the tall stranger. Bishop's hand dropped, easing the pistol from its holster behind his back. Only the single man exited the vehicle. Both his hands were visible—no weapon. That meant Bishop had the first shot if…

"Nigel, you son of a bitch, you scared the hell out of us!" Gillian was out of the car and making a beeline for the stranger. The man smiled and opened his arms in a welcoming gesture.

Bishop jerked his head in her direction, keeping the gun out of sight for the moment. "You know this guy?"

She ignored him, smiled sweetly, and strode to the man, giving him a hug. Then she pushed him back hard in the chest with both hands. She poked him in the sternum. "If you ever do something like that again, I'll kick your ass."

The man released an apologetic look and spoke with a British accent. "I believe you would, dear."

Gillian turned to Bishop, "We can relax now—Her Majesty's Secret Service is here. Troy Bishop, meet Nigel Goodwin from MI6."

Bishop slipped the hidden Sig Sauer back into its holster and strolled over to the man. Nigel appeared to notice Bishop's attempt at keeping the gun out of sight but didn't say anything. The Brit extended his hand. "Terribly sorry if I gave you a fright—just trying to have a bit of fun with the old girl." He winked at Gillian. "Are you a… friend of hers?"

Gillian interrupted. "Mr. Bishop is working on something with me —he's with the US DoD."

A knowing expression lined Nigel's face as he and Bishop shook hands. He stood a little over six feet—about Bishop's height—well-groomed black hair with traces of gray at the temples, and a few extra pounds around the middle. He had the look of an academic.

"Let's get out of this infernal rain and have a pint—my treat for behaving so badly," Nigel said. He ducked back into the Land Rover and pulled out a tweed Irish-style hat and white overcoat. Slipping them on, he waved his hand toward the ivy-covered pub entrance. "Shall we?"

Bishop and Gillian followed. She probably read his mind because she mumbled, "He can't help himself—he's English."

The pub had a *Cheers* feel: a local hangout with an established group of regulars and a few tourists sprinkled around. Nigel ambled up to the female bartender with his hat cocked to one side and pulled low on his brow and his white overcoat draped on his shoulders.

"Beastly weather we're having this evening. Could you fix us up with a table with some privacy?" He smiled and slid a bill across the bar.

She dropped her towel on top of it. "Sure thing, mister." She turned to a short, skinny man behind her. "Hey, Sam, seat these folks at the table in the back."

Sam motioned to them, and they followed. Nigel smiled at the bartender, tossing her a "Thanks, love" as she slid the towel and bill out of sight.

The round, wooden table sat in a quiet nook at the back of the place, so ancient it looked like it had been born there. Four comfortable chairs with red leather seats surrounded it. Nigel shook the rain off his coat and ordered pints of ale for everyone.

After the waiter left, Gillian asked, "Nigel, what brings you out here? I didn't receive any notification."

Bishop recognized this remark for what it was—a rebuke. Protocol demanded that allied intelligence services notify each other, and get permission, when they wished to operate on the other's turf. That's why Bishop's arrival in Victoria had been so carefully scripted. That's how Gillian knew she'd be working with him and which hotel he was staying in.

Nigel dismissed the reprimand with a hand wave. "No time for proper notification—that'll come later. They rushed me out here. Afraid we must beg forgiveness on that count."

She leaned forward on the table. "Don't tell me you were just in the neighborhood."

Nigel glanced around and lowered his voice. "Hardly—this is as official as it gets. We're looking into this dreadful pathogen business. Thought I'd drop by Belousov's for a chat when I saw headlights pulling out of his private drive. I didn't know who it might be, so I followed—turned out it was you."

The waiter returned with three pints and set them on the table. Nigel gave him a couple of bills as he flashed a full, toothy smile. "Don't let us go dry back here."

"So what's MI6's connection with this?" Bishop asked.

Nigel raked fingers through his damp hair and took a long swallow of ale before answering. "We intercepted traffic from Mainland China indicating their interest in this affair." He took another long drink and let the last statement sink in.

Gillian leaned a little closer. "What does China have to do with it?"

Nigel dabbed his mouth with a paper napkin. "Let's say for the sake of argument that we have a source who told us they might be involved. Would that be a large enough ante for MI6 to get into this game?"

Gillian turned to Bishop, and he nodded. She grinned. "Yeah, that'll get you in."

A loud cheer went up from the main bar area around the TV. Someone had just hit an outside-the-park home run.

Nigel rocked back. "We don't know any details yet, but we have suspicions Claudine Mercier is somehow involved."

"The person who owns Picard Island?" Bishop asked.

"Yes, big corporate type. Runs a pharmaceutical company," Nigel said.

Bishop and Gillian turned and stared each other. Nigel looked from one to the other. No one said a word.

His eyes pinched. "What?"

"And you wanted to talk to Belousov because he was a bioweapons expert and worked for her at Alo Vita Labs," Bishop said.

"Exactly," Nigel exclaimed. "But how did you…" A confused expression spread across his face. "Ah, yes, I see. You two haven't exactly been sitting on your hands."

"We scoped out Picard Island earlier today from the mainland," Bishop said.

"Interesting." Nigel shifted in the chair and whispered, "I'm afraid I'm also here running interference for the royal family. Damn bunch can't stay out of their own way these days."

"How are they involved?" Gillian asked.

"Claudine Mercier was once married to the younger brother of the Queen Consort's ex-husband. He died several years ago under mysterious circumstances—inconclusive autopsy, that sort of thing."

Gillian asked, "*The* Queen Consort—who's married to the British monarch? You've got to be shitting me."

Nigel flashed an embarrassed grin. "One and the same, I'm afraid. Claudine was a brilliant medical researcher before meeting him. After his death, she took over running his company, evidently got bored, and returned to supervising research. Had a bit of bad luck in the lab— somehow became infected with a pathogen she was working with and almost died. Old thing's face suffered terrible scarring from a flesh-eating bacterium. Hardly goes out anymore—became a recluse. Anyway, she's back running the company."

Gillian took a swallow. "So how does she fit in?"

"That's the trouble; we don't know. Our source indicates she'd been in communication with the Chinese Ministry of State Security. Something about biologicals. Possibly it's a legitimate state contract for some drug her lab produces. She has a production facility in mainland China, but any contacts with Chinese state security types are suspicious."

Gillian set her pint on the table. "You said her last name was Mercier."

Nigel finished his ale and slammed the empty glass on the table loud enough to be heard over the TV. "Yes, changed it back to her maiden name after her husband's death. If she's involved, I must notify London immediately so they can start damage control before it hits the press. The royals don't need another embarrassment."

The waiter arrived with three new ales and collected the empty glasses. Bishop waited until he left, then spoke in low tones.

"Sounds like we should take a closer look at Picard Island tomorrow."

Nigel perked up. "Mind if I tag along? I'll furnish the boat."

Gillian glanced Bishop's way and he shrugged. Turning back to Nigel, she said, "Okay, you bring the boat. Where are you staying?"

He raked a loose hair back into place. "At the Empress, of course. Only decent English hotel in the city."

Gillian made a low whistle sound. "Look at you. I don't recall you being so extravagant while on an expense account."

Nigel took a slow sip of his new ale. "I have a confession. This is my last assignment. I've put in my papers. Retiring after forty years in the service next month."

She smirked. "How will the Empire survive?"

"Don't know, but Meg and I will live out our years in Wales. Inherited an old cottage there a few years back—been fixing it up as we can afford to."

"Congratulations, Nigel," Gillian said.

It was hard keeping these two on task. Bishop leaned toward Nigel. "Back to our trip tomorrow—any chance of landing and taking a look around the island?"

Nigel's brow wrinkled, and he shook his head. "I shouldn't think so. My sources say she maintains excellent security on the place. Employs one of our former Special Boat Service types as her head of security. Nasty bugger—Stewart Anderson. We'd better stay on the water for this outing."

This wasn't the way Bishop worked. Dancing around a problem only made it worse and wasted time. Nigel seemed like a nice enough guy but wasn't prone to rush. Too much was at stake to waste time. Bishop suspected he'd have to figure a way to light a fire under him.

They finished their drinks while Gillian and Nigel caught up on intelligence service gossip. Bishop spent the time thinking. He needed to get on that island, but he wasn't sure how. Neither of his partners saw any urgency. If China was involved, that changed things. He needed to push *both* of them harder—but as a guest in Canada, he could only play by their rules.

TEN

Bishop was frustrated. After his shower that morning, he lay on the bed with a towel wrapped around his waist, fingers interlaced behind his head, and stared at the ceiling. It still bothered him about the lackadaisical way Nigel and Gillian approached the operation. Nigel understood he was on his last assignment and wasn't in any hurry for it to end. He seemed to relish the idea of doing things at a pace that made Bishop's teeth itch. Gillian had offered no objection last night when Nigel insisted on treating them to a curry buffet lunch at the Empress Hotel today. Bishop checked his watch—ten o'clock. Another hour and a half to waste. He'd risen early, done his floor exercises, and gone for a five-mile run, but was still restless. This seemed more like a vacation than a serious assignment.

The ringing of the secure phone drew him out of his malaise. He scrambled to get it by the third ring.

"How goes it?"

It was General Cook. Bishop filled him in on all the details they'd learned so far about Mercier and China.

"Is your phone set for encryption?" Cook asked.

Bishop glanced at the screen, which showed the letter zero with a red slash mark through it. "Yes, sir—we're good on this end."

A long pause ensued. Only the sound of rustling papers on Cook's end broke the silence. He spoke again. "I just received a call from Dr. Fletcher at USAMRIID—it's worse than we thought."

"How could it possibly be worse?"

"Dr. Fletcher's team's been conducting tests on the pathogen sample they found on the man's clothing. According to her, the stuff's been encapsulated in a cocoon or spore-like coating."

Bishop wasn't following Cook's line of thinking. "So?"

"So, Dr. Fletcher believes it will make the pathogen less likely to degrade in the environment and make decon a real bitch."

The revelation hit Bishop like a slap in the face. Of course—if someone designed the most lethal disease in history, it would only make sense to protect it against the elements. His mind drifted back to a briefing he'd received years earlier from the CIA. Most pathogens quickly degrade when exposed to the natural environment. UV rays and other weather conditions render most bacteria and all viruses inert over time. The exception was anthrax: because it produced spores, it was naturally encapsulated and protected from the environment. That was why it was so dangerous. It could dwell in the ground for decades before being inhaled and starting its life cycle over again.

"General, whoever made this stuff did it in a well-equipped lab with unlimited resources."

"That's the last thing Dr. Fletcher said," Cook responded.

Bishop recalled another thing from that briefing. Any country big enough to have a bio-medical plant could produce lethal biological agents—the list was endless.

"This Alo Vita Labs sounds interesting, if you ask me," Cook grumbled. "Do you have any background information on it, or that Mercier woman?"

"Yes, sir. The Canadian SIS are doing a full workup on them. I should get a briefing on the results in a couple of hours."

"Good. We'll also work up something on our end. I want any updates when you get them. If I have to work on a Saturday instead of improving my golf swing—I want something to show for it."

"Yes, sir."

"You need anything out there?"

"A good satellite shot of Picard Island would help."

Cook didn't immediately answer, but the sound of typing drifted over the line.

"You may be in luck. Looks like we have a bird tracking that sector later today. I'll shoot a call to NRO and see what they can manage."

"Thanks, General." Cook made it sound so easy. The truth was, getting the National Reconnaissance Office to track something usually took days and a stack of paperwork. It spoke volumes about Cook's clout that he could just "shoot them a call" and get a tasking in a matter of hours.

"Okay, stay in touch," Cook said.

The line went dead, and Bishop looked out his window at Victoria's Inner Harbor. Just then, a bright red cigarette boat sporting a white stripe raced past his window going about five times the speed allowed inside the protected waterway. Bishop squinted against the bright glare at the boat's driver. *Oh, no. Nigel.*

An hour later, Bishop stopped by Gillian's room and suggested they walk to the Empress Hotel. It was a beautiful day—clear skies, plenty of sunshine, and warmer temperatures. She embraced the idea, and they set out on the same Inner Harbor trail he jogged. Gillian wore a pale green strapless sundress and her large straw hat. She looked great, as usual.

"Find out anything more about Claudine Mercier or Alo Vita Labs?" he asked.

She dug in her oversize bag for something and mumbled, "Not much. Looks like Nigel was spot on about her, though. Everything I got backs up what he told us last night." Finally, she fished the 'Jackie O' sunglasses from her bag and slipped them on. "By the way, the RCMP and military are coordinating a coastline search, so we're allowed to just concentrate on Picard Island."

She popped a mint in her mouth. "One thing of interest in the report—the RCMP and the FBI already went to the island and interviewed that Stewart Anderson fellow."

Bishop slowed his pace. "Did they search the island?"

"Nope—just talked to Anderson and left."

He frowned.

"So, what do you think?"

"I think without a search we'll never know for sure."

"You mean a covert search, right?"

Bishop looked around to make sure they were out of earshot. "If we ask permission and they stall long enough to hide something, what good have we done?"

She didn't answer for a while as they kept walking, but it was clear he'd given her something to think about. She turned to him. "Getting the okay from my people might be a little tricky, but I'll do what I can."

"You guys have an excellent anti-terrorist black-op group. JTF2 could go in, take a look around, and get out without anyone being the wiser."

Gillian said, "I'll make a call."

The morning walk couldn't have been better. Victoria was awash in color. Potted flowers and vines hanging from every lamppost eased the transition from concrete to nature. The red snake trees and other sculpted shrubs led them to the entrance of the Boston-ivy-covered Empress Hotel. They strolled past the front desk and found the Bengal Lounge.

The hotel reminded Bishop of an old English museum. He hadn't visited the place in years, but little had changed. It remained airy and spacious, with antique fans slowly turning from the high ceilings. A pair of black marble elephants guarded each side of the entrance to the Indian themed lounge. The safari decor inside gave it a private English club ambience.

Nigel reclined against a couple of large pillows on a soft leather couch with a view of the Inner Harbor. He sipped his drink while flirting with a woman half his age at the next table. He laughed and said, "Good show," a little too loud, which drew a few disapproving looks from the early lunch crowd. Bishop and Gillian weaved their way through the tables toward him. He spotted them and attempted to rise but found himself too enveloped in the deep sofa.

"What will you two have?" He motioned for the waiter with his free hand.

Gillian ordered the Original Bengal Tiger and Bishop a Bombay Sapphire Tonic.

Nigel held up his glass. "Another Grey Goose martini, Bixby."

The smell of the curry buffet attacked Bishop's senses. Curry wasn't his favorite. Indian spices did nothing for him, but the atmosphere was relaxing and quiet. They talked over drinks until Nigel declared that the buffet beckoned.

After lunch, Nigel ordered a vanilla espresso, finally asked for the check, and threw down his American Express Platinum. Even with all he'd drank, he didn't appear the least bit wobbly. They took a cab to the marina and strolled down the steps toward a row of boats tied up at the end. A small crowd had assembled and was looking over the expensive, 39-foot red fiberglass racing boat with its two powerful engines. The look on Nigel's face reflected pure satisfaction—he loved this attention.

Bishop rolled his eyes. So much for being nonchalant. Nigel led the way past the admirers and boarded the craft. He held out his hand and helped Gillian aboard.

He dropped into the driver's seat. "I say, Bishop, would you mind?" He motioning to the mooring lines.

Bishop untangled the knots and jumped aboard just as the engines roared to life. The deep, rumbling baritone sound produced smiles of satisfaction from the bystanders. A couple clapped their approval.

"Nigel, how about letting me take her out?" Bishop hated the idea of getting into a thousand-horsepower boat with someone with a half dozen drinks under his belt.

"Sorry, insurance only covers me as the operator." Nigel winked and smiled.

Bishop wasn't sure whether to buckle up or leave the seat belt off— he might survive a roll-over if not buckled in. Gillian appeared totally enamored with the whole experience. She slipped into a white sweater, looking like a billionaire's wife. Nigel deftly maneuvered the craft out of the marina and through the Inner Harbor without incident, jabbering away the entire time. He eased through James Bay, and Gillian got a kick out of waving to the whale-watchers and other pleasure boats making their way through the area. Bishop loved the smell of salt water and enjoyed the seals at play near the rocky beach—but this was no way to do covert surveillance.

As Nigel entered the Juan De Fuca Strait, he dropped the hammer down and took off like a bullet. Bishop turned back and kept himself from laughing at Gillian. She held on to her hat while also fighting to keep her sunglasses from flying off—she wasn't smiling any longer.

"By god, this is wonderful!" Nigel yelled over the roar of the engines, as they ripped through the water at speeds Bishop didn't care to guess. The boat ran pretty smoothly for a rocket. Holland Point, Finlayson Point, and Clover Point flew by before Nigel slowed a bit at Ross Bay. "Worth every damn penny," he exclaimed, exhaling.

"You okay back there?" Bishop yelled.

Gillian jerked her hat off, ran fingers through her tangled hair, and glared at him. "Perfect!"

Bishop figured he'd just drop it—she wasn't in the mood for talking. Nigel swung north toward Oak Bay and set his final course for Cordova Bay. The water was calm, and the boat glided effortlessly through the dark blue depths. He pointed at a pod of orcas off the port side, and Gillian snapped a few pictures.

"That's it, dead ahead." Bishop motioned toward the tiny green speck rising out of the water.

"Right, how do you want to handle it?" Nigel asked.

"I'll get in back and use the telescopic lens and get what pictures I can from here."

"Right," Nigel said. "Ready for the camouflage, old girl?"

"Ready." Gillian stood and pulled the sun dress over her head. Underneath she wore a one-piece green bathing suit the same shade as the dress.

Bishop's eyebrows rose: Gillian had a much better figure than he'd imaged. The full breasts, firm hips, and narrow waist could belong to a movie star—not a spy. She rummaged around in her bag for a moment, finally pulling out a bottle of suntan lotion. Bishop grabbed his camera and joined her in the rear of the boat.

"Would you mind?" she asked, turning around and pulling her shoulder straps down. She held out the lotion bottle and he rubbed a couple of handfuls onto her back and shoulders. He allowed himself to fantasize about being with her.

"Thanks." She threw a beach towel on the aft deck and crawled on top.

He crouched low in the boat, with only the top of his head and camera showing. "Nigel, run east of the island and let me get some shots of the lagoon and yacht."

The pleasure boat traffic on this side of Vancouver Island was much sparser than around Victoria Harbor, so they stuck out like a gorilla at a beauty pageant. Nigel kept the speed steady, and Gillian rested her chin on her hands, alternating between looking at the ocean and Bishop. The hanging straps on her bathing suit hid little, and the more she squirmed, the more her breasts eased from around the edges of the top. Bishop found it hard to concentrate. She knew exactly what she was doing—and loved every minute of it.

As they motored just a hundred yards from Picard Island, Bishop pressed the shutter, shooting dozens of pictures. The powder blue yacht came into full view—the name on the stern, *Sea Angel*. One crewman worked on the top deck, but otherwise there was no one in sight. Nigel kept the boat far enough from the island that no one could see Bishop. Nigel made one slow loop around the place, like a sight-seer who didn't have a care in the world. Bishop mused, *Perhaps this was the perfect spy boat.* Who in their right mind would suspect spooks to be cruising around in a boat costing almost a half-million dollars?

"Okay, I got everything I need," Bishop said. "Let's go."

Gillian made sure she slid off the rear, got back into her dress, and sat down before Nigel dropped the hammer and blew out of there like the devil was on their tail.

The acceleration pressed Bishop back into the seat as Nigel ripped down the coast back to Victoria. *Oh, brother.* He hoped this was the last trip with Nigel at the wheel.

ELEVEN

Mercier listened to Stewart Anderson's report. "You're sure that was them?"

Anderson stood at the threshold of her bedroom. His concerned expression put her on edge. "Yes, ma'am. Our source in Victoria said they left in the boat less than an hour ago—that was them all right. They made a loop around the island then headed back toward town."

She stood and strolled to him. "Kill them—kill them all." She had a better idea. "No… bring one back here. Colonel Hong can interrogate that one. We'll need to find out what they know."

"Yes, ma'am." Anderson retreated back into the hall.

She poured another drink and stared out her bedroom window. The late afternoon shadows crept toward the house from the tall trees near the water. The waves lapped the rocks and rushed back toward the sea—so beautiful.

She lightly touched her cheek with her fingertips. The scarring felt rough, wrinkled, and dry. All so unnecessary. It didn't have to be this way. She could still have her beauty if not for the idiotic bureaucracy of the United States. Well, they would pay for their stupidity.

————

Bishop still considered himself lucky to have survived Nigel's boat ride as he downloaded the photographs to his laptop. Gillian was in her room taking a shower and had promised she'd meet them later for dinner. Nigel rocked back in a chair on Bishop's small balcony and nursed a whiskey. "Having any luck in there?" he asked.

"Just about got it," Bishop replied. When he finished the download, he heard a chime from the computer—he'd just received an email from Cook. It was classified TOP SECRET. No use trying to open it without encryption. He reached across the desk for a small black metal box with a tiny digital keypad. He input his six-digit code, and the lock released, the lid popping open. Nigel strolled back inside and refilled his glass, watching Bishop remove the strange-looking card from the box. Using a short piece of dark red wire with a round plug on one end and a USB plug on the other, Bishop connected the encrypted cell phone to the computer.

Nigel stared with apparent fascination while Bishop tinkered with the devices. "Sure you won't have one?" He held up the bottle of Glenlivet.

Bishop kept his concentration on the computer. "Later." He typed in his code and waited.

Nigel strolled around the desk and peered over his shoulder. "What the devil are you doing?"

Bishop sat back and explained. "My laptop contains an encryption program that's cleared for CONFIDENTIAL information only. If the information is classified SECRET or higher, I need to use the air card. It has a microchip that can unscramble SECRET and TOP SECRET emails."

Nigel sipped his drink and examined the computer screen.

"But," Bishop continued, "only by linking up the encryption capabilities of the cell phone am I allowed to send and receive TOP SECRET material."

Nigel pointed at Bishop. "That's exactly what I like about you Yanks—you have the best toys."

"I'm sure MI6 has the same thing."

Nigel mumbled, "Yes, but it's far more difficult than what you have," wiggling his finger at the laptop.

A red message banner scrolled across the screen announcing the TOP SECRET email could now be opened. Bishop stared at Nigel in silence, which engendered a "What?" expression in return. Bishop raised his eyebrows and Nigel finally took the hint.

"Oh, yes, I understand—forgot myself for a moment," Nigel sighed, strolling away so he couldn't see the message on the screen.

Bishop opened the email. *Your luck's good today—satellite photos attached.* It was signed *Cook.* Bishop opened the attachment while Nigel leaned against the patio door frame, staring across the harbor. The computer screen showed dozens of crisp color photos of Picard Island. Close-ups and obliques.

"Nigel, look at these." Bishop motioned for him to come over.

He and Nigel spent the rest of the afternoon examining the treasure trove of satellite pictures. Bishop played with the program and pulled up a 3-D image of the island. The last few sets of frames even showed them in their boat a few hours earlier. Gillian could be seen lounging across the stern in that sexy green bathing suit, while Bishop crouched near her, taking photos. The next to last one caught Bishop's eye. It was an oblique shot from the passing satellite.

He leaned forward and studied it with interest. Nigel had drunk enough by this time that he didn't notice the small glint coming from the upstairs window of Claudine Mercier's home until Bishop zoomed in. After cleaning up the resolution, he clearly saw the outline of someone standing at the window. He understood what the glint near the figure's head was—either a camera lens or binoculars. While they got their shots, they were also being watched. But by whom, and for what reason?

Nigel studied the image more closely and cleared his throat. "I suppose you know what that is?"

"Yup," Bishop said. "What do you think?"

Nigel set his whiskey on the desk and stretched. "I think I'll get cleaned up, dress for dinner, and be ready to dine in an hour." He ambled toward the door but stopped before opening it. "I also think I'll start watching my back."

A few hours later, Bishop and Gillian drove to Restaurant Matisse on Yates Street near the Inner Harbor. When Bishop told her about the person in the window, she frowned.

"Think they suspect something, or just a coincidence?" she asked.

"Don't know, but we should keep our eyes open from now on." A counter-surveillance program on the island was cause for concern. The White House, NSA, and Area 51 all had two things in common—strong counter-surveillance programs and hidden secrets. Why should it be any different with Claudine Mercier and Picard Island?

Nigel waited for them at a table near the back. The line of windows behind him afforded great views of Victoria's night lights. Bishop hadn't realized how hungry he was until he smelled roasted meat being served at a nearby table.

"What will you two drink?" Nigel waved at a waiter, who ignored him. Nigel whispered, "Had to bribe the wretched frogs for a table since we didn't make reservations. I think the buggers are ignoring me now—their grandfathers were probably Vichy French."

The waiter finally showed and took their drink orders after telling them about the evening's specials. He made it back in record time with another scotch for Nigel, white wine for Gillian, and a German beer for Bishop. After placing their orders, Nigel convened a dinner conference. Keeping the conversation low they discussed the operation.

"Well, frankly I don't see how we can make a final assessment of the place without having a look 'round," Nigel said, glancing at Bishop for his agreement.

Bishop fiddled with the salt and pepper shakers before answering. "We should check it out. It's time to either concentrate on, or exclude, Picard Island as a suspect location. Think we can get the RCMP to do a complete search?"

"Not likely," Gillian replied.

They both looked her way—it was her decision. She sipped her wine, the candle reflecting in her serious eyes. She set the glass down. "Too much politics. Mercier's too big a heavyweight. What would *you* need for a covert search?"

Bishop held up his hands. "Hold on—don't you guys want a Canadian team for this?" He lounged back. "I'm a bit out of my jurisdiction here."

Nigel eyed Gillian. "Speaking for His Majesty's government, I recommend we proceed immediately. Don't waste time dragging someone else into this—operational security and all that."

Gillian's brow crinkled. "If I request a Canadian team, it might take several days to deploy, that is if it was authorized at all. If I got permission, could you do it?"

Bishop didn't like the sound of this. Operating inside a sovereign, allied country as a declared agent was one thing, but doing a covert op there was another. "Yeah, but I'd need a few things, and authorization from my boss. I can tell you he won't like it."

She nodded. "I'm in the same situation. What would you need?"

Bishop leaned in closer. "Mask, fins, snorkel, dry suit, rebreather, buoyancy compensator, a compass—"

"Whoa, hold on… I can't remember that. Make me a list."

Nigel asked, "Think you can locate all that, old girl?"

"It's stuff the navy should have, right?"

Bishop sipped his beer. "Yup."

She scribbled into a small notebook. "I still maintain a good liaison with MARPAC. Besides, the home of Canada's Pacific Fleet is Vancouver Island. They'll loan me what we need."

Nigel raised his glass. "Then it's settled. We'll go tomorrow night."

Bishop now had to explain to Cook why he'd be the one going in. Just then, the first course arrived. He spooned down the lobster bisque, watching Gillian pick at her Caesar salad. Nigel burnt his mouth on his escargot bordelaise, invoking a curse on the cook. Bishop's mind drifted to the satellite shots and photos he'd taken from the boat. He had to figure out an approach to the island—it wouldn't be easy. This thing was escalating a little too fast now.

TWELVE

Stewart Anderson paced his office, smoking a cigarette. Who would die immediately and who later under Colonel Hong's interrogation? His source in Victoria informed him that of the three, the American might have the most information worth knowing, but he was also the most capable of putting up resistance during a snatch and grab. The woman would be easier, but she also probably knew the least. As for the old Englishman, he might or might not be of any use—probably not worth the effort. Anderson only had one chance, so he had to get it right. He'd go after the American—Bishop.

Another thing his source discovered: the American and Canadian woman paid a visit to Viktor Belousov. His drinking had gotten worse since he left the company, and he might have let something slip. Anderson would deal with the three spies after first paying Belousov a visit. Perhaps the old drunk might give him some insight into what the other side was up to.

A light knock came from outside his office door—Colonel Hong. Anderson answered it, and the short, middle aged Chinese man greeted him with his usual sneer. Aggravating bloat, his coal black eyes reminded Anderson of a shark. Since Hong's arrival a week ago, the guy had been circling, never seeming to sleep. He'd become the de facto security chief for the upcoming operation—whatever it was. Anderson assumed it had to do with the RCMP and FBI investigation, so it must be illegal.

"Colonel Hong, come in."

The little man did a quick head bow. "Thank you."

"Cigarette?" Anderson held out his pack.

"No… thank you."

Anderson sat on the edge of his desk. "What can I do for you?"

Hong remained perfectly still, almost at attention. "I have completed my security survey of the island and found it inadequate. I have instructed the security staff that until further notice they will be working twelve-hour shifts. We need additional people—especially at night for the perimeter."

Anderson wanted to wring the little bastard's neck. Island security was his exclusive purview. He understood he must relinquish some authority because of Hong's arrival, but the son-of-a-bitch could at least go through him before handing out new instructions to the staff. He allowed a smirk as cover for his anger.

"Okay, Colonel, I'll make out a new schedule. Say, I might need your help. There's a possible security leak on the mainland—one of our former employees. Would you be available tomorrow?"

Hong glared. "Perhaps, if I'm not gone from the island too long. What time?"

Cigarette smoke bothered Hong—the watering eyes and sour facial contortions delighted Anderson. He took a long drag and exhaled a stream of smoke in Hong's direction. "Oh, I don't care. How about one o'clock tomorrow afternoon?"

Hong let out a small choking sound. "Very well, I will go." He turned and retreated from the foul atmosphere.

"Colonel Hong?" Anderson said.

Hong turned back to him before Anderson said, "This leak might need to be plugged forever—you know, look like natural causes or an accident. Think you could handle that?"

———

Making his way down the hall, Anderson's last revelation surprised Hong. This Anderson fellow was more treacherous than he had been led to believe. But his request for death by *natural causes* gave Hong an idea. It would involve Dr. Tee, but that was the reason he was included as part of the team. Hong still bristled at the thought that, with additional education, he could have had Dr. Tee's job. But that was the way the system worked. His destiny had been decided by someone other than him, and that meant how much education he had received. Still, Dr. Tee could be useful. That black bag he carried everywhere had who-knew-what in it. It was always locked and by his side. Secret papers or deadly toxins—probably the latter. People did not call him Dr. Toxin for nothing.

———

Bishop was still sleeping when Colonel Maxwell, General Cook's deputy commander, called at 5:04 AM. Bishop rolled over and glanced at the digital clock on the nightstand and immediately regretted last evening's pub hopping with Nigel and Gillian. Nigel insisted on showing them his favorite Saturday night drinking establishments around town, and of course that involved a drink or two at each. Bishop finally begged off around midnight. One thing he didn't regret was being with Gillian. At each bar, she'd sat a little closer. She was interested but wanted time.

He fumbled for the encrypted phone in the dark, and finally found it in his open suitcase. "Bishop here."

"You okay? You sound sick," Maxwell said.

Bishop coughed, "I'm fine, sir. A little early here, that's all."

"Sorry for the wake-up, but the general wanted an update before going into the morning briefing."

Bishop needed to sell him on the idea of doing the recon on the island. "Well, we've been studying the photos, and have planned a covert search tonight. I'll be the one going in." He tensed waiting for the response. A long moment of silence followed before Maxwell answered.

"Alright, but no direct intervention—just a recon. The Canadians okay with this?"

"My contact's getting permission from them." Bishop changed the subject. "You got anything for me, sir?"

"Bad news—three of the coast guard crew died. The rest are critical."

A pang of guilt swept over Bishop. While he partied in Victoria, men died—time meant lives. "I'll let you know after we complete the search."

"I'll inform the general—good luck."

Bishop dropped the phone into his bag and tried to fall back asleep, but it was no use. He still wasn't enthusiastic about doing the covert operation. The Canadians had well-trained people for such jobs. All his senses told him they should wait for Canadian special ops, but if he insisted, they might have to wait a week or longer. The Canadians didn't see the urgency the US felt in getting this resolved. Could they afford to wait? He wasn't sure. What he did know was someone controlled a deadly virus and might deploy it at any time. Time to stop talking and start acting.

———

Viktor Belousov napped on his oversized chaise lounge after a late lunch. Avery rested on his lap; a soft purring sound filled the room. The loud knock at the front door startled the old man. He first thought it a dream, but it continued. Even Avery jumped to the floor at the commotion. Belousov pulled himself out of the chair and shuffled toward the door. As he looked through the peephole, Stewart Anderson waited. What did that asshole want? Belousov unbolted the door and swung it open.

"Good afternoon, Viktor," Anderson said. "Mind if I come in?"

Before Belousov answered, a short Asian man dressed in dark clothes stepped into view from around the corner of the house. Belousov didn't like the look of this. "What do you want?"

Anderson stepped over the threshold and pushed him back into the hall. "I have a couple of questions—that's all."

The Asian man followed, looking around the front yard before entering and closing the door.

"I don't understand—what kind of questions?" Belousov backed into the living area with Anderson following.

"Sit down and relax, Viktor—we won't take up much of your time," Anderson said.

Belousov plopped into his chair while Anderson strolled around the cluttered room. He ran his finger across the fireplace mantle and wiped the accumulated dust on his pants. Belousov drew a nervous breath—Anderson wore clear latex gloves. The other man wore black leather ones.

"You live like a pig, Viktor," Anderson declared.

Belousov didn't answer. His heart pounded.

"I said you live like a pig!" Anderson shouted. "Are you a pig, Viktor?"

Belousov shook his head. "No."

Anderson turned and faced him. "Do you know what a pig is?"

The old scientist stared back. "No." He shot a glance at the other man, who walked around the room near the back of his chair.

Anderson moved closer and bent at the waist, resting his hands on his knees. "A pig is someone who earned a good salary, who is drawing a good retirement, and who betrays the trust we placed in him."

Belousov squinted. "I don't know what you mean. What did I do?" He threw his hands up.

"What did you tell the American and SIS agent who visited you a few days ago?"

Somehow, he knew about the visit—better tell the truth. "They asked me about my employment with Alo Vita Labs, and I told them."

"What did you tell them? Did you tell them about the trip to Macau, about the research?"

Belousov's chest heaved. "No—nothing like that. I only told them about my work here in Canada on pharmaceuticals—that's all."

"Are you sure, Viktor?"

Belousov tensed. Anderson's evil smile scared him. "I swear— that's all." He searched again for the Asian man—he was almost directly behind him. The old Russian's breath came in short pants. Fear welled up inside him—this wasn't going well. From the rear he heard Avery's cry. He turned and the Asian man held his cat by the throat. The feline, gasping for air, attempted to scratch free. His efforts netted him nothing. The man held the hapless animal at arm's length as it fought for air, scratching the black leather gloves.

Belousov jerked his head back to Anderson, "I've told you the truth—let Avery go."

Anderson crossed his arms. "The whole truth, Viktor?"

"Yes, yes, the whole truth."

Anderson winked at Hong, who slung the half-strangled cat to the floor.

"Okay, relax. But I'm afraid you can no longer be trusted. You're a loose cannon, Viktor."

Belousov was only half listening, watching Avery scramble to his feet and race behind the sofa. "What... what did you say?"

"You heard me. I don't think you can be trusted any longer... probably never could be."

"No, you're wrong. I—"

The sting in the back of his neck stopped him in midsentence. The Asian man placed the cap back on the syringe and backed away. Belousov clasped the back of his neck. "What have you done?"

Anderson smirked. "Just a little insurance, that's all."

"What was that? Truth serum?"

Anderson took out his cigarettes and lit one. He leaned against the wall, watching Belousov. The other man walked back into view, dropping the empty syringe into the pocket of his jacket. The old man knew it wasn't truth serum, but feared what else it might be.

Anderson shrugged. "You're a biologist—having any symptoms that might give you a clue what we shot you up with?"

Belousov drew a frightened breath. Just as he'd feared—a biological agent. His heart raced, sweat formed on his face and neck, mouth dry. All signs of stress—not any kind of poisoning. "Call a doctor for me," he begged.

Anderson laughed. Even the grim Asian fellow smiled at his plea.

Belousov's worst fears were now confirmed: they meant to kill him, and there wasn't a thing he could do to stop them.

"You sure you told us the truth about the American and SIS agent?"

"I swear—I said nothing."

Anderson strolled around the room in silence for a few moments. He flicked some ash on the carpet, "I don't know, Viktor. Story sounds a little fishy."

Belousov squeezed the back of his neck, as if that might stop the poison from entering his bloodstream. "Please, Stewart. Don't let me die—not like this." The hand he used to hold his neck felt like lead—it dropped uselessly to his side. His mind wandered. *Paralysis of the extremities. My god, what have they done?* His vision blurred. He shook his head, but it didn't help. He'd offer one last plea—promise them anything. Before he spoke, the double vision set in, "Botulinum," he whispered.

Anderson stood directly in front of him with a cruel expression. He leaned forward and rested his hands on his thighs. "Viktor, you're a frigging genius. Actually, it's Botulinum Neurotoxin Type A. You know how it works. It paralyzes the nerves so the muscles can't contract. Muscles that control breathing and the heart."

Belousov could no longer speak. His chest tightened and his mind drifted. He couldn't concentrate. His vision shrank to a pinhole. Just before the pinhole closed, his body stiffened and relaxed—the slowing heart finally stopped.

THIRTEEN

Bishop finished his workout, had breakfast in his room, and then spent the rest of the morning studying the satellite and boat photos he took of Picard Island. The place was heavily wooded except on the very top, near the house. The one feature he'd noticed that might work to his advantage was the fissure. The split in the ground looked pronounced from the satellite shots. Ranging from about three to five feet deep, and just as wide, it ran perpendicular from thirty yards behind the house all the way down to the beach. He hadn't seen it from the mainland because it dumped into the water on the opposite side of the island. That would be his ingress and egress point. Approaching the house from any other location would expose him too much.

He still had no idea where Gillian was. She'd borrowed his SUV keys last night with the promise of picking up his shopping list at MARPAC today, but as morning turned into early afternoon, she still hadn't returned. He ordered room service for lunch, and later dropped off to sleep in the oversized chair with the laptop in his lap. Knocking on his door woke him. He checked his watch—2:17. Opening the door, Gillian marched in, dragging a large, green canvas dive bag. She threw her purse on his bed and dropped the bag on the floor, then collapsed in the empty chair and exhaled. "I had no idea it would take so long."

Bishop had suspected that hitting the Canadian Navy up for a loan of equipment on a Sunday morning wouldn't be as easy as she'd hoped. "Any problems?"

She sighed. "Most everything on your list was no sweat, and they handed it over without question. The last item gave them some heartburn, however."

He sat on the edge of the bed. "Did you get it?"

She stood and dragged the oversized purse to her. Opening it, she fished out a smaller OD-green canvas bag. "Here," she said, then flopped back into the chair.

He unsnapped it and peeked inside before emptying the bag on the bed to inventory its contents. Four 1.25-pound blocks of C-4, detonators, and two timers—exactly what he ordered.

Gillian crossed her arms. "To acquire the explosives, I had to get the director's approval. They're pulling so much heat over this thing, they didn't ask too many questions. They did order me to closely monitor you." Her right eyebrow rose in a provocative fashion. "So it looks like I'll have to stick close as long as you have those explosives in country."

Bishop loved that look. He'd grown too fond of her for his own good. "I can think of no one I'd rather be stuck with." He winked and began repacking the explosives.

She motioned toward the C-4. "What's your plan for that?"

Bishop slid each block back into the bag. "Nothing in particular at this point."

Her eyes pinched. "Then why have me go to the trouble of getting it?"

He looked up. "I like explosives."

She didn't bother commenting, but he got an eye roll for his flippant answer.

"Have you heard from Nigel?" he asked.

"He'll meet us at dinner and go over things. Since you're the one who's doing all the heavy lifting tonight, you get to pick the dinner location."

"Italian take-out in my room. We'll make this headquarters central."

She licked her lips. "Sounds like fun. I know just the place. I didn't know you liked Italian."

He closed the explosives bag and looked up. "Carbs. I need carbs for that swim tonight. Especially in cold water. I hate cold water."

He unpacked the diving equipment, laying each piece on his bed. Gillian poured a drink from the bottle that Nigel left behind.

"The supply officer said they just serviced the rebreather last week. Did a canister and cylinder swap and pressure check—whatever that means." She shrugged.

Bishop examined the closed-circuit rebreather and checked the oxygen valve and scrubber. "Looks good."

He pulled the black Gore-Tex dry suit from the bag and searched it for punctures. A set of thick insulated fleece underwear lay underneath, and two pair of heavy wool socks. Unlike wet suits, dry suits fit loose except at the openings around the neck, wrist, and ankles. While wet suits allowed a thin layer of water to enter, which the body could warm, dry suits permitted no water entry. Any warmth came from whatever clothes the diver wore under the suit. In the frigid waters around Victoria, it was the only option. He checked the arm length. "Looks like it'll fit."

Gillian bit her lower lip and grinned. "Want to model it for me, cowboy?" She had a mischievous look—the scotch must have relaxed her.

"Later," he mumbled, checking the night vision goggles in the darkness of the bathroom. Satisfied, he stuffed the gear back into the bag and zipped it. "Did you get the underwater sled and have someone check it out?"

"Yeah, the supply NCO installed a new battery and did a utility check—it's in the back of your SUV." She finished her drink, stood, and ambled to the door. "See you later."

At ten o'clock, Nigel and Gillian strolled in with the Italian take-out like two party goers ready for a night on the town. She served up the spaghetti and meatballs, lasagna, and ravioli, while Nigel opened the bottle of Chianti Classico—Bishop allowed himself one small glass.

Nigel kept them laughing with funny stories from around the world of his forty years of exploits in MI6.

When they finished, Bishop began the briefing. He explained the approach and the ingress and egress points. He went over emergency contingencies and communications.

Nigel tossed down the last of his wine before saying, "So you plan to go overboard at one o'clock, have a look around for a few hours, and be back at the pickup site by four?"

"That's the plan. Any questions?"

Gillian glanced at her watch. "It's almost midnight now. When do we leave?"

"Immediately." Bishop stood. "Think you can get us there in the dark, Nigel?"

He grinned. "I'll get you there, all right."

They slipped out the hotel's back door, and Bishop drove his SUV to the rear dock. He heaved the underwater sled and dive bag into Nigel's boat, then left Nigel and Gillian at the dock while he parked the SUV at the hotel. As he walked back down to the dock, something caught his eye—a red flash. He stared into the darkness: a vehicle sat in the shadows of the hotel on the north side. The motor was running, but he couldn't see the occupant. He didn't like it. He turned toward the car and picked up his pace. Probably just someone waiting to pick up a hotel employee getting off work.

As he approached, the vehicle rolled around the corner and up the hill with its lights off. When it got to the main street, it turned right before merging into traffic. Not a good sign. The red light flashing must have been a foot accidentally touching the brake pedal.

Nigel had the boat's engines purring when Bishop jumped in. They slid into polar jackets. It was going to be a cold ride. When they moved out of the marina, Bishop broke the news.

"I think someone may have been watching us back at the dock," he shouted over the engines.

Nigel turned. "Why do you say that?"

"Walking back from the garage, I spotted a car with its engine running and lights off. When I went to check it out, it drove away."

Gillian leaned closer. "See who it was?"

"Nope. Looked like an import. Maybe a Volvo—not sure."

"Tags?" Nigel asked.

"Couldn't see; its lights were off."

"Blast our damn luck," Nigel snapped.

"So, do we call this off or go ahead?" Bishop asked.

Nigel eyed Gillian and then Bishop. "Speaking for myself, I'd say it's your call, old boy. Could be just a coincidence, or something more sinister. You're taking the risk—you should make the decision."

Bishop stared at Gillian. She frowned. "I totally agree. If you have a bad feeling, then let it go—we'll find another way."

There wasn't another way—everyone knew that, and the clock was ticking. "I say we go," Bishop answered.

Nigel nodded in agreement. Gillian's expression showed what she thought. She still didn't like it. By the time they got into position on the far side of Picard Island, it was 1:03 Monday morning. Nigel cut his running lights and stayed in the channel, holding about five hundred yards from the island. Gillian helped Bishop into the dry suit, and held up the rebreather as he swung his arms through the nylon loops. He tightened them and checked the breather system one last time. Nigel lowered the sea sled into the water and held the anchoring rope.

With his head covered by the dry suit and sealed mask, Bishop could hardly hear a thing. He sat on the edge of the boat facing them and held up his right thumb and index finger making a circle. Nigel made the same OK sign and patted him on the back. Bishop turned to Gillian. She also gave the OK sign, and he did a back entry over the side into the dark, cold water. The calm water and clear outline of Picard Island made taking a final compass reading easy. He flooded the sled and slipped beneath the small ripple of waves.

There's always a certain amount of anxiety with all night dives, especially in an unfamiliar area. An orca might mistake him for a fat, juicy seal. The operational stresses and overall mission demands could drive someone crazy if they thought about it too long. None of these preyed on Bishop's mind. Only one thing worried him: who was in that car back at the hotel?

He kept a close eye on the compass. If he'd calculated it right, he should exit the water near the fissure. Showing no bubbles thanks to the rebreather, he cruised at an even speed. A few minutes later, he checked the digital depth gauge on the sled. Much shallower than a minute ago—the beach couldn't be far. A minute later, the blackness surrounding him give way to traces of light from the dim moon. He cut power on the sled and found himself in about four feet of water. A quick survey of the beach showed no activity. He took off the fins, climbed over the rock outcroppings, and dragged the sled ashore. He removed the pistol from its watertight case.

Bishop pulled off the rebreather, mask, and hood. He fitted the night vision goggles in place and listened, straining his ears for some unfamiliar sound. After a couple of minutes, he pushed the sled under a rock ledge and crept along the shoreline, looking for the fissure. About a hundred feet later, he almost stumbled into it. He lowered himself into the ditch and began working his way up toward the house. He wasn't certain what he was searching for or where he might find it. Anything related to the pathogen's production, transportation, or storage.

Where to search was the next question. Several locations looked promising. The boathouse by the dock, the garden shed, and the greenhouse could all hold something of interest. As for the main house and yacht, he wasn't sure if he could manage a decent search in the time allotted.

It was slow going, the loose pebbles underfoot constantly shifting. Every minute or so, he'd stop and listen. About forty yards from the house, a branch cracked in the dark forest to his left. He froze and flattened on the ground. Some limb falling off a tree? He waited another minute, listening—nothing.

The sound of a Northern owl floated through the thick forest from the far side of the island. Bishop crept on hands and knees. The sharp edges of larger rocks mixed in with the pebbles bit through the dry suit and his gloves, and he winced when one caught him on the kneecap. Sweat formed on his brow. The night wasn't warm. It was exertion and stress.

He raised his head just enough to see the lights of the house directly in front of him. The fissure would end in about another twenty feet. He'd have to skirt along the edge of the wood line after that. He assumed a crouched position and was preparing for a vault over the top when whispered voices filtered from the woods to his left. He slowly lowered himself flat on the ground. Yes, they were voices—soft tones—but definitely voices. Not speaking English, but some Asian language. His skin tingled and stomach churned. *This was a set-up.*

More muffled voices again to his left. From his right, a loud whisper echoed: "Shut up, you bloody idiots!" That whisper had a British accent. It sounded only yards away. The other voices stopped, and only the sounds of crickets again broke the silence.

Stewart Anderson wanted to kill the noisy bastards he worked with. He'd got a heads up about the American possibly sneaking on the island and had set up the perfect ambush. He could capture the man and get some answers about the government's knowledge of their operation before doing away with him without anyone becoming the wiser. But Hong's morons would spoil everything if they couldn't keep their mouths shut. If they'd been in his old SBS unit, he would have dismissed them. He checked the time. According to his beach watchers, the American had landed a few minutes ago. He should just be far enough into the trap by now. Time to join him in the ditch.

Bishop knew a setup when he saw one. The trap must have been laid soon after they'd left the hotel. A spy probably alerted the island. The thing that surprised him was how they knew he'd chosen the fissure as his point of ingress. Only Nigel, Gillian and he knew that—an expert must have put the ambush together. Someone with technical knowledge of how to run a special operations op. The guy probably identified the fissure as the island's main vulnerability. Nigel said Claudine Mercier's head of security was former British Special Boat Service. He probably orchestrated this welcome party. Well, this was one party Bishop had no intention of attending. They didn't know exactly where he was at this point. Otherwise, they would have already moved in.

Bishop still held a small tactical advantage and intended to capitalize on it.

Bishop silently twisted himself around toward the water. He eased down the slope, again stopping every few yards and listening. Directly in front of him, the fissure made a turn on its way to the beach. If he could get back in the water, at least he wouldn't be surrounded. A scary thought popped into his mind: if they suspected he'd use the fissure, why not intercept him when he left the water? They didn't want to kill him—they wanted him alive. A shiver traced through his body. If that was the case, they were probably waiting for him back at the beach.

Crunching rocks came from the area he'd just left. He slid around the corner of the fissure and peeked up the ditch toward the noise. A bush growing out of the wall gave him cover. The tall figure moved down the ditch toward him like a soldier, in a low crouch, with the assault rifle shouldered, and sweeping the area back and forth. The small green laser dot moved from side to side. But the worst part—the guy also wore night-vision goggles. Only the protection of the bush saved Bishop from being seen.

The sound of movements from the woods to his left and right signaled their intent. They probably realized he was somewhere in the ditch, and were pushing him back toward the water, where a team waited to jump him. Think it through—what did they least expect? Could he make it work? If the British SBS guy was in the ditch, and if he was the smartest in the group, that left the idiots topside. Timing would be everything—timing and a lot of luck. He rolled on his side and readied another twelve-round magazine for his pistol. This would take a lot of firepower.

He took another quick peek around the bush. The figure moved with the grace of a trained commando, the menacing green dot slowly sweeping the ditch ahead of him. Yup, he was the Brit. Bishop got to his knees, took a deep breath, let out half, and then swung the pistol around the side of the bush. Finding center mass, he fired three quick shots. The man stumbled back and dropped. Bishop stood and turned, firing five shots over the top of the ditch into the dark woods to his left, then twisted and fired another five to his right. A scream raced through the forest. Just as he'd hoped, both sides of the ditch erupted in gunfire. Not at him, but at each other. The night lit up with flashes of light as screams and shouts echoed around him.

Bishop ducked and dropped the empty magazine from his pistol. He slammed in the extra twelve-round magazine and sprinted down the ditch. He kept low and ran for his life toward the water. Just before the ditch opened up to the beach, two dark forms emerged from each side, blocking his path. They were perfectly silhouetted with the pale moonlight reflecting off the water behind them. Bishop tried to stop, but his feet slid from under him on the loose pebbles. One figure flicked on a flashlight and raised his pistol. Falling on his back, Bishop took aim and put two rounds in each before they fell.

No time for caution—the little distraction he caused wouldn't last long. Already the sound of gunfire in the woods was tapering off. He mumbled a prayer and dashed for the water. He kept the pistol in firing position until he made the right turn toward the sled. The coast looked clear, so he rushed toward the rock ledge where he'd hid it.

He dragged the sled into the water and refitted the dry suit hood, mask, and rebreather mouthpiece. A stray shot or two still came from the area around the fissure. In the darkness, a loud, angry voice yelled in a booming English accent. "I said hold your bloody fire!"

Either he'd miscalculated about the English guy being in the ditch, or his shots didn't kill him. Squatting low, Bishop pushed the sled in front of him and engaged the starter. It caught and silently pulled him out to sea. He scanned the dark water, looking for the boat—nothing. After about two hundred yards, he stopped and inflated his buoyancy compensator. Some cold water had seeped inside the suit where he'd failed to properly attach the hood while making his escape—he shivered from the chill. Looking around, he probed the blackness on each side. *Okay, here goes nothing.* The last thing they'd discussed in the briefing was emergency egress—he hoped they'd been paying attention.

Bishop slipped the six-inch cylinder from his buoyancy compensator pouch and unscrewed the top, breaking the watertight seal. He held it above his head and pulled the ring on the bottom. A muffled puff rang out as the red flare streaked into the dark sky. When it reached its apogee, he heard the rumble of an engine but saw no lights. An icy chill ran up his spine. Could Nigel run him over in the darkness? Damn right he could.

———

Stewart Anderson thanked god he was still alive. He rolled over to his side in the ditch and sucked in a deep breath. His chest felt like he'd been hit with a sledgehammer. He winced as the pain shot through it, wobbling to his feet. Bulletproof vests had their limitations, but they at least kept you alive.

The half dozen men from the island security force and another half dozen from Hong's team babbled like monkeys in the darkness. Loud moaning and a few screams drifted through the night. Anderson picked up the assault rifle and crawled out of the ditch. What a screwed up bunch of imbecilic fools to be stuck with.

———

Fifty yards to the left, a spotlight switched on, painting the ocean with its swaying beam. Bishop unhooked his mini-mag light from his belt and flashed it a couple of times in the direction of the spotlight. The boat coasted up beside him. He handed the sled to Nigel, threw the fins into the back of the boat, and scampered up the ladder. Nigel jumped back into the driver's seat as Bishop rolled onto the deck. He'd no sooner gotten to his knees than Nigel dropped the throttle, and the thing took off like a Saturn Rocket. He toppled backward before Gillian could catch him.

Bishop jerked the mask and hood off and sat up against the side of the boat. Gillian's embrace found him. She held him tighter than he'd ever been hugged before. Without thinking, he returned it, stroking her back.

"We heard shots," she said, her words barely audible over the roaring diesel engines.

"Looks like I was expected."

She pushed him to arm's length. "The car at the hotel?"

"That'd be my guess."

Nigel yelled something, the engine noise drowning out the words, and handed back a small pocket flask. Bishop unscrewed the top and took a long pull. The smooth scotch tasted good. He dried his hair and grabbed the polar jacket after slipping on a wool watch cap. He crawled into the front seat beside Nigel.

The Englishman yelled over the engines, "Bit hairy, eh?"

Bishop took another swallow from the flask. "Yes, a bit."

For the rest of the trip, Bishop slid low in the seat and nursed the flask, staring at the star-filled sky. Three issues troubled him. First, the mysterious car—who was it? Second, the fact they were no closer at getting a good look around Picard Island than they'd been earlier. And third, they'd clearly made their intentions known. It would now be harder to conduct any future covert operations against the island.

The clock read 3:20 AM when they docked at the marina behind Gillian's and Bishop's hotel. The stress and exertion, plus half a flask of scotch, made it difficult for Bishop to get up from the deep boat seat. He dragged himself out and tied off the boat, while Gillian backed his SUV down to the dock. He threw the sled and gear in and then turned to Nigel.

"Of course, you realize we're being watched here. We'll never know when or where, but someone's on our tail."

Nigel tugged at his left ear. "Quite so. Any debugging equipment about? I'd like to check my room. Swine might have planted something."

Gillian spoke up. "I've got one—I'll bring it over tomorrow."

"All right, I'll see you two for lunch," Nigel said, suppressing a yawn and walked up the hill.

"Need a lift back to your hotel?" Gillian asked.

"Not necessary, but thanks. That's why they invented Uber," Nigel answered.

Bishop and Gillian parked the SUV in the underground garage, and he pulled the dive bag from the rear, hauling it into the elevator. The halls on his floor were deserted when he inserted the key card into his door lock.

Gillian asked, "Mind if I come in for a nightcap?"

"Not at all, but I'm cleaning up. May as well wash this gear off, or the room will smell like fish in the morning." He dumped the equipment in the tub. "Make yourself at home."

Gillian poured a generous amount of scotch, flopped into a chair, and switched on the TV.

Bishop finished washing his hair and lathered his body. Next, he worked on the dive equipment. He rinsed off everything and ran hot water through all drain holes and valves. As he finished each piece, he set them outside to dry on the bathroom rug. The only things left were the mask and dive knife. That's when the shadow appeared on the shower curtain. Thoughts of the movie *Psycho* popped into his head. Keeping his eyes fixed on the shadow, he silently slid the knife from its sheath and braced himself before jerking the curtain back. There in the warm, curling mist of the foggy bathroom stood Gillian—naked as he. She grinned, set her empty glass on the counter, and stepped into the tub, letting the warm water cascade over her shoulders. She pressed her full, creamy breasts against him and took the knife from his hand, dropping it on the bathroom floor.

"I don't think you'll need that—as you can see, I'm not armed."

FOURTEEN

Stewart Anderson stood in front of his bathroom mirror and pulled the navy blue sweater over his head. He grimaced at the pain. How had it gone so wrong? He'd set up the perfect ambush in the fissure to catch the American as he approached the house, but his plan collapsed. He had two men wounded and two killed. They were imbecilic morons, but that's all he had on his team. With four out of commission, he'd have to do the job himself if he wanted it done right.

Anderson pulled the Velcro straps and loosened the ballistics vest enough to slide it off. He slipped out of the undershirt and examined the three dark purple bruises on his chest. The shot group was impossible. You could cover all three hits with a silver dollar. The guy didn't have a laser sight, shot in total darkness from at least twenty feet and under stress. Even with night goggles, the marksmanship was unheard-of. Who could shoot that well? A US Navy SEAL or member of Delta, that's who. He lit a cigarette and realized he'd grossly underestimated the opposition. He'd not make that mistake again.

And to top it off, Mercier called and bitched at him for half an hour about the whole affair. Perfect. He still wanted the American alive, but first he needed sleep. Exhausted, his shoulders sagged and legs felt like lead. When he got up, he'd have to make new arrangements.

It was time for extreme measures, and that's one thing Anderson was well versed in.

————

Bishop awoke in the dark room to the slamming of his door. He rolled over and reached for the Sig Sauer on the nightstand. With the curtains drawn, the room remained mostly black, but traces of sunlight eased around the curtain edges. His hand found the weapon, but something felt different. Wedged between the trigger and trigger guard was a piece of rolled paper. He switched on the lamp, wiped his face, and read the note.

Meet you in the lobby in an hour—Gillian.

Bishop dropped his head back on the pillow. Thoughts of last night raced through his mind. If he'd ever had had a better lover, he couldn't remember one. They'd explored every inch of the other's body— nothing had been off limits. He rolled over, and her scent lingered on the soft sheets.

An hour later, the drive to the Empress Hotel seemed strained and awkward. Bishop spoke first. "About last night—"

Gillian finished the sentence. "Hope you didn't mind me interrupting your shower." Her mischievous smile cracked the tension.

"You missed a spot while you were scrubbing my back."

She placed her hand on his thigh and squeezed. "Then I'll make sure I get it tonight."

When they strolled into the Empress bar, Nigel sat slumped in a chair at the back. "What will you have?" He began motioning at the waiter.

"Canadian beer," Gillian said. "I feel patriotic this afternoon."

Bishop helped her with her chair. "I'll have the same."

"Two Molsons, Billy," Nigel yelled.

Nigel looked like hell. Dark, puffy circles hung under both eyes, and he wasn't quite his old chipper self.

"Rough night?" Bishop asked.

Nigel finished his whiskey and waved for another. "Dreadful—dreadful. Hardly slept a wink. Kept going over things, trying to figure out what our next move should be."

Bishop leaned closer. "I called my people and told them what happened. They weren't pleased but understood there wasn't anything we could do."

"What are your people thinking?" Gillian placed her hand under the table on his leg.

Bishop lounged back. "They left it up to me."

"At what point do we turn the thing back over to the RCMP and tell them they should execute a search warrant?" Gillian asked.

Nigel started to speak, but the waiter arrived with the drinks. After he left, Nigel straightened up in the chair and whispered, "I believe they'd need probable cause to get a magistrate to issue a warrant."

Gillian took a swallow of beer. "What about the fact they tried to kill Bishop last night?"

Bishop said, "What proof do we have of that? I'm the only witness. Hard for me to swear out a complaint when I violated the law by landing on their island, uninvited, in the middle of the night. They'll just say an intruder landed on the island and shot the place up. No, we can't go the law enforcement route on this one."

Gillian removed her hand from his leg. "So we're back at square one."

Nigel studied his glass. "Not quite—let's not forget our mandate. We don't operate strictly within the law. Has the military or RCMP had any luck with their expanded search of the coast?"

Gillian shook her head. "No."

Nigel pursed his lips. "Since the RCMP, military, and FBI can't come up with anything, we seem to be the last hope. Anyway, what's for lunch?"

They were half-way through the club sandwiches when Gillian's phone rang. She swallowed a mouthful of half-chewed food and answered it.

"When? By whom? Okay, I'll meet you there." She hung up and stared at the pair. "Belousov's dead."

Nigel glanced at Bishop then back to Gillian. "What happened?"

"Not sure. One of his old drinking buddies found him about two hours ago—at home."

"Heart attack?" Nigel asked.

"Possibly. He wasn't exactly the poster boy for men's health."

They both turned to Bishop. "What do you think?" Gillian slid her hand back on his leg.

He exhaled. "Interesting coincidence, don't you think? The man lived for seventy-five years, then two days after our visit, he dies."

"They said there didn't appear to be any signs of a struggle or foul play," Gillian whispered.

Bishop pushed his half-drunk beer aside. "I ignored a coincidence last night with that parked car, and it almost got me killed. We know what that bunch on the island is capable of."

Nigel downed the rest of his drink. "Let's go."

FIFTEEN

Traffic was light on the road to Sooke. The shaded highway offered a peaceful drive, except for the fact they were going to visit a dead man. Bishop checked email messages from the passenger seat and Gillian drove. The soft sound of Nigel's snoring filled the back of the car.

When she made the left turn on the gravel road, Bishop shook Nigel's knee. "Nap's over."

He groaned and stretched. "Wasn't sleeping—just resting my eyes a bit."

Belousov's small yard overflowed with vehicles: two police cars, an ambulance, and a pickup truck. As they pulled up, a gurney accompanied by two EMTs popped out the front door. It was followed by a uniformed constable. Gillian flashed her ID and introductions were made. Bishop unzipped the body bag for a look. Belousov's pale face greeted him. Except for his eyes being slightly open, the old man looked peaceful. He zipped the bag up and turned toward the entrance.

Gillian and Nigel followed the constable back into the house. Bishop checked the front door for forced entry as he walked in. The sound of the constable's voice echoed from the living area. "...and nothing to indicate anything out of the ordinary. A friend of his, Mr. Phillips, found him. Guy had a key, and when Belousov didn't answer, he came in. He was dead in the chair."

"Whose truck is that in front?" Gillian asked.

"Belousov's—Phillips borrowed it a few days ago and was returning it."

Bishop strolled around the cluttered living room, checking each window. "Were all the windows locked?"

The constable glanced over his notes. "All doors and windows except the one in the corner," he said, pointing to the window behind Nigel.

Nigel squatted and examined it as Bishop knelt beside him.

A police photographer walked in from the bedroom to join them. "Got all the photos, sir. Will there be anything else?"

"That's it, thanks." The constable turned to Gillian, "Any questions, folks?" The man looked like someone who'd missed his lunch and wanted to get out of there.

"Did you find his cat?"

"We did. Turned him over to the CSPCA."

Gillian glanced at Nigel and Bishop. They both shook their heads and walked to the door. She and the constable followed as the officer locked the front door and pocketed the keys.

"Did Mr. Belousov have any local relatives?" Bishop asked.

Gillian answered before the peace officer got the chance. "None—they're all back in Russia."

"I think that concludes my investigation," the constable said, locking the front door. He nodded before walking toward his SUV.

After the police car disappeared, Gillian turned to the two guys. "Well?"

Bishop and Nigel eyed each other, both apparently thinking the same thing. "Request an autopsy," Nigel said.

She cocked her head at Bishop.

He paused a second, studying the cabin. "Someone killed him."

"How do you know—did you see something in there?"

"No, it's just a feeling. I don't know how they did it, but someone killed him. An autopsy might tell us how."

Stewart Anderson could have gone all day without the visit from Claudine Mercier. She'd been drinking heavily again. And on those occasions, when she was in a particularly black mood, she sought him out as a punching bag. He hated the bitch and intended to give his notice. She'd promised him a huge bonus, and he'd use it to live on until another job came along. A man with his skills, and totally ruthless, could make as much money as he wanted if he didn't mind taking a few risks. He'd taken a lot more for a lot less money during his days serving the Crown.

It was early evening, and for the third time she stood in his office doorway and stared at him. They'd again gone over what went wrong the night before. She wouldn't let it die.

"You know what your problem is, Stewart? You're too damn optimistic." She took another swallow of gin and wiped her mouth with the back of her hand. She waved the glass his way. "My late husband was optimistic, too. But of course, like you, he was British." Her eyes narrowed, and her voice slurred. "What makes you bloody British so cheerful, anyway?" Before he could answer, she smirked. "I don't see anything you have to be cheerful about. Your piss-ant little island has lost all its colonies. You have no real natural resources or serious exports, with the exception of bland food and ugly women with bad teeth."

After saying "ugly women," her hand drifted to her terrible facial scarring. She frowned. "And it's a mystery who you English think you're snubbing anymore. You're an international joke, a hollow shell of a great empire, wallowing in glorious memories of days gone by." She was shouting, and her eyes had that glassy, faraway look.

She touched her face again and whispered, "I was beautiful once, Stewart." Her head shot up and eyes fixed on his. "Did you know that? I was beautiful."

He wanted to hate her, but somehow felt only pity. Yes, she had been quite lovely, once. The oil painting and photographs throughout the house reflected a woman of striking beauty. But all that changed after the lab accident. He'd not been in her service then, but he'd heard the stories.

"Yes, ma'am." He sighed.

She wavered in the threshold with a confused expression. She let the glass fall to the floor, and jumped when it broke. Turning her back, she said, "I'm going to bed, Stewart. You need to smoke less. This room stinks—smells like an ashtray. You smell like an ashtray, Stewart."

Bishop understood they were being watched, so just to make sure a listening device hadn't been planted, he, Gillian, and Nigel spent the rest of the day meticulously de-bugging their rooms. Gillian had a small RF detection meter, and after a half hour scanning and searching Nigel's and her rooms, declared them clean. Nigel watched as they ran the detector over every wall of Bishop's room, waiting for the flashing red light and the high-pitched whistle to indicate a transmitting device had been discovered. Nigel drifted off to sleep every few minutes in the comfortable, oversized chair.

Gillian whispered, "Looks like he's in for the evening."

Bishop stopped searching the closet and stood, bumping his head on the top rod. "Damn." He rubbed the sting away and glanced at Nigel. "Yeah, it'll be an early night for him."

She grinned and pulled his face toward hers. After a quick kiss, she whispered, "And a late night for us?"

"Yes." And he went back to work.

A few minutes later he turned the scanner off and sat on the edge of the bed. Gillian poured scotch for three and handed him one. She shook Nigel's arm and his eyes cracked open. After handing him the glass, he perked up.

"Ah, perfect way to wake from a nap. Cheers."

Bishop rested his elbows on his knees. "I don't get it. You were right, Nigel. There should be bugs in at least one room. Unless they're depending a hundred percent on their spies."

Nigel sat up and took a sip, wiping a dribble from his chin. "Any ideas?"

Bishop shook his head. "No."

"Then I say we make dinner plans," Gillian said. She glanced at Nigel. "Any suggestions? I feel like Chinese."

Nigel swirled the drink in his glass and muttered, "You don't look Chinese. Think I'll take a rain check this evening." He held up the glass. "Have all the nourishment I need. Believe I should catch up on my sleep." He stood and downed the last of the drink, then took a few unsteady steps toward the door. "You kids don't stay out late—early day tomorrow."

"What do we have to do?" Gillian asked.

He yawned. "I'll figure out something by then. Good night," he said, just before the door closed.

———

General Cook settled back in his chair and relaxed to the soft sound of classical music. It was late, and his wife had retired, but he still had a stack of briefing material to wade through. If he didn't waste any time, he could be in bed before midnight. He popped the cap off the yellow highlighter and prepared to go to work when his secure phone rang.

"This is Cook."

"Sorry for the late-night call, General, but I've been looking over an official email from the Canadian Ministry of Intelligence, and have a couple of questions," J. Thomas Fuller said.

What was the national security advisor still doing at work at this hour? Anything to do with Canada probably had something to do with Bishop.

"Yes, Mr. Fuller, what can I do for you?"

The sound of rustling papers preceded Fuller's voice. "According to reports coming to the Ministry, there was a bit of a ruckus last night in Victoria." Fuller paused. "Says a large number of what appeared to be gunshots were heard coming from Picard Island. The local police investigated but were assured it was only fireworks. Is your man up there involved in any way?"

Cook leaned over and sat the briefing material aside. "Yes, sir. Our man, as well as the local SIS and MI6 agents, attempted a covert recon of the island last night. They met with considerable resistance. We believe there's surveillance going on against our people but haven't been able to identify the source as yet."

The line remained silent, and Cook fidgeted. Fuller was a good ally, but also very much a politician. His close personal friendship with the president could be a plus or minus.

"Doesn't sound too covert if your man walked into a shitstorm."

"No, sir."

The line went silent again. Cook knew Fuller—he must be thinking of the possible fall-out from every angle.

"All right, just needed a clarification of the facts."

Cook let out a sigh of relief. "Anything else, sir?"

"I trust you realize the prominence of the inhabitant of Picard Island. Some loose connection with the British Royal Family."

"Yes, sir."

"Okay, sorry again about the late night call."

"Good night, Mr. Fuller."

As Cook hung up, he made a mental note to call Bishop tomorrow. He had a bad feeling about this. Something didn't add up. What was he missing?

———

Canadian Vice-Admiral David Collins sorted through the remainder of his official correspondence and adjusted his glasses, squinting at the small type in the ship-to-shore message. He'd have to have his prescription updated or go blind reading such rubbish.

The door opened, and Lieutenant Parker stuck his head in. "I've completed the rest of the ops order, sir. Care to see it?"

"Just drop it in the pile with the rest." Collins motioned toward an inbox.

"Will there be anything else, sir?"

"No, thank you. See you tomorrow."

Collins wished he could also leave but had to wait for his next visitor. Commander Foster and his team had been flown in from the fleet. He checked the time—8:15 PM. Should be here any minute. He studied the Ministry of Intelligence request and dropped it back on the desk. Since it had been cleared by the minister, there was little he could do.

That didn't mean he had to like it, however. He was somewhat old-school in his belief that JTF2 personnel should confine themselves to only anti-terrorism and military matters. Every time they were called to assist the Ministry of Intelligence, they always came out on the short end. He'd been the commanding officer for JTF2 for the last four years. He sometimes put its interest too high for his own good, but he refused to submit to the whims of every damn politician who happened to swing into office for a short spell. His special commandos should only be used how and when he felt it necessary.

A solid knock sounded from the cabin door.

"Come," Collin shouted.

The husky, red-haired man ducked through the doorway and saluted smartly. "Commander Foster reporting as ordered."

He knew Foster. Former Navy Special Forces, good service record, highly decorated.

"At ease." Admiral Collins retrieved the Ministry of Intelligence's request and looked over it again before speaking.

"You and your team have been ordered to report for a special assignment to the Security Intelligence Service. It's my understanding you've worked with them in the past?"

"Yes, sir."

Collins glanced at the paper. "You've been instructed to report to SIS agent Gillian Hathaway in Victoria for whatever purpose she finds for you."

Foster frowned. "A woman?"

Collins sighed. He also thought the idea absurd. It was bad enough a JTF2 commando should work for a civilian, but never a woman civilian. He hid his disgust with authority. "That's the orders. Do you object?"

Foster snapped to attention. "No, sir."

Collins handed him a plain white envelope. "Good. Here are the official papers. Did your team travel with you?"

"Yes, we flew in together. They're in the mess."

"Round them up, contact this Hathaway woman, and see what in the hell she wants."

"Yes, sir."

Collins studied the younger man a moment. "Tell me, how long have you been in the military?"

"Almost fifteen years, sir."

"Sounds like you plan to make a career of it. Is that correct?"

"Yes, sir," Foster answered.

Collins met his eyes. "Then don't screw this up."

———

Gillian insisted on Chinese take-out, so Bishop ordered from a restaurant across the harbor. He probably sounded paranoid on the phone, but insisted he'd meet the delivery man at the hotel's back dock. He didn't want any more people knowing which room he occupied than necessary. He even regretted that RCMP Inspector Koner knew. Bishop took the last swallow of his drink and started to get up, but Gillian playfully pushed him back into the chair. She began a striptease as she prepared for her shower.

She pranced across the room and slid one piece of clothing off after another, humming some lounge melody while pulling her cotton turtleneck blouse over her head and slinging it toward him.

Bishop considered skipping dinner. What he had in front of him was better than anything he'd get from a restaurant.

Pulling off her jeans, she whirled them around a few times and released them in his direction. By her grin, she clearly enjoyed this. She moved closer and he reached for her leg. This engendered a slap of the hand and a "No touching the merchandise" remark.

She danced around until her bra and panties were the only things left. When she unsnapped the bra, she leaned over and pinned him to the chair, giving him a long, wet kiss.

He pulled her onto his lap and caressed her back. She broke the kiss and asked, "Did you order dessert, too?"

"Fortune cookies."

She pouted. "I hate fortune cookies." After another deep kiss, she whispered, "I'll give you my special dessert. I guarantee you'll like it better." She grinned, jumped off his lap, and sprinted for the bathroom.

Bishop found his wallet and Sig Sauer, slipping both into place before leaving to collect the food. On the way out, he stuck his head into the bathroom. She stood adjusting a shower cap onto her short hair. "Put the chain on after I leave," he said.

She followed him to the door, and the last thing he heard was the chain sliding into place. He strolled through the lobby and took a left out the front door. An orange plastic construction net stretched across the stairs, blocking the shortcut to the back dock. He took a right and followed the trail around toward the water. Music from Victoria's Inner Harbor greeted him as he walked down the paved driveway toward the dock. The edge of the moon had just started to rise—another beautiful evening in Victoria, but not quite dark yet.

The delivery boat pulled up when he rounded the corner. He waved and picked up the pace. The kid handed him the takeout bag and Bishop slipped him forty Canadian dollars. "Keep the change," he said, heading back up the path leading to the lobby. The smell of the food made his stomach rumble. He worked his way up the path and opted for the side door instead of negotiating the construction mess. The hotel's exterior lights switched on as dusk approached.

As he made the turn toward the side lobby, he saw them—two young men standing near the door. They had that oversized, pro-football build. Looked like they were waiting for someone. They noticed him at the same time. One nodded to the other, and they began walking down the vehicle ramp toward him. *This feels like a snatch and grab.* Everything was in place—two mean, bully-boys with thick necks and low brows, a quiet, less-traveled area of the property, and no witnesses. The only thing missing was the pickup vehicle ready to whisk away the unsuspecting victim to god-knew-what fate.

The sound of an engine behind him caused the hair on the back of his neck to bristle. He didn't turn around. He didn't have to. He glanced at the shiny bumper of the hotel courtesy bus parked directly to his left: the reflection of a white panel van with no headlights slowly rolled up behind him.

———

Back in the room, having finished bathing, Gillian examined her naked profile in the foggy mirror. She sucked in her tummy and ran her hand across it. Not bad, but she still wanted to lose five more pounds. She wrapped the towel around her and cleaned the mirror before brushing her hair several times. She thought she heard the snap of the door safety chain. She turned off the bathroom vent fan and heard it again. "Hold on and I'll unchain the door." She stepped into the hall and reached for the chain as the door rattled.

She laughed. "I said hold on and I'll unchain it."

A black gloved hand lunged inside the crack and slid its way up to the chain.

Gillian released a surprised yelp and jumped back. She gave the door a firm kick. A man's scream sounded from the hall as the hand jerked out.

———

In the hotel's side driveway, Bishop's stomach knotted—the odds stunk. The two goons were only about thirty feet away. The van behind him eased to his left rear, and the sound of the side door sliding open could be heard over the engine. How many were waiting to jump out and grab him? If he went for the pistol, would they shoot him from behind, or would one of the two in front nail him first? With nowhere to run, he had to fight, but he had to fight smart.

His timing would need to be exact. He ran toward the two thugs in front. It was clear from their confused expressions, they'd not expected this. They were used to having people flee when they approached. The thought of someone charging was totally foreign. He took full advantage of their hesitation. Throwing the bag of Chinese food at the one to his right, he pivoted on his left foot and delivered a perfect side kick to the other's groin. The guy dropped to his knees, grabbed his crotch, and gasped.

The other guy quickly recovered and rushed him. The giant swung his right fist, and Bishop blocked it and ducked. The sound of several sets of feet hitting the pavement came from the van behind him. He didn't look—he had enough to handle with this one. He came up with a hard uppercut and felt the man's jaw crack. He did a front snap kick and made solid contact with the fellow's left knee—that cracked also. The man screamed and fell.

Now he faced the mob. There were three—one more than he'd expected. They weren't as big as the first ones, but two had clubs. He took a step back to gain distance and study them. Only the middle one looked to be in shape—the other two, with the clubs, had scared expressions. The one on his right jumped at him, swinging wildly. Bishop dropped and did a spinning leg sweep, sending the man falling hard on his backside. He yelled when his tailbone smacked the concrete.

Bishop sprang up and circled to his left, again to gain distance. The other two followed, but no one pulled a gun. With the van no longer behind him, it was time to put the odds in his favor. His hand slid to his back for the Sig Sauer pistol. As he drew it, the remaining two just stood there with stupid expressions.

He had seen that look before. *The fight was over.* These two weren't going to push their luck. The driver had already helped the two big ones inside the van and scooped up the one with the broken tail bone. Bishop slowly backed up, keeping his eyes on them, until his heel found the driveway curb near the hotel entrance. The last two jumped into the van and it whisked past him, out of the drive, and swung toward the street. He got the license plate number before it disappeared around the corner.

At that exact moment, two elderly couples exited the side door. Their dress indicated a quiet dinner at an elegant restaurant. Their laughing stopped at the sight of spilled Chinese food, drops of blood and Bishop, red faced, looking like he wanted to take on all comers.

Their collective mouths gaped open when he walked toward them slipping the pistol back into his waistband.

He smiled. "Had a little accident with my dinner." He brushed himself off and strolled into the side lobby door.

When he got to his room, he fished in his jeans for the key card and slid it into the lock. After the familiar click and green arrow, he pushed on the door, but the chain was still in place.

"Gillian, unchain the door," he said through the crack. When there was no response he yelled, "It's me, Bishop—unchain the door."

There were sounds of movement from the other side, but no reply. A second later, the rattle of the chain drifted through the door crack. When the door swung open, she fell into his embrace, throwing her arms around his neck and hugging him.

"Someone tried to get into the room." Her voice had that frightened edge.

He undid her grip and pushed her to arm's length. "Who?"

"I don't know."

"See anyone?"

She wiped a wet strand of hair from her face, "When I looked through the keyhole, there was a short Asian man dressed in black. There was something sinister about him." Bishop's puzzled expression must have engendered her next question. "Did something happen?"

"Several guys jumped me outside. Wanted to take me for a ride. Sounds like they planned to search the room, but you stopped them by being here."

"What do you think?"

"I think I'd better check on Nigel." He picked up his phone.

———

"…and I'm not sure when I'll be back. Things aren't going as I'd hoped," Nigel said into the phone. "Oh, I have another call beeping in. Talk to you tomorrow—bye, love."

He disconnected and reconnected with the incoming call. "Hello."

"Are you okay?" Bishop asked.

"Of course. What's wrong?"

"I almost had a snatch and grab pulled on me about five minutes ago, and someone tried coming into the room while Gillian was there."

Nigel shifted his stance. "Is that so?"

"Yeah, so watch yourself tonight. Block your door at least. Do you have a weapon?"

He cleared his throat. "I might be able to find one around here somewhere."

"Good. Call if there's trouble—see you in the morning."

Nigel hung up and stood by the bed a moment. It seemed the tables had turned. Before, they were the hunters. Now they were the hunted. He strolled to his briefcase on the desk. Opening it, he picked up the semi-automatic pistol. He dropped the magazine and inspected the bullets. Satisfied, he inserted it back, laid it on the nightstand, and then slid a chair under the door handle. Yes indeed, the worm had turned. That could only mean one thing: they were getting a little too close to the truth for someone's comfort.

SEVENTEEN

General Cook waited in the anteroom of the national security advisor's office and mentally went over what he wanted to say. Fuller wouldn't like it, but it had to be said. In the middle of the night, after Cook's brain relaxed, it came to him like a clap of thunder. It was the only choice.

Finally, after over half an hour, he was ushered in. Fuller sat at his desk, having a phone conversation he clearly thought boring. His eyes rolled with frustration as he waved at the general to have a seat. He interrupted the caller. "And thank you, Mr. Secretary, for sharing that. I'll have someone look into it."

He dropped the receiver back into its cradle with an exasperated sigh and leaned back in the chair. "So, Harry, what's the thing that can't wait?" Fuller lifted the coffee cup and took a sip.

Cook scooted to the edge of the chair and met eyes with him. "We have a major problem in Victoria."

Fuller's brow furrowed, and he set the cup back on the desk. "Problem?"

"Sir, last night an attempt was made to snatch our man up there. It looked professional. Our agent is okay, but I have a very bad feeling about what might happen next. Somehow our involvement has been leaked."

Fuller exhaled and stood.

Anytime Cook delivered bad news, he'd noticed Fuller didn't want to hear about it sitting down. The national security advisor jammed his hands in his pockets and strolled to the window, probably subconsciously putting distance between him and the trouble. He turned and stared at Cook. "What do you need, General?"

"Our man, Bishop, has requested the services of our technical and surveillance people to back him up."

A relaxed expression swept over Fuller. "Don't the Canadians have similar resources?"

Cook held his gaze. "Yes, but we have better equipment and more experience in that sort of business."

Fuller must have felt confident enough to reclaim his chair. He rocked back. "Very well. I'll see the proper diplomatic niceties are observed—go ahead and send them."

Cook stood. "There is one other thing."

"What's that?"

"When Bishop went to Canada, he arrived as a declared agent. Since he's been there, he's been dogged with failure after failure, and now they're after him. This support team should be undeclared."

Fuller's head snapped back like he'd been slapped. "Are you suggesting that…"

Cook held his hands out. "Hold on. Since we don't know who's working against us, we don't know who to trust. I'd recommend the prime minister and director of the Canadian Intelligence Service be the only ones briefed. Our undeclared team won't be armed and won't be involved in any direct actions."

Fuller dropped his elbows on the desk, dragged his hand down the length of his face, and groaned. "I can't authorize that. I'd be skinned alive. They are our allies, after all. The president will have to okay it. Are you sure there's no other way?"

"How many of the Coast Guard crew have died from the virus?"

"The last one died Monday night."

"So it killed them all within ten days of exposure—even with the best medical treatment available?"

Fuller exhaled and stared at the desk. "Point taken, General. I'll push it through with the president."

———

Bishop finished shaving and prepared to start Tuesday morning. The earlier call from Cook about the Coast Guardsmen depressed him but gave him the opportunity he needed to press for sending the support team. Gillian grumbled over it, believing the Canadians could do the job without Big Brother's help, but let it pass.

The bathroom door opened, and she stepped inside. Her hair was still messed up from sleeping, and that gave her a wild, sexy look. "You'll never guess who just called."

Bishop brushed the towel across his face one last time. "Who?"

"My section chief. It seems we're getting more reinforcements than either of us realized."

"Oh?"

She moved beside him and touched his chest, raking her hand across an old scar. "Yeah, they're dispatching a Canadian JTF2 commando team. With the group your people are sending and our Special Forces unit, we'll have a small army—so much for low profile."

He took her in his arms and pulled her closer. "We might need all of them before this is over. Perhaps the time for low profile has ended. The bad guys seem to know who we are—our cover's blown. Any luck on the license plate off the van?"

Her hands caressed the small of his back. "The plate came back registered to a stolen vehicle. The local cops are handling it." Her lips slid across his.

"There is one thing we have to watch out for." His right hand slipped under her nightshirt.

She pulled back a little. "What?"

"Whoever they are, since they were unsuccessful in grabbing me, probably won't let it go."

"Don't say it."

"If they want me out of the way, the next time they'll try and kill me."

She playfully slapped his chest. "You're a pessimist."

He held her closer and whispered into her ear, "No, I'm not. If I were, I'd have said they'd try and kill you."

Her body stiffened in his embrace. She rested her head against his shoulder. "Don't let them do that."

———

Stewart Anderson finished giving his report and waited for her response.

Claudine Mercier stood in front of her study window, and the sunlight flowing through gave her an almost spiritual look. "Not very satisfactory." Her voice had that tone he hated, that condescending, inquisitional edge which told Stewart Anderson of her disapproval.

He shuffled his feet, feeling like a kid late with his homework. *Damn, I hate her.* "The one called Bishop appears to be more talented than we'd realized. It won't be easy getting to him—especially now. I say we just kill him."

"We still need to know what they know. What about grabbing one of the others?"

He reached for his cigarette pack before remembering where he was. His hand dropped back to his side. "It'll be tough—they're on their guard."

"Can it be done?"

"Yes."

She set the cup and saucer on the desk and stared out the panoramic window. She crossed her arms and stood as still as the mannequin of her sitting in the chair in the corner. The mannequin creeped Anderson out. Why would anyone commission a full-sized wax statue of themselves? It could not have been a more exact likeness... except that it showed her face as it had been prior to the accident.

She whirled around and eyed him. "Grab one of the others. By this time, they all know the same thing, anyway. Kill Bishop—do it your-self." A sly smile crossed her face. "If you can. Otherwise, I'll have Colonel Hong do it."

Anderson exploded. "I'll damn well finish it."

She grinned. "I know you will, Stewart. I know you will."

EIGHTEEN

Gillian had a meeting with the commando leader, so Bishop and Nigel decided on an outdoor bistro near the Inner Harbor for lunch.

Nigel wiped his mouth with the napkin and looked up. "I'm moving to your hotel today. They've found room for me on your floor. Best we all stay in an area where we can support each other."

"Why?"

"This business of traveling back and forth to each other's hotel has become an unacceptable risk. Better to consolidate our resources—tighten things up."

Bishop downed the last sip of cola. "Makes sense. Should we try and get Gillian on our floor?"

"Whatever for? She spends her nights in your room—doesn't she?"

Bishop blushed. "How did you know?"

"I've been observing people and making decisions about them for years. I can tell the way you two interact—there's something there."

"Nigel, I…"

"No need to explain. If I were twenty years younger and not happily married, I might give it a go myself. She's a beautiful girl."

"Yes, she is."

"I just have one concern, however. If this is just a road fling, be careful. I've known her for years. Doesn't give her heart easily. I think of her like a daughter. Wouldn't want to see her get hurt."

Bishop met his gaze. "It started out that way, but now…"

"Enough said, old boy. Not my business, in any case." Nigel stood and dropped a wad of money on the table. "Have a couple of errands to run before I make my move this afternoon."

"Watch your six today, Nigel."

Nigel grinned and pulled back his jacket, revealing a small semi-automatic pistol. "I always watch my six, Bishop. You be careful. It seems you're their main person of interest."

"I have to meet our surveillance team leader." Bishop also stood. He said his farewell to Nigel and meandered down the sidewalk.

The surveillance team leader was a fanatic about security, so Bishop planned on spending the next couple of hours strolling around the Inner Harbor shops. If he was being watched, he had to lose the tail in advance of his meeting with Hal. To the casual observer, he looked like any other tourist. In reality, he was constantly running a surveillance detection route. A good, well-staffed surveillance team would be difficult to shake, but he knew how to do it.

Finally, after almost two hours, he checked his watch and wheeled back toward the Empress. Walking past the hotel, Nigel's words echoed. *Gillian isn't a road fling.* Bishop wasn't sure what his feelings were toward her. With all the excitement and intrigue of the assignment, he'd not taken the time to really consider it. After this thing was over, he'd see what developed.

The BC Parliament loomed straight ahead. He'd always considered it one of the most beautiful public buildings in the world. Fronting the Inner Harbor, the Neo-Baroque, brick-and-granite structure spread across the vast, immaculately landscaped front lawn. He walked up the sidewalk past the statue of Queen Victoria toward the door. Two uniformed officers manned the entrance and gave each visitor a hard look.

After entering, most people took a right or walked straight ahead to other areas of the building. Bishop checked his bearings, studied the signs, and took a left toward the restrooms and water fountain. He pretended to examine the photos on the wall while strolling past several benches en route to the men's room.

Before lunch he'd received an encrypted email from Hal, the surveillance team leader. He was the one person in the P2OG that really scared Bishop. It wasn't the fact that the guy was almost twice his size. But Hal was just so good at his job. When General Cook staffed the Protective Preemptive Operations Group, he realized that having a top-tier surveillance/counter-surveillance unit would be critical. After asking around, he decided on Hal, who was working surveillance for the CIA. Cook had no qualms about stealing him from the Agency, because he knew they'd stolen him from the FBI.

Hal started recruiting his old buddies from the CIA, FBI, Secret Service, and several other top-line intelligence and law enforcement organizations. Rumor had it that, after Hal's recruitment, Cook's phone rang constantly with enraged complaints from agency heads about his crude recruiting methods—he offered more money. By the time the surveillance unit got fleshed out, Cook had the best in the business.

Hal called his group the Ghostbusters—more spirit than flesh and blood. When they were on your tail, you never knew it. Foreign intelligence services occasionally suspected they were operating in their countries but could never catch them.

Bishop looked both ways before slipping into the men's room. He checked his watch—right on time. Now all he could do was wait. He crossed to a urinal and stood there as a cover in case someone came in. The cool quietness of the place soon became maddening. He checked his watch again. Where was Hal? The door opened, and an older man wearing shorts and a t-shirt edged to a urinal beside Bishop. Bishop flushed and moved to the sink and mirror. He washed his hands, waiting for the older man to finish up. By the time he made it to the sink, Bishop had finished drying his hands and killed more time by checking his hair. The old guy left, and Bishop turned and leaned against the sink.

He'd been in this john for almost ten minutes. Where was Hal? Something must have happened. He'd have to just make contact later. He headed for the door and a gruff voice from a nearby stall said, "My wife doesn't spend as much time in front of a mirror as you do, Bishop."

"Hal?"

The big man stepped out and extended his hand. Bishop shook it. Hal's grey eyes matched his short gray hair. They made him look sinister. "Thought that old guy would never leave. Did you check for tails?"

Bishop grinned. "I'm black, no tails."

Hal led the way out into the hall, and they stepped around the corner near a utility closet and exit. Bishop briefed him on all that had happened. Hal made a few notes and asked several clarifying questions.

He closed his notebook and gave Bishop a serious look. "Our orders aren't to get involved in any direct actions."

"That's fine—we now have local Canadian talent to handle that. Just get these guys off my back long enough for me to do what Cook sent me here to do."

Hal's beefy hand shook his. "I'll be in touch—good luck."

As he turned to leave, Bishop asked, "How were you able to get to Victoria so fast? It took me almost all day."

Hal shrugged. "After you and Cook talked this morning, he put us on an executive Learjet. We waited on the tarmac at Andrews until Fuller got presidential authorization—the flight took no time."

Bishop shook his head and walked back down the corridor. No one could figure out how the general always got what he wanted. An executive jet—a new high, even for him. Then Bishop had a second thought. A Learjet for Ghostbusters and a cargo plane and ferry for him after leaving Andrews in the middle of the night? *Figures.*

NINETEEN

It was late afternoon before Bishop got back to his hotel. Since his assignment in Victoria had been billed as a liaison-type mission, he'd not taken any specialized equipment. In situations like this, he used a simple trick to determine if his room had been entered. He started this after a nasty surprise in a Gaza hotel several years ago. He would tear off a short strip of paper and roll it into a ball. This, he'd place under the room door when departing. Upon returning, he'd peek inside before going in. If the paper had moved, the room had been entered. If the paper was gone, it was likely housekeeping had cleaned the room and removed it—housekeeping noticed things like that.

Okay, it wasn't foolproof, but it was low-tech and could be utilized anywhere. Besides, he always assumed his room had most likely been rifled during his absence. He slid the key card in the door lock, and the green arrow symbol flashed before the click. There was no sign of the paper when he stuck his head in. He opened the door wider and stuck his head in a little farther—still no paper. He fully entered the room and closed the door. A nightstand lamp shined against the opposite wall. Did he or the maid leave it on? The light cast a faint, unfamiliar shadow. He stopped and studied it for a second—then the shadow moved.

———

Gillian finished her meeting with the JTF2 commando leader, Commander Foster. She sat in her car and went over the call she'd just received from her section chief—it was weird. Why had he asked all those questions? *"Are you sure you have this, Hathaway?" "The prime minister and director have concerns. Sure you're up to it?"*

After a few minutes' reflection, it all made sense. *Oh my god, they're thinking about pulling me off the mission because of my lack of experience.* No one had expected this op to blow up like it did. They didn't trust her enough to do the right thing. Could she do anything at this late date to change their minds?

She reached for her cell but pulled her hand back. No, calling would be the wrong move. A sick, hollow feeling rolled through her. Better to wait for the final verdict.

———

Bishop drew the Sig Sauer from his waistband holster, keeping his eyes on the moving shadow in his room. Whoever it was stayed in a crouching position just around the corner—ready to spring. From the outline, it looked as if they had something in their hand. Bishop's heart raced as he carefully moved with the pistol in the combat shooting position around the corner. His finger tightened on the trigger. Getting off the first shot in a gun fight was key.

Making the turn, his weapon came to rest on a man crawling between the wall and bed. A pair of oversized earmuffs with a set of wires ran from the man's head to a softball-sized silver paddle in his left hand. All this was attached by other wires to a dark blue suitcase on the bed—opened to reveal a host of dials, meters, lights, and switches. Andy wasn't really a stranger. He kept crawling, holding the silver paddle against the baseboard near the carpet. He'd not noticed Bishop only a few feet away.

A couple of seconds later, he stopped crawling and appeared to stare at Bishop's shoes as if trying to figure out why they were in his way. He looked up and Bishop grinned, about to greet him, but before he could get a word out Andy shook his head and put his index finger to his lips. He pointed to his watch and held up a finger—indicating one minute. Andy went back to the scan of the baseboard while Bishop holstered the pistol and waited.

Bishop had met Andy years earlier, after General Cook appointed him to head the Technical Operations Support Group within the organization. With only a half-dozen assistants, Andy supported P2OG operations worldwide. Bishop didn't know how he did it—probably by working the ten-hour days, six-days-a-week schedule. Cook had once ordered him to take a vacation, but he had sneaked back into the lab after closing each day and tinkered.

The tall, skinny Andy stood and slid the earmuffs off. He tossed them and the silver paddle onto Bishop's bed and stretched his back.

"You know I almost shot you," Bishop said.

Andy grinned. "You couldn't hit the floor with that thing—I'm not afraid."

He was the cockiest guy in P2OG. Bishop liked him. "Find anything?"

Andy motioned at the desk to a Plexiglas box about the size of a cigarette pack. He picked it up and held it out for Bishop. The top of the box had a built-in magnification lens. Inside rested what looked like a three-inch strip of lead from a mechanical pencil.

"Where did you find it?"

"Behind the wood frame seam of that picture." Andy pointed to a garden landscape on the wall by the desk. "Didn't see it at first, but I kept picking up a faint signal from the area. Took me half an hour to find it wedged between the print and frame."

"High tech?"

"Very, probably state-sponsored. Can't pick one of these up in a spy shop."

Bishop examined the bug with interest. "I guess our Canadian detection equipment wasn't up to par."

"What did you use?"

Bishop pulled the Canadian device from Gillian's equipment bag and handed it to Andy.

He smirked and tossed it back to Bishop. "Seventy-nine ninety-five on eBay." He touched the device in the blue suitcase on the bed. "And $67,881 from Lawrence Berkeley National Laboratory." Andy's eyebrows rose. "Get what you pay for."

Andy was a geek, but in the best way. One of the civilians in the outfit, he'd gained the respect of everyone from General Cook on down. A young man with physics, chemical, and electrical engineering degrees from MIT, he could write his own check anywhere, but Andy chose P2OG. Rumors said Cook made him a deal.

Bishop laid the case back on the desk. "So am I clean?"

"Yup, but I need to check your friends' rooms. And by the way, you're not fooling anyone with that stupid paper-on-the-floor trick. Anybody in the business for long knows it. I'll drop off something better for entrance detection tomorrow."

Bishop frowned at Andy's comment. "I'll set it up so you can debug my friend's rooms."

After Andy left, Bishop showered and dressed in dark navy chinos with a light gold sweater. He'd just sat back with the national news and two fingers of scotch when the door opened and Gillian strolled in.

"How did the meeting go?"

She dropped her bag on the floor and drained the last of Nigel's scotch into a glass. "Fabulously. The guy seems especially sharp— think we can make good use of him and his team. Says he knows you."

Bishop did a double take. "Knows me?"

"Yup—says you were part of a Delta team that gave him training in combating terrorism when he was brand new to the outfit."

"Yes, I came up here while recovering from that ass-kicking in Afghanistan. What's his name?"

"Nathan Foster."

Bishop shook his head. "Doesn't ring a bell."

Gillian flopped in his lap and ran her hand up the inside of his sweater. She kissed him hard, showing more passion than he'd expected. "Will you remember me after you leave?"

He grinned. "Who says I'm leaving?"

Her brow relaxed and she opened her mouth to speak, but her cell rang. "Hello, Nigel." Her eyes drifted over to Bishop. "Yes, we were just talking about dinner. Sure, come on over and we'll have a drink before we leave." She glanced at the empty bottle. "Oh, could you possibly pick up some more scotch on the way?"

The sound of Nigel laughing boomed out of the phone before Gillian hung up.

"He'll be right over. I'd better clean up." She jumped off his lap and headed for her room.

Thirty minutes later, Nigel exclaimed, "Good god—you're joking," after hearing Bishop's story of Andy finding the bug.

"No, someone's heard every word we've said in here from the outset."

Gillian lowered her head and blushed. Bishop figured she'd just recalled their first wild night together and who might have been listening. "So why didn't my detector pick it up?"

"Not enough signal strength being emitted, according to Andy. Very high tech, latest generation stuff."

Nigel downed the remainder of his drink and poured a smaller one. He looked Bishop's way. "So, did you meet with your surveillance people?"

"Yeah, they're operational as of now. Did you get moved into this hotel?"

"Yes, I'm down the hall on this floor—awful downgrade from my last room."

Bishop handed each of them a note with only a phone number. "The next time you're going to be out of your rooms for a few hours, give this guy a call—his name is Andy. He'll sweep your rooms and install a jamming device to block any further bugging attempts."

Gillian studied the note. "How do we get him a key to our rooms?"

Bishop grinned. "You'd insult his abilities by offering him one."

Nigel folded the paper and dropped it into his pocket. "Love these gadget types. What's for dinner? I'm starved."

"Wharf Steak and Seafood. It overlooks the Inner Harbor," Bishop answered.

Gillian and Nigel stared at each other. This was the first time he'd offered a restaurant suggestion since meeting them. A smile crossed their lips—they'd figured it out. The surveillance team leader had picked the restaurant, not Bishop. He'd have half his team set up at the hotel and follow anyone who followed them, and the other half waiting in cover at the restaurant to catch suspects that showed up there.

They took Gillian's car and drove at a leisurely speed, not wanting to lose any tails.

"Should we continue to work out of the hotel or move the whole operation to the navy base?" Gillian said. "We could guarantee maximum security there."

"Move? I just got settled in," Nigel protested.

"What do you think?" She looked at Bishop.

"I work without a net most of the time—makes it easier. If we move to the base, we'd have better operational security, but could suffer other unintended restrictions. I say stay where we are for now. We've already neutralized the bugs in our rooms, so that only leaves the bad-guys surveillance team to report on our comings and goings. Once we identify them, we'll have your new commando buddies neutralize that bunch, leaving the opposition deaf and blind to our intentions."

She shrugged. "Okay, sounds like the majority votes to stay."

Nigel sprawled in the back seat. "Besides, all the decent restaurants are close to our hotel. Every eating place near the Navy base is beastly."

Bishop glanced at her and winked. She cracked a grin as they pulled up to the restaurant. The valet parking guy gave them the chance to linger at the front a moment, chatting before going in. Any tail would have to be blind to miss them, and this would give Hal's boys an opportunity to identify the bad guys.

Walking inside, Gillian looked great in the low-cut royal blue sweater and black skirt. Bishop paused and sniffed the air before entering. The evening appeared to be taking a turn for the worse. A cool north wind had kicked up, and the smell of rain drifted past his nose.

———

In the restaurant parking lot, Hal watched them walk in. "Okay, who's got the eyeball?" he growled into the encrypted radio mic.

"I do."

"Then talk to me, Pete. What's going on?" Hal rocked back in his car seat as the first rain drops streaked down the windshield.

"Three good guys being seated—one bad guy watching from the bar."

"Did he show up with the team that followed them from the hotel?"

"Yes," answered another voice, "just walked in."

"You sure about that, Grant?"

"Yup."

Hal considered the report, and then keyed the mic. "Okay guys, they probably have two teams operating. One at the hotel and one here. Stay alert to counter surveillance." He took a large bite of tasteless protein bar and stared at the rain. Whoever they were, they knew their stuff.

———

Bishop just finished the first bite of shrimp before answering the cell call.

"You have at least two guests at the restaurant. One in and one outside. Watch what you say at the table. Call me before you leave." Hal's deep voice echoed before the line went dead.

Nigel sipped his Burgundy and glanced at Gillian.

"Well?" she asked, turning her attention to Bishop.

He slid the napkin from his lap and ran it across his mouth as he spoke. "We have a couple on us—one's inside, somewhere, most likely the bar."

Gillian lifted her wine glass, blocking her lower face. "Think they can read lips?"

"Wouldn't put it past them," Bishop said.

The remainder of the meal was spent in small talk about nothing in particular. Anything to avoid discussing the operation. They had after-dinner coffee until Nigel called for the check.

"This one's on me, tonight."

"You're too good to us," Gillian whispered, touching his arm.

Nigel beamed with satisfaction. "Yes, I know."

While he signed the credit card receipt, Bishop shot a call to Hal. "About to saddle up, buckaroo."

"Giddy up," Hal answered. "We're ready."

Gillian drove slowly back to the hotel because of the slick streets and pouring rain. "Where'd all this come from? Today was beautiful."

"Low pressure system from the north," Nigel groaned from the back seat. "Should blow out by tomorrow."

After Gillian parked in the underground garage, Bishop felt sure Hal must have identified all the tails by now. No doubt there'd be one hanging around the hotel to confirm their final return. He looked forward to getting back to the safety of his room.

Once inside the lobby, Gillian headed toward the gift shop. She turned back to Bishop, "You two can go on up—I won't be long."

"Be on the lookout," Bishop said.

"Don't be silly—I'll be fine. Just need a couple of toiletries. See you in a minute." A smile traced her lips.

Bishop didn't want to leave Gillian alone as she walked away, so he stood staring at her.

She looked back and frowned. "Don't go getting all protective of me—now get."

He stepped back into the elevator and glanced at Nigel. "Night cap?"

Nigel thought about it for a second but waved the idea away as the doors opened to their floor. "Not tonight." He yawned, strolling out of the elevator. "See you in the morning."

Bishop turned in the opposite direction and fished for his keycard. He found it just in time to slip it into the slot without missing a step. Cracking the door open, he glanced in, looking for the piece of paper. He still liked using it—old habits die hard. It had been pushed back further inside the room. Someone had opened the door since he'd left. The bed had been turned down, so it was probably the maid. Why hadn't she picked up the ball of paper? His hand slid behind his back to retrieve the Sig.

He stood perfectly still holding the pistol and listening. Could they have figured out he'd located the bug and decided to plant another?

He edged into the entry area and flicked on the bathroom lights. Glancing into the mirror, he saw no one hiding. He moved deeper into the room, weapon in the shooting position, past the corner where Andy had been crawling earlier. Nothing there, either.

Bishop had just slid the pistol back into its holster when he detected a burnt tobacco odor in the room. *Cigarette smoke.* The hair on the back of his neck stood up—it smelt like an ashtray. He again reached for the pistol, but he was a second too slow.

Someone sprang from the far side of the bed. The muscular, brown-haired man wielding a knife leaped straight for him. Startled, Bishop pivoted while trying to draw the pistol. His left foot caught the leg of the desk chair as he turned and lost his balance. He fell backwards to the floor with the man following him down. They hit hard and Bishop's head bounced off the carpet, but he managed to catch the hand holding the knife only inches from his throat as the assailant put all his weight behind it.

Bishop pushed with his right leg in an effort to roll the man off, but the tight quarters between the desk and bed allowed no room for movement. The killer's red face edged closer as he threw all his strength into the murderous task. The smell of stale tobacco breath blew into Bishop's face. Bishop's strength began to wane, and the cold steel slipped an inch closer. He pushed hard with his left leg to throw the man off, but to no avail.

TWENTY

ess than a second later, a crash and explosion of glass
smelling of scotch showered Bishop's face. The attacker's grip
went limp for a moment, and Bishop pushed with everything
he had, shoving the guy to the floor beside him. Bishop still controlled
the guy's knife hand and wasted no time banging it against the desk
until the man's grip released. Gillian stood behind Bishop, holding just
the broken neck of Nigel's scotch bottle. The jagged edges protruded
like a claw. Her hair had fallen into her wide eyes watching the
struggle.

"Thought you could use a hand," she said.

Before Bishop could answer, a fist caught him under the chin, and
he fell backward. The fight was back on. He got to his feet first. The
man tried to stand, but Bishop did a short leg sweep and caught him
behind the left knee. He crashed to the floor onto the shards of broken
glass. The guy bounced back up and charged like a bull. Gillian
jumped and rolled across the bed to get out of the way as the man's fist
swung in Bishop's direction.

She fell to the floor and grabbed the handle of the sliding glass door
to pull herself back up while Bishop and the man fought their way
toward her. She staggered to her feet just before the guy threw a

roundhouse at Bishop. He blocked it, grabbed the attacker's arm, and swung the man in her direction while delivering an elbow between the shoulder blades.

She fell backwards, still holding the door handle, and the glass door slid open to the cold, wet balcony. The attacker recovered and charged again. Bishop landed a kick to his right knee, and a punch to the face. The assailant fell onto the balcony with Bishop in pursuit. The man jumped back to his feet just before Bishop delivered a side kick to the gut. The fellow lost his footing on the wet concrete and fell backwards over the edge.

To Bishop's surprise, he didn't complete the fall. Four fingers and a thumb were wrapped around the top of the steel pipe railing. Moments later, another four fingers and thumb slapped into place about shoulder width apart from the first.

Bishop glanced into the room at Gillian. She peered out, raked her hair away from her eyes, and stared at him. He caught his breath and they eased to the edge and looked over the balcony. A light rain still fell as they stared at the fellow. He hung there, face bleeding, wearing a curious smile—almost a defiant smirk.

"I've never fought a man and woman before. Must make a note not to try it again," he said, matter-of-factly in a British accent.

"Who are you?" Bishop asked.

The guy looked over his right shoulder at the ground four floors below. He repositioned his grip and said, "Help me up, and I'll tell you. This wet railing isn't easy to keep a grip on."

Bishop touched the inside of his lower lip and tasted blood. "I like you right where you are for now. Who are you?"

The man stared over his shoulder again and back at Bishop with a twisted grin but didn't answer.

"If you don't tell me, I'll let you hang there until you fall. There's no one out on a night like this. No couples strolling by for you to shout to. I can wait as long as you can while you're trying to keep a grip on that rain-soaked railing."

To prove his point, Bishop pulled a balcony chair under the overhang and took a seat. He could only see the hands from where he sat. He winked at Gillian. She had an *I don't know if this is such a great idea* look. Her nervous eyes watched the hands and she started to say something. Bishop's index finger shot to his lips, and he shook his head. She eased over and stood beside him, resting her arm on his shoulder. Several minutes passed, and the hands repositioned themselves a couple of times on the wet railing.

"Hey, you still here?" came the voice from the other side of the balcony.

"We're still here," Bishop said. "Ready to talk?"

"I'm ready," a defeated mumble answered.

Bishop and Gillian looked over the edge into the face of the beaten man. His wet, brown hair had matted from the rain and hung limp across his right eye, which had started to swell, and blood still trickled from the right side of his head where Gillian had clubbed him with the bottle. From his expression, he was at the end of his strength, and couldn't hold on much longer.

"What's your name?" Bishop asked.

The man tried to answer, spat out a combination of rain and blood, and said, "Stewart Anderson."

"Why were you trying to kill me?"

He squinted, and then smiled. "Orders. Nothing personal."

"Whose orders?" Gillian asked.

"My employer—Claudine Mercier."

Bishop and Gillian exchanged glances.

Bishop scowled. "Okay, sport, I'm going to pull you up so you can answer some more questions in the comfort of our room." He slid the pistol from its holster and pointed it at Anderson. "This lady will kill you if you make any move on me. Understand?"

Anderson grimaced. "Hurry, I'm slipping."

"So, how do you want to do this?" Gillian asked.

Bishop put his arm around her shoulder and walked back into the room. "First thing—take off your panties, hurry."

She did a double take. "Do what?"

"Take off your underwear—panties to be exact," he repeated, "unless you want to hold him down after we pull him back in. I don't have any flex-cuffs."

"Use your belt."

"Belts tend to slip, especially when wet." He had rope in the dive bag but didn't want to waste time digging around for it—Anderson couldn't wait.

She frowned before dropping on the edge of the bed and slipping out of the sheer baby blue, white-laced thong. The fact they were still warm made Bishop smile as he picked up Anderson's knife and cut them on each side, leaving only the crotch to hold them together. He stuck them into his pocket and walked back to the balcony.

"You still there?" He glanced over the edge.

The strained voice answered, "Not for long."

"Here, hold this," Bishop said handing Gillian the pistol. "If he tries anything as I'm pulling him in—kill him."

Gillian accepted Bishop's pistol; her lips thinned with tension.

Bishop hung as far over the edge of the balcony as he dared. He gripped the railing with one hand and used the other to stretch, catching the back of Anderson's belt. He began lifting the dead weight straight up. The limp bulk of the man pulled hard on his shoulder. His right arm felt like it would slip out of the socket. He rocked back and used his body leverage to get Anderson chest-high to the top of the balcony. Anderson swung his foot over and caught the rail. Bishop let out a groan, and with one final tug, dropped him onto the rain-soaked balcony.

Light rain continued falling as the man lay there, breathing hard. Bishop knelt and pinned him, binding his hands behind his back with the panties. Lifting him with his collar and the back of his belt, Bishop dragged him inside onto the carpet near the bed. Gillian closed the door and moved away. Bishop raised Anderson to a seated position with his back against the sliding glass door.

"Give Nigel a call. I want him in on this."

She grabbed her cell phone and walked into the bathroom for privacy.

Bishop picked up Anderson's knife and examined it. "Microtech, double edge, tactical, fixed blade, eh? Is this what the Special Boat Service is issuing now days?"

Anderson's eyes fixed on the knife and his body stiffened.

Bishop smiled. "You know, I did some cross-training with SBS a decade ago. Were you still with them or had you moved on?"

Anderson showed a morose stare. "I'd moved on."

This was good. Get the guy talking about something non-threatening first, and then transition to the tougher questions.

Behind him Gillian cleared her throat. "Nigel's on his way."

Bishop sat on the edge of the bed and wiped the rain off his face.

"Who were you with?" Anderson asked with a questioning stare.

"Delta."

Anderson shifted to a more comfortable position and stretched his legs, allowing a slight grin to sweep across his lips. "I should have known—you were the bugger on the island the other night."

"That's right, Stewart."

Anderson looked down and smiled again. "Figures, from the way you were shooting. Nailed me pretty good."

"That was you in the ditch?"

"Yeah, until you put those three rounds in my vest."

Things were progressing better than Bishop had hoped. Anderson seemed to have a desire to talk. *Keep him going. Don't push it—let it flow for a while.*

Two short knocks echoed from the door. Gillian looked through the peephole and unlocked it. A disturbed expression lined Nigel's face when he surveyed the condition of the room and Anderson sitting on the floor. Gillian pulled him into the bathroom, and soft voices drifted out as she explained what happened.

"You're still bleeding a little from the head." Bishop touched the same side of his own head to show Anderson where. "We'll get you patched up in a minute."

Anderson snorted. "You kicked my ass pretty good, mister. Guess I'm a little out of shape. Too many years of easy living."

Bishop made a show of rubbing his jaw. "I don't know—you landed one or two good ones on me."

"Lucky hits—that's all," Anderson grumbled, lowering his head.

Nigel and Gillian walked over and stood beside the pair. Anderson glared at the two. He turned back to Bishop.

"Call the cops. I'm ready to go now."

"We have a few more things we'd like to know, Mr. Anderson," Nigel said.

"Well, you're not going to get them from me—I want a lawyer before I say another word."

With the arrival of Nigel and Gillian, the mood had taken a definite turn for the worse.

Nigel knelt beside Anderson. "We're not the police. And we're not going to call the police until we get our questions answered. And we're under no obligation to furnish you anything."

Anderson stared hollow-eyed at the edge of the bed and didn't answer.

Nigel stood up and gazed at Bishop. "A word, please." He motioned toward the hall with his head. "You, too, my dear," he said to Gillian.

The group walked across the room to the short hall leading to the room door. Nigel turned and whispered, "Well, what do you want to do?"

There was indecision in Gillian's face. She bit her lip and stared at Anderson. "What do you think, Bishop?"

"We have to find a place for interrogators to work on him for a while."

"RCMP?" she lifted an eyebrow.

"No, this is an intelligence operation. Bringing the federal police in changes it to a law enforcement thing. We have more flexibility by keeping the cops out," he whispered.

"I have a plan, but I need to make a few calls first," Gillian said. "Keep an eye on our friend—I'll be right back."

She left while Bishop and Nigel lingered near the door, both eyeing Anderson with contempt. Bishop dug into the dive bag under the bathroom sink and found the coil of nylon rope and duct tape. He tore a six-inch piece of the tape from the roll and stuck it to his shirt. He strolled toward Anderson, making a tight loop in one end of the rope.

Nigel leaned against the door with a concerned expression. "If you do this, we might come off looking like criminals."

"I don't like being lied to, especially by an assassin." Bishop's threatening gaze drifted back to the man bound on the floor. Bishop wanted to engender fear and doubt in the man's mind as to what he was up to.

"What are you going to do?" Anderson's breaking voice croaked, as Bishop and Nigel approached.

Bishop didn't answer but slapped the duct tape over Anderson's mouth. Nigel held him while Bishop tied and looped the rope around Anderson's ankles. Anderson struggled as Bishop tightened the slack and dragged him onto the balcony. He tied the opposite end of the rope to the rail and checked the knot for tightness.

Anderson fought against being stood up until Bishop delivered a hard blow to the gut. All the air rushed from him, and he bent double, struggling to catch a breath just through his nose. His knees buckled and he dropped forward. Bishop caught him in mid fall, lifted him to an upright position, and pushed backward, hurling him over the balcony railing. The rope caught with a snap and a muffled grunt from Anderson as he reached the end of his short bungee jump.

Looking over the edge, Bishop jerked the rope a little. "Hey, Stewart, I'm going to wash up and maybe grab a snack. If you want to talk when I get out, we'll see about pulling you back up. If you don't, you're of no use to us. I'm cutting you lose. Think it over, pal."

He turned to Nigel and winked. "I'll be out in a few minutes."

Ten minutes later Bishop finished combing his hair and stuck his head out of the bathroom. Nigel leaned against the sliding glass door frame watching the rope. Walking to his side, Bishop slipped his watch back into place and whispered. "Think he's had his 'come-to-Jesus' moment yet?"

Nigel shrugged, "I would."

Bishop picked up the knife and strolled back to the edge of the balcony. He peeked over the rail and looked into Anderson's terrified eyes. Bishop examined the knife and ran his thumb down the edge.

"Boy, this thing's sharp. I wonder how many times I'd have to saw on this skinny-ass rope before it let go?" To emphasize his point, Bishop rested the blade edge on the rope, and, without applying any pressure started a sawing motion.

Anderson let out a sorrowful, muffled sound through the tape, and his eyes closed. Bishop leaned a little farther over the edge, keeping the edge of the knife on the rope.

"What's that, Stewart? Couldn't quite make that out? Could it be you want to talk?"

Anderson opened his eyes, nodded, and let out a pleading groan.

Bishop shook his head. "I don't know. You didn't do so well last time. Said you'd answer our questions, but then chickened out at the last minute. You're not going to chicken out again are you, Stewart?"

Anderson quickly shook his head in silence. His eyes were closed again—he'd finally broken.

"Okay, I'm giving you one last chance. If you fail to answer any question, back over the rail you go. Understood?"

Anderson nodded.

Bishop looked at Nigel. "Give me a hand."

Pulling Stewart up turned out to be a lot harder than pushing him down. It took back-breaking work just to get his lower legs up over the rail. Nigel had to sit down and catch his breath while Bishop grabbed Anderson's jacket lapels and hoisted him back onto the balcony. The guy dropped like a sack of rotten potatoes on the concrete floor. Bishop stepped under the overhang and let out a long breath. The light rain had turned to a chilly drizzle.

"Okay, you're back on terra firma. Time for another little chat."

Bishop dragged Anderson back into the room, and Nigel closed the door. He sat Anderson upright with his back to the glass and jerked the tape off. The man shook with fear, cold, and exhaustion. His eyes had a wild, feral look.

"Let's start again, Stewart," Bishop said.

Anderson dropped his head and took in a labored breath.

"How long have you worked for Mercier?"

Anderson took another deep breath. "Four...no, five years, now."

"Why does she want to see me dead? I've never even met her."

Anderson's right eye had almost swollen shut. He blinked a couple of times to focus and leaned his head back against the door. "She's afraid you might interfere with her plans."

"What plans would those be?" Nigel asked.

"Some deal she's working with the Chinese."

Nigel's concerned expression reflected Bishop's.

"Tell me about it," Bishop said.

"Not much to tell. She kept me in the dark. Said it wasn't my concern and not to ask any questions."

Anderson's voice had grown gravelly, and he maintained a morose stare, the mark of someone whose mental and physical reserves were depleted.

"I'm not buying it." Bishop took a seat in the desk chair. "You know more than that. Tell us what you found out from snooping around or listening at doors. You look like the curious type. You know things you weren't officially told. Right?"

"Yeah, I found out stuff," Anderson spat. "For the last few weeks, they've been receiving crates on the island. About four or five come in every five days or so."

Bishop leaned toward him. "What kind of crates? From where?"

"Wooden. Don't know from where."

"What size?"

"About one and a half meters long and a half meter wide."

Bishop did a quick calculation and looked at Nigel. "Around four and a half feet by one and a half feet?"

Nigel nodded.

"Any markings on them?"

"No."

"What's inside?" Nigel asked.

Anderson shifted his gaze before saying, "Don't know. That's something you'll have to ask Mercier or Colonel Hong."

Bishop glanced at Nigel, then back to Anderson. "Who's this Hong guy?"

"He and another guy, Dr. Tee, arrived just before the first shipment. Story is, they work for the Chinese Ministry of Public Health. Hong and Tee are involved in whatever Mercier's up to."

"Describe them," Nigel said.

Anderson leaned his head back against the glass door and took a ragged breath before saying, "Hong's short, slim, with a scar across the bridge of his nose—always dresses in black."

"And Tee?" Bishop asked.

Anderson shook his head. "He's in charge, I think—strange guy. Tall, scraggly goatee, wears black wire-rim, tinted glasses. Oh, and always carries a black briefcase. Never seen him without it. They brought about a half-dozen other guys with them. Don't know what they do."

Bishop's cell rang—it was Gillian. He didn't answer—wanted to finish the interrogation first. He looked down at Anderson for several seconds, then squatted next to him and spoke, his voice holding a menacing tone. "Stewart, pay attention, this is the most important question of the night. Are you ready?"

The man's expression darkened. "Yeah."

"Within the last couple of weeks, did anyone get violently ill on the island?"

Anderson's eyebrows knitted together. "Not to my knowledge."

"Did anyone leave the island unexpectedly?"

"Now that you mention it, yeah."

Bishop picked up the rope still tied around Anderson's ankles and fingered it lightly. He stared Anderson's way. "Tell me about that."

Anderson kept his eyes on Bishop's hand and the rope. He took a deep, shuddering breath. "Well, last week, we had a big ruckus one night. One of Hong's men came up missing. Everyone got involved in the search, and we covered every inch of that island—never found him. One of the small sailboats was also gone. I figured the Chinese guy must have taken it and it was just a defection to Canada."

Bishop's mind drifted back to the small Asian man on the autopsy table. The bloody teeth and dark skin.

"Who was he?" Nigel asked.

"One of Hong's men—that's all I know."

Bishop dug out his phone to call Gillian back just before she strolled through the door, followed by two EMTs pulling a gurney. Another guy accompanied the group. The tall, dark-haired man with graying temples wore a business suit and a serious demeanor.

"That's him, Doctor." She pointed toward Anderson.

Without a word, the man walked over and knelt beside him. He set the black medical bag on the bed, took a look at the gash on Anderson's head, then slipped on a pair of latex gloves. He grunted and turned Anderson's head from side to side while holding his chin. With probing fingers, he parted Anderson's hair and examined the cut. The man opened the bag and withdrew a pair of surgical scissors.

Anderson's eyes widened. "What's this?"

The tall man didn't answer but cut Anderson's jacket and shirt sleeve up to the elbow.

"Now, this won't hurt a bit. Just a little something to make you more comfortable during the ride." The tall man removed the syringe from the bag.

Anderson did a quick shift and tried to stand. Bishop put him in a headlock. "Okay, Stewart, hold still."

The mysterious man did his work with precision. Who was this guy? Gillian hadn't bothered to tell Bishop or Nigel her plan.

The man removed the cap from the syringe and poked it into Anderson's lower right arm. "That's a good fellow." He caught Bishop's eye. "You can release him—he's not going anywhere now."

Bishop let Anderson go and overheard Nigel laugh from the bathroom. "Capital idea, old girl," he hooted.

He and Gillian had been talking in low tones while Bishop and the tall guy did their work on Anderson. Anger flashed in Anderson's eyes, and he cursed. Taking little notice of the outburst, the man placed his implements back inside the bag, slipped off his gloves, and stood. He and Bishop walked to where the group waited near the bathroom door.

"He'll be out in a couple of minutes. I'll be in the ambulance."

Gillian extended her hand. "Thank you, Commander Alford—I really appreciate it."

Alford smiled. "My pleasure."

After he left, Bishop joined Gillian in the bathroom while Nigel chatted with the EMTs.

"Mind telling me what's going on?"

"I called my office and got permission to have him transferred to the navy base. They have facilities to hold him incommunicado while we send in an interrogation team."

Bishop grinned. "You're not just another pretty face, are you?"

An expression of satisfaction swept over her. "Nope."

"Okay chaps, looks like he's cashed in his chips for the evening," Nigel said to the EMTs.

Bishop glanced at Anderson. He sat perfectly still, chin on chest, drooling with his eyes closed. They wasted no time loading and restraining him on the gurney. Bishop untied Stewart's hands and feet, searched his pockets and wallet, and dropped the loose papers, keys, cell phone, and wallet into a clear plastic bag. Bishop handed it to Gillian, and then motioned to the EMTs. When they wheeled Anderson out, she turned to him and Nigel.

"I'm riding in the ambulance to the base to make sure he gets checked in without any problems. Don't wait up—I'll take a cab back."

Before either could answer, she left and closed the door. They just stared at each other.

Bishop broke the silence, "I wish we'd had another five minutes with him before they showed up. Mercier has a pharmaceutical plant in China. What's the chance this is a legitimate business deal they don't want leaked out until they release a new drug or something on the market?"

Nigel sniffed. "I've no doubt it's a business deal but seriously doubt it's legitimate." He walked back to his favorite chair and flopped down. "I know what my people will demand as soon as I tell them about this."

"Probably the same thing mine will," Bishop said. "Find out what's in those crates."

TWENTY-ONE

Wu Chen strolled through the underground tunnel connecting the Ministry of Public Security and the Ministry of State Security in Beijing. His life consisted of going from one meeting to the next. A far cry from his youth in rural China. Chen had been one of the lucky ones. Born to peasants but blessed with brains, that's how his superiors described him. But he also possessed a cunning and cleverness few realized until too late.

He understood at an early age how the Chinese Communist Party worked. This gave him an advantage. Chen became the youngest Youth League leader in history. His fanatical adherence to party doctrine and bold style rocketed him into national leadership positions. At university he adopted his country's desire for a new China. After graduation, his appointment at the Ministry of State Security, Ninth Bureau, alerted all doubters: this was a man to be reckoned with.

Now, twenty-two years later, as minister of state security, he faced his greatest challenge. His reputation and career rested on the outcome of the next meeting. The party's general secretary, and the nine-member standing committee of the Politburo, wanted an explanation. Operation Black Jade had been compromised, and they needed answers. Chen had retrieved the top secret documents from his safe before the meeting. After being ushered into the third-floor conference room of the party congress building, he paused and drew a breath. The general secretary and nine Politburo members waited.

When the double doors closed, the general secretary welcomed Chen. A high-back chair at the end of the long conference table was reserved for him. He bowed to the assembled group and laid his notebook on the table before taking his seat. His throat went dry when he scooted his chair into position. He made a show of opening the notebook and removing the top secret documents. Chen casually poured a glass of water from the carafe and took a sip. No one asked a question or uttered a word. The dead silence held its own fear.

Chen cleared his throat, studied his prepared remarks, and began. "Almost a year ago, the premier instructed me to instigate plans directed at collapsing the United States economy. They believed the US was its most vulnerable since the Great Depression. A number of ideas were put forth, and each was extensively researched. After much debate, we decided that shutting down all US Pacific ports from Seattle to San Diego would be the best solution."

Chen paused for effect and took a peek at his audience. Surprise and shock traced across the faces of all present, except the general secretary. He had been in on the plan from the outset. Chen gave the members a chance to absorb it further, and when the low mumbles and whispers trailed off, he continued.

"The plan has the added benefit of not only shutting down all US Pacific sea commerce, but also increasing *our* foreign trade. Without the competition of the largest economy in the world, we could sign contracts, securing all of Asia, Australia, New Zealand and India as exclusive trading partners for the foreseeable future."

Again, this news caused much whispering and exchanging of glances among the members. Before Chen could continue, Wen Chi raised his hand.

"Excuse me, comrade Minister, but you said all West Coast sea commerce?"

Chen fixed his gaze on him. "Yes, comrade."

Chi folded his hands. "And how many ports would be affected —total?"

Chen glanced at his notes, but he already knew the number. He only wanted to buy some time. His stomach twisted and his right leg shook. He must settle down. "Twenty-nine, comrade," he answered.

Chi stared at the fellow on his left. Yongkang, known as the father of the standing committee, had been there the longest. His influence stood second only to the general secretary's, and he was consulted on almost every important issue. Yongkang didn't speak, but an unsettling smirk crossed his lips. The general secretary had probably leaked the details to him. Many a bureaucrat had fallen to Yongkang's questions. Losing face before the standing committee led to loss of office and power. Yongkang delighted in destroying careers.

Chen directed his attention back to his notes. "We considered different methods for accomplishing this daunting task. We needed a plan to not only shut down the ports but ensure they could not reopen in time to save the US economy from a deep depression. A complete destruction of the facilities was out of the question because our fingerprints would be associated with such an attack.

"And you found such a method?" The gravelly voice spoke up, belonged to Yongkang.

Chen set his notes aside and directed his full attention to the senior standing committee member. "Yes, comrade."

Looking at the other members, Yongkang waived his hand. "Please, share it with us." The evil expression the old man flashed scared Chen. If he already knew about the plan, this could be a trap. Chen swallowed hard and dabbed sweat from his brow.

"We consulted with the Tenth Bureau, and they recommended contamination of the ports with a highly contagious biological agent—a virus—as the best way to accomplish the goal."

A loud murmur came up from the table. Soon everyone became animated, talking at once. Everyone except Yongkang. Another smirk crossed his lips, and he eyed Chen. He had probably planned this all along. Finally, Yongkang held up a hand for silence. When the room became quiet, he leaned forward and met eyes with Chen. "Please continue."

Chen referenced his notes once again—to buy a few seconds and settle his emotions. "We contracted the operation through a third party, thereby removing ourselves from any suspicious activities with the incident. Since the Wuhan lab COVID-19 incident, the World Health Organization and the CIA watch every move we make as far as biological activities."

"What exactly does this third party know about our involvement?" the general secretary asked.

Chen faced the man. "They know only that they are being paid a half billion US dollars by a Chinese man. They must suspect state sponsorship, but there's nothing to directly link us with them after the mission has been accomplished."

"And this third party can carry out the operation without our involvement becoming known?" Chi asked.

"Yes, comrade," Chen answered.

Yongkang folded his hands and said, "Tell me, if we wreck the US economy and all their trade, as well as our ownership of their Treasury bonds—what happens to our economy?"

This had been the question Chen dreaded. The Chinese economy would also take a nose-dive. Estimates varied widely as to how much it might cost the country. The most optimistic prediction indicated a small short-term pain for an even greater long-term gain.

"It would cause a temporary recession in our country. The loss of so big a trading partner can't help but push us into an economic downturn, but we project that, with the US ports out of commission, the Pacific Rim will have little choice but to turn to us. They must trade with someone, and we are the biggest market they can access. It might be a year or more before US ports could be brought back up for shipping. By then we could have established favorable trade agreements for the next decade."

Several members nodded their heads in agreement. Chen relaxed at the positive response shown by the men. He let out a long-held breath. The odor of his perspiration made him a bit nauseated.

"But comrade, what about all the US debt we hold in their bonds?" Chi asked.

"We have calculated that. Over the last year, we've quietly been unloading US bonds at a discount in smaller, secondary markets." Chen cleared his throat—the dryness had returned. "Unfortunately, it will be necessary to write off a substantial amount so that it appears we possessed no forewarning of the incident, but we can afford it with the additional revenue acquired through the new trade agreements. We have tripled our cash reserves in recent months."

Heads bobbed around the table and whispers broke out between members. The general secretary tapped on his glass with a pen. "Gentlemen, this meeting is not to discuss the plan, but to determine whether it should go forward. It may have been compromised. Chen, please explain what happened."

As the suspicious and curious eyes fell on Chen, his stomach tightened again. "We commissioned production of the pathogen at a pharmaceutical plant owned by the third party. The pharmaceutical plant is located in Macau. Twenty-nine canisters of the pathogen are being shipped to Canada. They are disguised as scuba tanks. The third party will load them on their yacht, and sail in a few days from Victoria to Seattle.

"The motor launch from the yacht will disburse the airborne pathogen from it's stern while it shuttles from ship to shore at each port down the US seaboard. The pathogen has been processed into a fine powder, which is indistinguishable from the exhaust of the motor launch. It will infect people miles inland and completely contaminate the port facilities. With an incubation period of a week to ten days, we should easily be able to infect the last port before symptoms are seen in the first one."

The group sat open-mouthed at the revelation. A plan so simple, yet so diabolical. Chen addressed the group again. "A problem arose when one of our men became infected. Before we acted, he fled in a sailboat. The US Coast Guard picked him up, and while he died soon after his rescue, they are now alerted. Their police and intelligence agencies are investigating. We've not come under suspicion. I believe the operation should continue."

Chi's brow crinkled. "Comrade Minister, you speak of this third person. Who is it? Why are they helping us?"

Chen gazed at the general secretary and allowed him to answer the question.

"Gentlemen, the mysterious person is the pharmaceutical mogul,

Claudine Mercier of Alo Vita Labs. Her reasons are personal as well as pecuniary."

The men exchanged whispers, and several private conferences broke out around the table. Chen sat back and let them discuss it, glad to take a rest from talking. Yongkang asked the next question.

"What steps have been taken so no additional problems will arise? If we are found out, it would constitute an act of war."

Chen leaned forward. "We've sent our two best people. Dr. Tee will handle the biological aspects as well as supervise the release of the pathogen, and Colonel Hong will oversee security."

Heads nodded. This appeared to garner much appreciation from the group. Both men worked in the Scientific and Technological Tenth Bureau. Both were well-known and respected.

Yongkang's brow folded. "Excuse me, but I thought Dr. Tee's expertise was biological toxins, not pathogens. Isn't that why they call him *Dr. Toxin* at the Tenth Bureau?"

Several around the table nodded. The rest had confused expressions.

Chen released a quick grin. "Partly correct, comrade. Dr. Tee is most experienced with toxins. His poisons work so well few toxicologists can unravel what killed the victim. But he also has great experience in pathogens. You will recall he headed up our test with weaponizing the plague and smallpox last year."

Yongkang shrugged. "If you say so."

Chi rested his forearms on the table and interlaced his fingers. All heads turned in his direction. "Comrade Minister, I'm no scientist, but even I see a flaw you've not addressed."

Chen was ready. This old inquisitive bastard always looked under every rock and behind every door to pull out something to challenge a good idea. Chen had baited him to force this question. Now he could deliver the coup de grace.

Chi smiled at the other members. "If this virus is as deadly as you've described, what will keep it from infecting everyone—another worldwide pandemic?" He sat back with a satisfied smirk as the members erupted in agreement.

Chen also rested his forearms on the table. "Forgive me, but I failed to mention the fact that when we engineered the virus, we included an extra DNA and RNA strand which has allowed us to develop a vaccine. We have nothing to fear from the virus and can market the vaccine to the world at an inflated price."

Chi frowned and seemed to bite back a response.

The general secretary again pinged his glass. "I will not allow Operation Black Jade to go any further without a consensus from the committee. We take a risk here. Our actions *do* constitute an act of war, if discovered. We will vote now if there is no further discussion." He looked around the table at the nine men. "I will not vote, so a majority of five is necessary to pass it. All in favor of cancelling the operation, raise your hands."

Chen's skin felt as if it would crawl off his bones, watching the hands rise. Four votes of no confidence in him. Any of the five remaining members could refrain from voting. He needed all of them for the thing to pass. The general secretary recorded the four *no* votes in his binder, then lifted his head.

"All in favor of continuing the operation, raise your hands."

Four hands rose, including the inquisitive Wen Chi's. Yongkang did not move but stared at Chen. Finally, as if a heavy weight hung from his wrist, he slowly raised his hand in dramatic form. A slight smirk crossed his lips when the general secretary recorded the vote. The operation would continue.

Chen sat back in the chair. The old devil had made him wait. Probably wanted to see him sweat a little more. Well, he got his wish—soaked and completely drained, Chen relished another victory.

TWENTY-TWO

Bishop's room was still a wreck, so he took a change of clothes to Gillian's. He crawled into bed a little after midnight—about ten minutes before she returned. She snuggled beside him, and they dropped into a deep, peaceful sleep. The thought kept running through his mind—he owed his life to this woman. Some people might have frozen with panic, but not her. Even though she was young and inexperienced, she had something you couldn't teach. Courage and the will to learn were essential qualities in any good intelligence officer. Combine those with her natural intellect and you have a powerful force.

The next morning, they met Nigel for breakfast in the hotel restaurant. Bishop and Nigel filled her in on what Anderson told them the previous night.

"So, what's our next move?" she asked.

Bishop leaned closer. "I should hear from Hal sometime today. He'll let me know about the surveillance operating against us last night."

Nigel looked in deep thought. He finally joined the conversation. "I believe we've turned an important corner. If Anderson and the surveillance team were Ms. Mercier's eyes, now she's almost operating blind. If the listening device in your room was her ears—now she's deaf." He sat back with a satisfied expression. "I'd say we've taken the advantage away from her."

"I have an appointment to meet the interrogators. They're flying in later this morning," Gillian said.

"I'm still troubled by something," Bishop whispered.

Nigel and Gillian stared at him in silence.

He blurted, "Why?"

"Why, what?" Nigel asked.

"Why is Mercier involved in such business? Why is there Chinese involvement? What do she or they possibly expect to gain from this? She's already filthy rich, successful, and wants for nothing. Why would someone like that risk everything? Doesn't make sense."

Nigel dabbed his mouth with the corner of his napkin and looked across at Gillian.

"Beats me," she said. "Perhaps the interrogators can fill in some blanks."

"Well, if you'll excuse me, I have a few calls to make." Nigel rose from the table.

Gillian checked her watch and also stood. "The interrogators will arrive in less than two hours. Wouldn't hurt to spend a few minutes schmoozing some of the brass at the base. Never know when I'll need another favor."

"Want someone to go with you?" Bishop asked.

Gillian winked at Nigel. "Like someone with a gun?"

Bishop had been waiting for her to bring up the fact he had a weapon in her country without proper authorization. He smirked. "Yeah, someone like that."

She never missed a beat. She reached over and gave Nigel a one-armed hug. "You stay here and protect poor Nigel. I'd hate to think of anything happening to the old boy."

"Perish the thought," Nigel agreed.

Bishop joined the group as they left the restaurant. He couldn't shake the thought they were still missing something—something important. For all the high fives and backslapping over last night's success, he still had that feeling. He knew just who he needed to call.

He slid the electronic key into his door and peeked inside. He'd forgotten to set the piece of paper on the floor last night as he'd left to sleep in Gillian's room. It was just as well, because the first thing he saw was Hal's huge frame, sitting in the large comfortable chair by the window.

He was reading the paper with a Grande cup of Starbucks in his meaty paw.

"I really don't know why I even bother locking this damn door," Bishop said by way of greeting. "Everyone who wants to seem to come in on their own."

Unperturbed, Hal lowered the paper. "Morning, Bishop. Looks like you had a hell of a party last night." He surveyed the lamp lying on the floor and broken glass at the end of the bed. "Place smells like a bar."

Bishop pulled the desk chair over to the sliding glass door and sat across from him. "Had an uninvited visitor." Bishop waved his hand around the room. "This was his calling card." He handed over Anderson's black commando knife.

Hal examined it with interest and let out a low whistle. "Ugly thing."

"Yeah. Did you come up with something?"

Hal pulled two sheets of paper from his inside coat pocket. "We were able to spot two vehicles and four suspects tailing you. Here are the vehicle descriptions."

"Any ID on the guys in the cars?"

"Second page. We couldn't get great descriptions of the occupants because it was dark and only one went into the restaurant. We shot a few photos, though. Might have the Canadians and SIS run them through their facial recognition software." He handed Bishop a microdisc in a small plastic bag. Hal pursed his lips. "There is one odd thing worth mentioning, however."

Bishop looked up. "What?"

Hal shifted in the chair and took another sip of coffee. "They were an older crowd."

"Huh?"

"The guys tailing you last night were an older crowd. I'd put the youngest at about 55 or 60. You'd expect maybe one guy, the boss, to be older, but not the whole team. That type of work is a young man's game. Old-timers don't hold up too well in that kind of crazy shift environment. Living out of cars on surveillance work isn't what these guys should be doing at their age."

"Were you able to find out anything about them?"

"We followed the vehicles to houses in the suburbs after they finished tailing you. Looked like some place your average neighbor would live. Nothing suspicious or sinister to mention. The addresses are at the bottom of the second page. Shouldn't take much detective work to figure out who they are."

Bishop again scanned the paper. "Great work."

Hal pushed his bulk up from the chair. "Let us know before you go anywhere. We'll give you cover." He strolled to the door.

Bishop studied the papers a long time. Lots of questions, very few answers. If they expected to get to the bottom of this, they needed to start filling in the blanks, fast. He dialed the encrypted phone and leaned back in the chair.

"This is Lesa."

The voice sounded all business. He knew better. "Sure is nice up here."

"Is that you, Bishop?"

"Who else?"

"Where is up here?"

"Victoria, British Columbia."

Her sensual groan floated into his ear. "I love it there—spent one of my honeymoons in Victoria," she cooed.

Lesa changed husbands as often as she changed agencies. She'd last worked for the National Security Agency until Cook stole her from them. There wasn't a better intel analyst in the country. Her databases overflowed with information.

"I have a problem that needs solving."

Her voice took on a business tone again. "Okay, shoot."

"This is going to be an easy one for you. I need as much information on Claudine Mercier as you can come up with. She owns Alo Vita Labs. Lives here in Victoria, at least part time."

"Am I looking for anything in particular or just a general info flush?"

He thought for a second. "Yeah, see if you can figure out why she would be involved in nefarious activity against the interest of the US or Canada."

"Is that it?" she sighed.

"That's all for now."

"Will you bring me back a souvenir?"

"Sure, what do you want?"

"A rich Canadian," she said, just before hanging up.

With Nigel and Gillian occupied for the moment, Bishop had little to do but wait. He opened the sliding glass door to get a breath of fresh air. The oppressive smell of thick scotch still hung in the room. He'd have to tip housekeeping especially well. As he stepped onto the balcony, the warm sun bathed his skin and the swish of waves splashing on the rocks below made him more restless. It wasn't smart, but he wanted to take a long run to clear his head. If he stayed near the water, on the walking trail, he could deal with whatever might come his way. He'd be damned if he'd be held prisoner in this room.

He changed and wrapped the Sig in a hotel face towel, then slid it and his cell phone into a small backpack and looped it over his shoulder. He called the front desk and apologized in advance for the mess in the room, dropped a hundred on the pillow, and using the back stairwell, sneaked out of the side entrance near the trail. As he began his run on the path leading to the downtown inner harbor, the clear morning air was rich with the aroma of blooming flowers.

Turning the first corner, he slowed because of two landscaping guys working in an area just off the path. The older white guy was explaining something to the younger Asian kid. They wore identical dark green overalls with the name of the landscaping service on the back. The older man attached a high-pressure hose to what appeared to be a steel scuba tank. The last words Bishop heard him say before he got out of earshot were "compresses insecticide."

Ten minutes later, Bishop blew into the crowds milling around the inner harbor shops. He started back down the trail toward his hotel, dodging a mime on stilts juggling bowling pins. When he got back to the turn where the two men were working, the older man stood directly under a snake tree. Its red bark had turned a copper green color.

The fellow held the opposite end of the hose that was attached to the scuba-tank-looking canister. He was covered from head to toe in a Tyvek suit, gloves and goggles, and wore a respirator. An almost-invisible mist spraying from the nozzle of the hose drifted high into the old tree. The kid noticed Bishop staring and waved an agreeable hello as he passed.

Just then, two men stepped onto the trail from an adjacent path. They walked toward him, apparently discussing something serious. The pair looked in good shape and were dressed in stylish business casual. They weren't the same guys who tried to kidnap him a few days earlier, but it seemed clear they had something on their minds other than a morning walk. Their eyes met his as they strolled closer. He couldn't tell if their coats hid weapons. Their hands were visible, and their arms swayed in time with their pace.

TWENTY-THREE

Bishop came to a full stop. There wasn't any exit from the trail. Water to his right, and a small patch of ground to his left with a tall wooden fence blocking any escape. He slid the backpack off his shoulder and unzipped it, never taking his eyes off the approaching men. They stopped and glanced his way, then turned to each other in quiet conversation. Bishop eased his hand inside the pack and found the grip of the pistol. The two men continued their approach until one reached out and touched the other's hand. They stopped and gazed at each other. The next second one guy put his free hand on the other guy's cheek, and ever so gently gave him a long kiss on the lips.

Bishop let out a breath he'd held too long just before the couple turned, hand-in-hand, and strolled in his direction. Well, if this was a setup it was the best he'd ever seen. Bishop shifted so he'd be on the land side of the trail as they passed. He kept his hand on the Sig inside the backpack—finger on the trigger. The two never paid him any more attention, giggling about some private joke. He zipped up the pack and walked the rest of the way to the hotel.

By the time he made it back to his room, he had formulated a plan. He dialed Hal and threw out the idea he'd been thinking about on the trail. Hal loved it. Bishop dialed Gillian's number. She said the interrogators had just landed at the base. He explained his idea to her. She seemed a little less enthusiastic than Hal but agreed to at least think about it.

Next, he called General Cook and gave him an update on last night's activities. There was concern in Cook's voice about the crates. They agreed 24-hour satellite surveillance on the island would be in order. Bishop then explained what he wanted to do that evening. Cook's initial silence caused concern. He agreed it would be the next logical step and gave his blessing.

Bishop did his usual sit-up and pushup routine, showered, and called Nigel.

"Want to grab a bite?"

"Sure."

"Meet you in the hotel restaurant in ten minutes."

When he arrived, Nigel waved him over to the window table.

"Waiting long?" Bishop took his seat.

Nigel only shook his head—something troubled him. The scowl and furrowed brow looked too out of character.

"What's wrong?"

Nigel looked from side to side and leaned in closer, barely whispering. "I contacted HQ earlier and provided an update."

Just then a waiter approached with a couple of menus. He handed one to each and motioned for another staff member to fill their water glasses. "We have several specials today. I'll give you time to look these over and tell you about them in a minute." He turned toward another table of four.

Nigel waited until the fellow was out of earshot, then leaned in close to Bishop. "The Canadian Security Intelligence Service is considering replacing Gillian on this assignment."

Bishop sat back. "Where did you hear that?"

Nigel touched the side of his nose with his index finger. "My sources inside the community."

"But why? She's doing a good job. What happened?"

Nigel shifted and straightened the silverware on his napkin. "Some rubbish about her being too young and inexperienced for a high-profile case like this—ridiculous, really."

Bishop's emotions flared. It would break her heart. It might break his, as well. He'd allowed himself to become too involved with her.

"Do you agree with them?" he asked.

Nigel's head shot up. "Heavens no. Wouldn't hear of it."

"So, what do we do?"

"Well, I put in my two cents with the office. They might make a call on her behalf—if we're lucky." Nigel stared out the window.

A teenager with a carafe of water walked up and filled their glasses. Bishop's big appetite was gone, and he only had a little clam chowder and sourdough bread.

While they ate, he briefed Nigel on his plan. After the plates were cleared, Bishop's cell rang.

Gillian's voice had an excited edge. "Where are you?"

"Nigel and I just finished lunch at the hotel."

"Good, bring him to your room. I'll meet you there in fifteen minutes."

Had she received the notification she was being recalled? "What's wrong?" Bishop asked.

"You were right about Belousov. I just got a call from the medical examiner's office. He was murdered."

Bishop glanced at Nigel and grinned. "Well, isn't that interesting."

Fifteen minutes later, in Bishop's room, Nigel asked, "Murdered? How?" He'd claimed the large chair near the window and sat there like a king on his throne, silhouetted by the bright light washing through the room.

Gillian flopped down on the edge of the bed before answering. "Botulinum, one of the deadliest toxins known." She leaned forward and rested her arms on her knees. "The pathologist said it didn't come from anything he ate or drank. The contents of his stomach showed no trace of it."

Nigel made a face at the suggestion of analyzing the contents of a man's stomach and gently laid his hand over his own.

"So, why do they think he was murdered?" Bishop asked.

Gillian got up and walked to within a couple feet of him. She reached around and softly pinched him behind his neck. "Right there, at the base of the hair line, they found a little welt. They believed the toxin was injected in that area."

Nigel steepled his fingers. "Let's see. Big pharma mogul with access to all kinds of nasty bacteria, viruses, and toxins. A willing henchman in the form of Stewart Anderson, and an old retired, alcoholic employee like Belousov who talks too much. Yeah, I might see a connection."

"Me too," Bishop said. "Give this information to the interrogators. They can use it as leverage when talking to Anderson."

"Already done." She sat back down. "I had an interesting call from my director earlier."

Bishop held his breath, waiting for the next sentence. He could feel the same tension emanating from Nigel. Was she being relieved?

A puzzled expression crossed her face. "He asked me what I thought about the way the investigation was progressing, and if I believed we should just turn the whole thing over to the RCMP."

Bishop prayed she had answered correctly. If they were considering replacing her on this assignment, they'd want to know if she was fully committed to following it through. If they suspected she was the least bit wishy-washy, she'd be gone.

Nigel had a worried, nervous expression. "So, what did you tell him?"

She strolled to the mirror of the dresser, made a few adjustments to her hair, and checked her lipstick. She turned and faced the pair. "I told him I'd be damned if I'd even think about giving this to the RCMP. They had their chance, as did the FBI. Just because neither could come up with a clue doesn't mean we have to do their jobs for them and then let them take the credit."

Nigel's eyebrows rose. "You told the old man that?"

"I sure did." She dropped back on the edge of the bed and crossed her legs. "And then I told him just what Bishop said last night when I thought we ought to turn Anderson over to the RCMP for interrogation."

Bishop tried to remember what he'd said, but he was too slow.

"I told him this inquiry had left the law enforcement side and passed to the intelligence end, and we weren't giving it back. We were making progress and planned to finish it."

That wasn't exactly what Bishop said, but whatever he'd said obviously inspired her to stand up to her director like a twenty-year veteran.

"Well done, girl," Nigel blurted out. "That's giving the old sod his due. What did he say to that?"

"Believe it or not, he asked me if we had everything we needed. Offered to send in more SIS agents. I declined—said we could handle it." Gillian looked Bishop's way. "Did I do good?"

He relaxed his shoulders and smiled. "No—you did great." Bishop briefed her on his idea for tonight, and she agreed.

She grinned, lay back on the bed, stretched, and yawned. "I feel like a nap."

Bishop picked up the papers Hal gave him earlier and dropped them on her face. "You can sleep when you're dead. We still have work to do before tonight."

She didn't touch or try to remove the papers. "What's this?"

"The vehicle descriptions and addresses of the people following us last night."

She bounced up, grabbing the papers as she stood. "Hal got them, eh?"

"He got them," Bishop confirmed. "Can you have your people run the tags and addresses?"

"I'm on it." She dug for the phone in her purse.

"A note of interest." Bishop held up a finger.

She stopped searching and turned his way.

"Tell the analysts that the names belong to people in their 50s and 60s. Don't know if that makes any difference, but it might be useful for their purposes."

"Are we talking about the over the hill gang?" she asked.

TWENTY-FOUR

Claudine Mercier drummed her perfectly manicured nails on the desk and phoned Stewart Anderson for the third time—she was worried. He hadn't returned last night and wasn't answering his phone this morning. He wasn't the sort to avoid her. His British Commando machismo wouldn't allow that. Where could he be? Had he skipped out? No, she'd promised him a big bonus once the operation concluded. She knew he'd stick around for that. Probably tied one on and got a hotel on the mainland for the night—wouldn't be the first time. He'd show up later.

She glanced at the desk calendar. The last shipment was due any day. Once it arrived, the *Sea Angel* could sail the next morning. She loved her yacht. The thought of using it for such a nasty purpose made her angry, but it was the ideal cover. Known by all in the West Coast maritime crowd, there'd be no suspicion seeing it sail down the US West Coast. Her mind briefly turned to the morality of what she was about to do, but the bitterness crept back in. She couldn't let it go—she wouldn't let it go. It was what sustained her. The thought of getting even, of making someone pay, poisoned her soul a little more each year. Everything was going so well until she was infected. She couldn't change the past, but extracting her revenge would start to make it right.

This would be her only chance. That's why she'd initiated contact with the Chinese. The plan was hers. They'd refined it, worked out the logistics, and insured the items were smuggled into Canada, but she gave herself credit for it. It wouldn't bring back her face, but at least it would even the score. As for the half-billion payment she'd receive, she couldn't have cared less about the money. It was just a number she'd thrown out to see if they would bite. They bit hard—just what she'd wanted.

———

Bishop lounged on the bed with the laptop, checking for encrypted emails. Gillian had some shopping to do, and Nigel had disappeared for less than half an hour before returning to Bishop's room with a fresh bottle of scotch. He set it on the dresser and sniffed.

"They got most of the smell out of the carpet. Do try and dissuade Gillian from breaking this bottle over someone's head." He opened it and poured a generous portion in a glass. "To your health," he said. "Sure you won't join me?"

Bishop shook his head and kept typing.

Nigel took another drink and smacked his lips. He found his favorite chair and lowered himself into the soft cushion. "I think I've figured you out," he pontificated, staring at Bishop.

Bishop ignored the taunt.

"You're too much of a Puritan for your own good," Nigel declared.

When he failed to respond, Nigel took another sip and continued. "I'd bet my pension your ancestors came over on the Mayflower and never touched a drink in their lives."

Bishop finally released a grin as his gaze drifted Nigel's way but said nothing.

Apparently, Nigel was just warming up. He slouched lower in the chair, propped his feet on Bishop's bed, and studied the ceiling. "Let's see now, you probably originally sprang from the loins of a Calvinist minister, I should think."

"Okay, okay—stop it; you're killing me. Give me a short one or I'll never get any work done," Bishop said.

Nigel leaped to his feet and poured Bishop a large one. "That's the spirit. Glad to see you've come to your senses. When I imbibe alone, amidst company, it makes me think maybe I have a drinking problem." The traces of a grin cracked the corners of his mouth.

Bishop accepted the glass, took a quick sip and went back to his computer until his cell rang.

"Hello, Lesa. Got something I can use?"

"I hope you appreciate me working overtime for you," she grumbled.

"Of all the people who work overtime for me, I always appreciate you the most."

"I've been drilling into Ms. Mercier's background for the last few hours. She's an interesting character, you know?"

"Really? Tell me."

"Well, for starters, she used to be married to the Queen Consort's ex-husband's…"

"Younger brother," Bishop finished her sentence.

"Right," she said. "The old boy died a decade ago, and there was talk in the gossip columns about something fishy pertaining to his death. Seems it all got neatly swept under the rug with British efficiency. Anyway, she inherited all his money and the pharmaceutical company. Instead of running it, she went back to medical research— her first love—at the company's California lab."

"How many labs do they have?"

"Do you mean research or production?"

"Both."

"Let's see…" Lesa hummed "California Dreaming" under her breath. She always hummed when she thought hard about something. "Five," she answered. "Two in the US, one in Canada, one in England, and one in China."

"China?" The labs had been mentioned in the briefing material Cook gave Bishop. He'd made note of them but didn't think any more about it until Stewart Anderson's revelations last night about the Chinese guys visiting Mercier.

"Yes, in Macau," Lesa said. "The labs specialize in research and development of vaccines and drugs to treat highly infectious diseases."

"Like Ebola?"

"Exactly. The US, England, China, and a dozen other countries have contracts with them to produce vaccines. Most of what we receive gets sent to the CDC's Strategic National Stockpile. You know, the stuff we keep under wraps until there's a biological attack?"

Bishop's mind raced, trying to connect the dots. All the pieces were there, but the motive still wasn't clear. Nigel's head rested against the pillow cushion of the chair, and his eyes were closed. His glass was empty and dangled loosely in his hand. An occasional snore drifted through the room.

"Bishop, are you still there?"

"Yeah, just thinking about something."

"If you meet this woman, don't forget to address her as 'Doctor'— she has a PhD in bio-chemistry. A respected researcher in her day."

"Okay, did you come up with anything on why she may have a beef with the US or Canada?

"Yup." He perked up and shifted the phone. The sound of papers shuffling and humming preceded her answer. "Doctor Mercier left the company CEO position to become the head of research. She still owned the thing, but apparently hated the business end of it. Hired a company president, kept her seat on the board, and in reality, ran the company from the shadows. Anyway, back in 2010, she and her team were working at the California facility when she almost died."

"Flesh-eating bacteria research?"

A long silence followed. "Bishop, do you have a damn camera hidden in my office?"

He took the rebuke with as much good nature as possible. She was tired and wanted to go home. "No, ma'am."

"Then kindly let me finish telling my story."

"Sorry."

"As I was saying, she became infected with the stuff they were researching. She demanded to be flown to Canada, but her condition was too grave, and her doctors wouldn't release her. The CDC got involved and, because she remained highly infectious, they ordered her into isolation."

"I'm not following you."

"Here's the kicker, Bishop. The flesh-eating bacteria was on her face. She knew her own lab in Canada had an experimental drug that might treat it, but the FDA wouldn't approve its use in the United States and wouldn't allow her to leave. Before her doctors could bring it under control, it had destroyed half her face—horrible, horrible scarring. After recovering, she tried suing the FDA for half a billion dollars, but the case went nowhere. Left California and hasn't returned to the US since."

"So, are you saying what I think you're saying?"

"Yup. She has no problem with Canada, and, if she wants to see anything bad happen to the United States, it's for one reason —revenge."

"Thanks. I'll get back to you." Bishop lay back on the bed. Of all the motivations he might have considered, revenge never crossed his mind. Of course, he wasn't an insanely wealthy and beautiful woman whose face had been destroyed. He'd been in Victoria almost a week, and had a good case built against Mercier. But none of it would hold up in court because he had no direct evidence of her involvement. He cast the idea aside. He wasn't a cop; he was an intelligence officer. He'd briefed his agency and let Gillian brief hers. The politicians would decide when and how to act. Dealing with Mercier had passed from their hands. If there was no direct threat against the US or their allies, he may as well start packing his bags.

He still intended to go through with the plan tonight, but figured sooner or later, the Canadians would intervene and he and Nigel would be relieved.

He jumped at the loud rap on his door. Nigel stirred from his nap, held the empty glass to his ear, and said, "Hello—Nigel here."

"Nigel, it's the door," Bishop whispered, sliding off the bed.

Nigel pulled himself to a more formal sitting position and ran a hand over his face.

Bishop looked out the peephole at the big man with close-cropped red hair. He didn't know the guy, but the face looked familiar. He swung the door open, and the large fellow jumped.

"Can I help you?"

"Mr. Bishop?"

"That's me."

The man's eyes darted from side to side. "I was instructed to meet Ms. Hathaway here at five."

Bishop looked at his watch; it read five o'clock on the dot. "Who are you?"

"Lieutenant-Commander Foster, sir." He blushed a little before saying, "We met a few years ago when you gave a lecture to our group on terrorism."

"I see you two have met." Gillian's voice floated down the hall as she approached.

"Somewhat," Bishop said.

She lowered her voice and nodded to Foster. "This is Nathan Foster —JTF2."

Bishop shook hands with him. "A pleasure, Foster—good to see you again. Come in."

Nigel stood and Bishop introduced him to the newcomer. "Aren't you chaps modeled after our SAS?"

"Yes, sir," Foster said.

Nigel blushed. "Good lord, don't call me sir. I'm too young and certainly not deserving of the title." Nigel lifted the bottle. "Would you like a drink?"

"No, thank you."

Another knock sounded from the door. Bishop checked the peep hole and let Hal in. More introductions were made before everyone but Bishop and Hal found a seat. Bishop walked to Foster's side and laid a hand on his shoulder.

"We've had people on our tail since we arrived a week ago. Tough to conduct the kind of investigation we're doing with a crowd." Bishop glanced at Gillian. "Any info on them yet from your people?"

She shook her head.

He continued. "Hal here can identify them. They follow us every time we leave the hotel. They've never made any threatening gestures, so it looks like they're used for surveillance only." Bishop strolled back to the bed and sat on the edge. "But they've become a real nuisance. It's time to take them out. We're not involving the local cops on this one—strictly an intelligence matter."

Foster grinned. "Right."

"We three will be the bait." Bishop pointed to himself, Nigel, and Gillian. "Hal and his boys will point out the guys we want neutralized while they're surveilling us. That'll be you and your team's job."

Foster's brow furrowed and he pursed his lips.

"You okay with that?"

"Yes, I'm fine with it. Just one thing."

"Yes?"

"What do we do with the bodies?"

Nigel broke down in uncontrolled laughter and exclaimed, "On that note, I need another drink."

Bishop grinned. "Perhaps I chose my words poorly. When I said *take them out and neutralize*, I meant take them prisoner and hold for interrogation."

Foster turned a shade of red that matched his hair. Bishop, not wanting to add to his embarrassment, poured a small scotch for each. He handed one to Foster and held up the other in salute. "I love working with commandos." He turned and nodded to Hal. "Now explain the plan."

Hal leaned against the far wall and cleared his throat. "We've looked around Victoria, and Beacon Hill Park appears to be the best location for what we have in mind. It has everything we need in a good snatch-and-grab site. First, it's isolated, but close to downtown. Second, it's a big place. Over sixty-two acres for me and Foster to commit all sorts of skullduggery. And third, there are lots of places to set up surveillance unnoticed. It's not uncommon to see cars parked around there day and night.

"We'll wait till around nine o'clock to give traffic a chance to thin out. Bishop and Gillian will pick up Nigel at the front of the hotel to make sure the bad guy's surveillance team sees them." Hal pointed to Bishop. "Then all you have to do is drive to the park, making sure you don't lose any of the tails. If you want, you could even stop at some location along the way for a minute just to ensure all the bad guys have caught up. We want to bag the whole group at once. This allows me and my men time to identify the cars following you. We'll put Mr. Foster and his team to work as soon as the bad guys settle down and start their surveillance." Hal slid both hands in his pockets and looked around the room. "Any questions?"

"I have one," Foster said. "Are any of the targets armed?"

Hal looked at Bishop.

"We have no idea. Assume they are—no need getting hurt out there."

"Anything else?" Hal asked.

"You have a location you'd like us to park," Bishop said.

"Oh, yeah." Hal took a city map from his jacket and spread it on the bed. Running his finger down the map, he stopped and tapped it. "Take Belleville and enter the park at this north entrance here, off Douglas Street. Follow it around and park at the southernmost tip, here on Dallas Drive." He tapped the map again. "It's a large area with plenty of cover for someone who might be watching you. "Don't park too close to either side of the overlook, but right in the middle. That'll force them to park between Victoria Point and Finlayson Point if they want to cover you. That's where we'll be waiting. Foster, if you'd like to come along, we'll do a quick recon of the area before it gets dark."

"Good enough." Foster stood.

Gillian spoke up. "After you nab them, we'll transfer them to the naval base for interrogation."

"Understood, ma'am," Foster said.

Bishop opened the door. "Okay, then. See you all later."

As Hal and Foster left, Gillian dropped on the bed, stretched and yawned. Nigel just sat there, sipping his drink. Bishop stood by the door, holding it open for several seconds before Nigel took the hint.

"Oh, I say," he stammered. "Think I'll go have a proper nap before tonight's excitement. Shall we say pizza to go at nine?"

TWENTY-FIVE

Colonel Hong stared at Claudine Mercier as she paced before her office window. He understood the reason she'd called him, but refused to acknowledge anything until she brought it up. At last, she did.

"It's after five and I still can't reach Stewart. Something's happened —I know it."

"Perhaps Mr. Anderson decided to leave."

She jerked her head in his direction. "Don't be a fool. He wouldn't just up and go. There's a reason."

Hong didn't reply.

"Don't you think there's a reason?"

Hong shrugged. "You know him far better than I." The scarring on her face turned a peculiar shade of pink when she became angry.

She stopped pacing and caught him with an icy stare. "When in the hell will the last shipment be here? We can't wait forever."

He shrugged again. "According to Dr. Tee, it will arrive when my government deems it safe. Coast Guard activity has increased over the last week. Avenues once open to us have been closed."

She whirled around and faced the window. "You're useless. Get out. I'll call Stewart's contact on the mainland. He might know something."

Blood rushed to Hong's face. The pulse on his left temple beat faster as he turned to leave. The fact Anderson was missing did disturb him, and it further complicated a delicate situation. If he could not be found, then he'd be a loose end. Hong's reason for being on the island was threefold: to supervise the storage and security of all arriving shipments, assist Dr. Tee in overseeing their disbursement, and ensure there were no loose ends at the conclusion of the operation.

This foolish woman should have known the results of her actions, but she thought herself too clever. Did she actually believe they would leave her alive with the information she had? He would make her death slow and painful—no loose ends.

———

After the others left, Bishop and Gillian lay in bed a long time. His arm cradled her, and her shallow breathing relaxed him. He'd lain there for almost an hour but couldn't nap. His mind went over every detail of the plan. Foster's question about the targets being armed kept popping back into his head. What if they were? What if they decided to attack? He didn't want Gillian in the car, but she was part of the group. Her absence might arouse suspicion.

She shifted and hugged him a little tighter. A groan slipped from her lips, and her hair tickled his cheek. He closed his eyes, and finally a fitful sleep enveloped him. He awoke when her body jerked. She broke from his embrace, sat up, and stared around the room like she was looking for something.

"Are you okay?"

She brushed the hair out of her eyes and shook her head. "I just had a dream… a bad dream." She touched him on the shoulder and then ran a hand down her face. Like she was making sure they were both real and not part of the dream. She slid off the bed and staggered to the bathroom, her steps unsteady.

He got up. "You all right?"

"Fine, just fine." The sound of running water drifted from the bathroom.

He followed her. Peeking around the corner, he caught her staring into the mirror. Her face was wet, and the tips of her hair dripped with water. She braced herself with both hands on the sink. Something in her eyes made him shiver. He'd seen that look before. Not on her, but on the battlefield. It was doubt. That doubt that cloaked itself around someone like a fog. That doubt caused people to make bad decisions—or worse, no decision—and freeze.

She noticed him and grabbed a towel, brushed it across her face, and grinned.

He pulled her to him and rubbed her back in large, slow circles. "Want to talk about it?"

She looked up. "Have you ever dreamed you were going to get killed?" Before he could answer, she rested her head back against his shoulder and exhaled.

"No," he whispered, "I never have. Was that your dream—that you were going to get killed?"

Her body tensed before she turned her face back up to his. "No, I dreamed you were."

———

Gillian went back to her room for a shower. She stood under the warm spray and sucked in a lungful of hot, wet air. Why did she have the dream? She wiped water from her face and leaned both hands against the wet tile wall. She'd been an intelligence analyst most of her professional life, first in the navy and then with SIS. With a push for additional women, she'd been approached to fill one of the available agent slots and accepted. That was probably a mistake. She wasn't ready. She'd felt the uneasiness of this knowledge throughout her training, but never expressed her self-doubts. That would have meant immediate dismissal. She loved her analysis job and now regretted being lured into a world of danger and suspense only fit for spy movies.

It was a little too late for recriminations at this point. She couldn't let anyone know of her fears and doubts—not now, not here. She wasn't a hero but had heroes working with her. Whatever happened, she'd see it through. She wasn't a quitter. Her biggest fear—her own agency suspecting she wasn't up to the task. She could handle anything but that.

———

Back in his room, Bishop watched the national news. The evening shadows cascaded through the sliding glass door, and lights across the harbor automatically switched on. He took a shower and studied the park map until his phone rang.

"Everything still a go?" Nigel asked.

"Yeah, we'll meet you in the front driveway. Bring along that gun I suspect you have."

"Gun. Me?"

Bishop chuckled to himself. Same old Nigel. "Right, see you then."

Hal called a few minutes later. "Okay, Foster and I finished our recon, and my guys met his."

"Good, we'll pick Nigel up at nine in the hotel's front driveway. Be on station by then."

"Will do," Hal said. "And Bishop?"

"Yeah?"

"Don't sweat anything. Foster's guys are all top notch. We'll keep you safe."

It was as if Hal had read his mind. "I never had any doubt," Bishop said.

Gillian called a few minutes later. "I'll meet you in the lobby in ten minutes."

"You okay?"

"Sure, ten minutes. Bye."

Bishop slid the pistol into his back waistband holster and grabbed a couple of extra magazines. He put on his jacket and checked himself in the mirror. The outline of the gun could not be seen. Satisfied, he headed for the lobby.

Gillian was just walking out of the gift shop. She grinned and strolled over to him.

"Ready?" he asked.

"Yup."

They took the stairs to the basement parking area. Five minutes later, they pulled up to the front of the hotel. Several cars were either dropping off or picking up passengers. Bishop left Gillian in the driver's seat and got out, making a show of looking for someone while standing with his door open. Just then Nigel strolled through the front door and looked from side to side, like he was expecting a friend to arrive. Bishop reached over, tapped the horn, and waved. Nigel waved back.

Nigel slid into the back seat and let out a sigh. "Well, if our watchers missed that performance, they're blind."

Bishop turned to Gillian. "Take it slow and easy to the park. Don't speed, don't roll through any yellow lights, and be sure to give signals before any lane changes. We don't want to lose anyone."

She licked her lips. A bead of sweat rolled down her temple. "Okay."

A minute later, Bishop's cell rang—it was Hal.

"You guys are looking good. We have three cars with bad guys following you. Two people are in one car and one in each of the other two."

"Thanks, Hal." He looked at Gillian. "Where are we stopping?"

"Gino's—it's around the next corner."

"Can't believe we've dropped from five-star dining to takeout pizza," Nigel moaned.

Gillian smiled for the first time and seemed to relax a little. "Okay, here we go," she said, turning on her right signal. "I called ahead, so it should be ready."

The hole-in-the-wall pizzeria with the red and green neon sign came into view. Nigel jumped out almost before she came to a full stop. He strolled inside and up to the counter.

Bishop's phone rang. "One bad guy car drove past and is parked the next block down waiting for you to leave. The other two cars pulled into the strip center lot just behind you. Don't look around— they're watching you guys like hawks."

"Okay, Hal, thanks for the update."

Gillian's gaze caught his eye. She wiped her sweaty palms against her jeans in a nervous gesture. *She needed to relax.*

Bishop stared straight ahead and slid a comforting hand across the seat on her leg and gave it a soft squeeze. "Be cool, they're all around us."

"Who's all around us? Hal's men or the bad guys?" she whispered.

"Both."

A minute later, Nigel ambled toward the car with a large pizza box and a bag of drinks. Gillian backed out and turned right onto the street, her lips drawn into tight lines.

Just before they entered the park, Bishop's cell rang. He put it on speaker and answered. "Hal, I have you on speaker. Are we still okay?"

"No problems. All three target cars are behind you—we're behind them. We've got the whole bunch in the bag. Park at the overlook, enjoy your pizza, and we'll do the rest."

The tension in Gillian's face melted. She released a familiar grin.

"Thanks, Hal—keep us in the loop."

The park road was well lit, and they had no problem following it to the overlook along Dallas Avenue. Large boulders and tall, stately trees lined the way. Gillian parked exactly where Hal described and turned off the car. Moments later, two vehicles coasted by at slow speed. Less than a minute later, another car pulled to the side of the road about a hundred yards up the hill. Its lights disappeared, but they had no illusions. Whoever drove it was watching and didn't want to be seen.

Bishop let his window down, slipped the pistol from its holster, and placed it in his lap. He looked over his shoulder at Nigel. "Pass me a slice."

Gillian dropped her hand over the back seat. "Me first."

Just then, another vehicle cruised past. Was it a bad guy, or just a local taking a drive through the park? No one turned to look, but three sets of eyes followed it from the car's rear mirror.

Bishop half-turned to Nigel. "How did you come to work for MI6?"

Nigel lounged in the back and waved the question away with his free hand, "Accident—pure accident." He slid low in the seat and nibbled at his pizza. "I was a child of privilege. My father's parents were quite wealthy. Not much left of the fortune for me—bad investments by parents and grandparents—so I had to get a paying job. Through old family connections, I attended Sandhurst and entered military service. After a couple of years, I was recruited into military intelligence. Made a few community contacts, and one day a friend of a friend called and asked if I wanted to make intelligence a career. Told him I'd never really considered it, and he told me to think it over and call him back. I did, and that's how I entered the spy game."

Bishop's ringing phone interrupted the conversation.

"Okay, all the bad guys have settled in. Did you see that car that stopped up the hill?" Hal asked.

"Yeah, we saw it."

"He has the eyeball on you. Just one guy in the car. He's only using binoculars—no night vision equipment."

"You sure?"

"Yeah, 'cause I have an eyeball on him with my night-vision. He's not using a parabolic mic, so it's okay to talk—he can't hear you."

"Where are the other two?"

"They're both well past you, near Victoria Point."

"Okay, we're just going to sit tight and let Foster's men do their work," Bishop said.

TWENTY-SIX

Eugene Carrier scratched his chin and held the binoculars steady, trying to spot any movement in the car. The radio on his console crackled.

"What are they doing?" Charlie's voice asked.

Eugene keyed the radio. "Damned if I know. They parked at the overlook and shut the car off. No one's gotten out. They're just sitting there. Hard to see, but best I can tell they're eating pizza."

"You got a good eyeball?"

"Yeah."

"Okay, we drove past them and are parked near Victoria Point. Give us a shout when something happens. We can't see them from our location."

"Right, I could go for some of their pizza right about now. Think they'd share?"

"Not likely," came the chuckled response.

Eugene dropped the hand-held radio onto the console and leaned back in the seat. With the moon up, he really didn't need the binoculars. What were they waiting on? Were they meeting someone? He squirmed to find a more comfortable position—damned prostate acting up again. The doctor said sitting too long aggravated it. Nothing he could do about that. He hated extended surveillances, and this one had gone on too long. But the money was good, and it wouldn't last forever.

He checked his watch. Over two more hours before getting-off time. He knew one thing for sure: he couldn't hold that piss for another two hours. He looked around to make sure no vehicles were coming and made his decision. Charlie's insistence about disconnecting the interior lights in the surveillance cars had been a stroke of genius. Opening the door, he slipped out into the darkness to the rear of the car and dropped his fly. He thought he heard something and jerked his head to the right. Nothing—his mind must be playing tricks. *What was that?* He caught something out of his peripheral vision—just a shadow close to the ground.

His next sensation could hardly be described. It was as if he'd just urinated on a live electrical line. His body convulsed as the current raced through his limbs, and his knees buckled. He tried to yell but had no voice. As he fell forward, someone caught him. No sooner was he down before a piece of tape was slapped over his mouth, a bag jerked over his head, and flex-cuffs bound his wrists behind his back. A vehicle pulled up. He lifted his head and tried to scream. Two pairs of strong hands tightly gripped his arms and legs. The motor sound gave way to a door sliding open. Muffled voices whispered something, but he couldn't understand what they were saying. He realized they were lifting him just before he was slammed down on a cold, metallic surface. A hard object rested against the back of his head. From behind, a man's voice growled, "If you want to live, lie still and don't make a sound."

That seemed like a pretty good idea to Eugene right about now.

———

On the opposite end of the road, the two men relaxed and listened to *The Zone* at 91.3 FM. Charlie liked modern rock, even though it wasn't Fred's favorite. But Charlie was the boss.

"What do you figure they're up to?" Fred asked, finishing off a bag of nuts.

Charlie glanced his way. "Who knows? Something's screwy. Doesn't make any sense. First night they've done anything like this."

Fred wadded up the empty nut bag and tossed it onto the back floorboard.

Charlie glared at him. "Does my car look like a trash can to you?"

"Sorry, I'll pick it up before I get out. Are you mad about something?"

Charlie shook his head and grunted. "Naw, just tired—ready to go home."

"Me too—never thought this thing would go on for a week."

Charlie held out his hand. "Give me the radio."

Fred fumbled around in his seat and handed it to him.

Charlie keyed the mic. "Hey, Eugene, when you need a break, let us know. Don't have any idea how long they might be here. Could be planning to meet someone." He unwrapped a stick of gum, waiting for the reply. He popped it in his mouth and held out the pack. Fred shook his head. Charlie tried again. "Hey, Eugene, did you copy?" Charlie glanced at Fred, then tried a third time. "Eugene, you hear me?"

"Maybe his batteries went dead," Fred said.

Charlie keyed the mic. "Jerald, you copying me?"

"Loud and clear," the voice said.

"Okay, swing by Eugene's location and check on him—he's parked on the side of the road just before you get to the overlook. Be careful: he's only about a hundred yards from the targets."

"Will do," the voice said.

Charlie adjusted his headrest and stared at the moon's reflection on the waves. After five minutes, he grabbed the radio again. "Jerald, is Eugene okay?"

Only a long silence answered. He glanced at Fred and tried again. "Eugene, Jerald, are you guys all right?"

Fred shifted in the seat. "What's happened?"

Charlie got a bad feeling. Radio troubles weren't common. Only something else could account for this. He held the radio closer to his mouth. "Eugene, Jerald, are you guys receiving me?"

Fred looked at him but didn't speak. His stare seemed to be centered on Charlie's chest. Charlie gazed down at the green dot on his shirt. His gut tightened, "Oh, shit." He turned to Fred. A similar dot had bloomed on the same area of his chest. The outlines of two figures dressed in black stood beside their car. The dark outfits, helmets, bug-like night vision goggles, and machine guns made him think of a Special Forces movie.

"Out of the car and on the ground, now!" the voice boomed as the doors jerked open.

"Let me see those hands!" another voice yelled, just before Fred was swept from the seat and thrown hard to the ground.

Charlie raised his hands, rolled out, and dropped to the gravel, spread-eagled. He'd never been on the receiving end of such treatment. His heart pounded and he felt dizzy. Who were these men? Drug cartel? Criminals? He closed his eyes and said The Lord's Prayer out loud.

———

Everyone had stopped talking, and only the silence of the summer night surrounded the car. A van had driven past about two minutes earlier, and Bishop's head followed it as it disappeared down the park road. When his cell rang, Gillian jumped. He checked the phone—it was Hal. Bishop put him on speaker.

"Are we good, Hal?"

The gruff voice filled the car. "Got 'em, Bishop—got 'em all."

Gillian released a breath and hit the steering wheel with her palm. "Yes!"

"Great work guys. Any problems?"

"One guy pissed all over himself when they hit him with the Taser —that's about it."

"Okay, we'll meet you at the base in a few minutes," Bishop said.

"Hey, there's just one other thing." Hal's voice had a tone Bishop didn't like.

"What's that?"

"Remember we talked about these guys being an older crowd, but professional?"

Gillian stopped smiling and leaned closer to the phone.

Bishop probably wasn't going to like what Hal said next. "Yeah, I remember."

"Well, when we tossed their cars, we didn't find much."

"What does that mean?"

"No surveillance logs, no surveillance action plans, no advanced monitoring equipment—nothing. Their stuff is crap—flying by the seat of their pants. You could get that equipment at any decent sporting goods store. This group isn't connected with the bunch that planted the bug in your room. And they're too old to be part of that gang that jumped you at the hotel."

Bishop didn't answer. His mind jumped back and forth, trying to make sense of what Hal just said.

"You hear me, Bishop?"

"Yeah, I heard."

"Okay then, we'll meet you at the base. Foster just called—they're expecting us."

"Thanks, Hal. See you there."

Gillian said, "I don't get it."

Bishop glanced over the seat at Nigel. His thumb and index finger rubbed his lower lip. He stared back. "Something's wrong."

Bishop turned to Gillian. "We'll figure it out at the base. Let's just—"

Gillian's cell stopped him mid-sentence.

"This is Gillian." She listened for a second. "Hold on, I'm putting you on speaker." She covered the phone with her hand and whispered, "It's my intel analyst getting back to me on the registration of the bad guys' cars. Okay, I'm back. What did you come up with?"

The female voice answered, "I'm sorry it took so long to run this, but there were software problems at the indices database—not our fault."

"That's all right. What did you find out about the names?" Gillian held the phone between Nigel and Bishop.

"Not much. No criminal records, all have lived in or near Victoria for decades. They pay their taxes, don't have any overdue library books, vote in every election, and have little or no debt. About the only thing they have in common is they're all cops. Well, they were all cops —retired now."

Gillian's head snapped. "Did you say cops?"

"Yeah, two were former RCMP, one a Victoria municipal policeman, and the other a Saanich officer."

"Thanks, Sara." Gillian dropped the phone into her bag. No one said a word, but they all probably had the same thought. If the local authorities were compromised, where did that leave them?

Nigel broke the silence. "Oh, dear. Not at all what we'd expected."

You could always count on him to deliver the day's best understatement.

TWENTY-SEVEN

The sprawling Canadian Forces Base, Esquimalt, is the home port to Maritime Forces Pacific and Joint Task Force Pacific Headquarters. The 10,000-acre facility rested at the southern tip of Vancouver Island on the Strait of Juan de Fuca.

When Bishop and party arrived at the Naden gate at a quarter till eleven, two uniform naval police were on duty. One sat in the well-lit checkpoint building, laughing into a telephone, as the other approached their car. Gillian rolled down the window and handed him a base pass and her SIS identification.

"Good evening." His eyebrows rose when he reviewed the credentials. "Where are you going?"

She smiled. "The brig."

He handed her back the papers and bent down. His glare fell on Bishop and Nigel. "These two with you, ma'am?"

"Afraid so."

He grinned. "Okay, just stay to the left after you go through the gate. Brig's on the right after you make the first turn—it backs up to the water—can't miss it."

She followed the road as it curved and parked in front of the two-story red brick building. Hal stood under a light pole talking to Foster.

Gillian, Bishop, and Nigel congratulated the pair on a successful operation. Gillian filled them in on what her analyst said about the guys being ex-cops.

"This stinks," Hal blurted out.

"If you'll follow me." Foster motioned toward a side door.

He slid a plastic card into the slot to the right of the door and input a code on the electronic keypad. A loud click followed, and the metal door released. They walked down a brightly lit corridor that smelled of Lysol, into a cramped office with a small wooden desk and only two chairs. One wall of the office was a huge two-way mirror. It looked into a larger, all-concrete room. The room held no furniture, pictures, or anything resembling comfort.

A heavyset man dressed only in boxer shorts sat on the floor. His hands were bound behind his back and a black hood draped over his head. Directly above him, a spotlight illuminated the immediate area.

Foster said, "Guy's name is Charlie. As you know, Mr. Bishop, we can handle this in a number of ways."

Gillian turned to Bishop. From her expression, she'd never sat in on an enhanced interrogation. He didn't want to shock her any more than necessary, but he didn't intend to start out too soft, either. A little scare always seemed to break the ice. "Let's be fair with him," Bishop said. "Try a level two first."

"You're nicer than I am," Foster replied, and then left. A few moments later, he reappeared in the concrete room carrying a two-gallon yellow plastic bucket. He wore a black mask and black leather gloves.

His footsteps scraping across the concrete floor echoed from speakers thanks to the hidden mic. Gillian's mouth gaped open. It looked like she was holding her breath. "What's he going to do?"

"Get us some answers, I expect," Nigel whispered.

Foster paused and glanced toward the group in the office.

Gillian's cold fingers grabbed Bishop's bicep.

Foster drew the bucket back and threw the contents at the man. When the water hit him, his body stiffened, his head snapped back, and he screamed. Foster immediately jerked the guy's hood off and put his mask-covered face inches from the man. With only slots for the eyes, nose and mouth, Foster must have looked like a monster to the poor fellow. He tore the tape from the man's mouth. "Why were you following them?" he snarled.

The expression of total shock and fear on the older, balding man caused even Bishop to wince. The wide-eyed creature jerked his head from side to side. His chest heaved, trying to catch his breath. "Don't kill me—please don't kill—"

Foster yelled, "Why were you following them?"

Bishop watched the performance and agreed with the technique—fear followed by intimidation. Under level two interrogations, Foster could do nothing to cause physical pain. The water bath and threats were as far as he could go. Given enough time, mind games, sleep deprivation, and temperature variances would break most people. The deep, dark recesses of one's mind could paint a much more haunting reality than most interrogators. Only a professional could resist. But in the end, if enough pressure was brought to bear, almost everyone talked.

Gillian's nails dug into Bishop's arm as the older man broke down. He reeled back from Foster's gaze and wept. "Please don't hurt me. My wife has cerebral palsy—I love her—she can't even walk."

Foster drew his pistol and cocked the hammer, taking care not to point it at the man—that was not allowed under level two. He held it at his side and circled the fellow a couple of times, letting the guy settle down.

Gillian twisted Bishop's arm tighter when Foster stopped in front of the fellow. He reached down, grabbing the last few scraps of hair on the almost bald head, and pulled back. Foster again got eye-level and raised the gun to within inches of the man's face with the barrel pointed toward the ceiling. The guy stopped crying; his eyes fixed on the pistol. His lower lip quivered, and his whole body shook.

In a menacing whisper Foster said, "Last chance. Why were you following them?"

The man looked at Foster as if he'd just heard the question for the first time. "My job—it's just my job."

"Who do you work for?"

"A private investigations agency," he whimpered. "Please don't hurt me, please." He hung his head and began to sob.

Foster walked behind the man and holstered his pistol. He turned and faced the two-way mirror. The eyes behind his mask seemed to lock on Bishop.

Bishop peeled Gillian's fingers off his arm and stepped to the mirror. He tapped on the glass a couple of times, and Foster nodded. Before leaving, he covered the man's head with the black hood but didn't tape his mouth.

"Mind if I have a go at him?" an unfamiliar voice asked.

Standing behind Bishop and Gillian was a short man in his fifties, dressed in jeans, a black turtleneck, and herringbone sports jacket. He had a neatly trimmed gray beard and intelligent eyes. He must have slipped in during the height of the questioning.

"Phil," Gillian said. "When did you get in?"

"Few hours ago—HQ sent me over. Thought I might be of use."

Gillian touched his shoulder. "Everyone, this is Phil Lester. He's the senior interrogator from SIS. He's been grilling Stewart Anderson for us. We call him Doctor Phil—he has a PhD in psychology."

Just then, Foster walked in. He said, "Didn't expect that kind of answer. Why would he lie about something that simple? He may just be a private investigator."

"What's his name?" Phil asked.

Foster dug into his pocket and handed him a driver's license. Phil examined it for a moment and handed it back.

"I'll ask him a few questions, if that's all right." He glanced at Gillian.

"Be our guest."

Without a word, Phil left and soon reappeared on the other side of the two-way mirror. He walked around the man on the floor. The guy must have heard him, because the hooded head followed his footsteps as he circled. Phil stopped behind him and laid a hand softly on his shoulder. The man tensed at his touch. In a quiet, calming voice, Phil asked, "Did he hurt you?"

The head twisted in his direction. "What?"

"Did he hurt you?"

"No… that is, I—"

"You don't need to worry about him anymore," Phil whispered. He strolled around, knelt in front of the guy, and lifted the hood. The man blinked several times. Phil laid a hand on his knee.

"Hello, Charlie. Mind answering a few questions for me?"

Bishop nodded: this was classic good cop-bad cop interrogation. The irony was that, in his terrified and excited state, Charlie didn't recognize it for what it was. When fear took over, you reverted back to basic principles—friend or enemy.

The fellow's expression turned from terror to confusion. He blinked again and licked his lips. "What do you want to know?" He swallowed hard and his nervous eyes widened.

Phil's voice remained quiet and calm. He kept his hand resting on Charlie's knee—maintaining that human contact. "You told the other man you worked for a security company or something? Tell me about that."

Charlie took a deep breath. "Yeah, an investigative agency."

"That's right, an investigative agency," Phil corrected himself. "Does it have a name?"

"Atlas—Atlas Investigations."

"Okay, but you never said why you were following those people. Were you planning to harm them?"

Charlie's jaw dropped at the suggestion. "No, no—I only followed them. I don't want to hurt anyone. It's just my job. I'm a private contractor Atlas hired to run surveillance on them."

Phil raised an eyebrow. "But why? What did they do that they needed to be followed?"

Charlie's answer caught Bishop off guard. "They're involved in a big blackmail thing. Aren't you with them?"

Phil smiled. "No, Charlie."

"Well then, if you're not with them—"

"Let me ask the questions," Phil interrupted. "So, who told you they were blackmailers? Who ordered you to tail them?"

Charlie shifted and stared at him. "One of the co-owners of the company briefed us about them."

"Co-owner, huh? What's his name?"

"Edward Koner."

The name caused Bishop's stomach to churn. *Oh, hell.*

Just then, Gillian repeated the name and pulled out her phone. She began scanning old emails.

Phil stood and looked down. "This Edward Koner fellow, who is he? A co-owner of the company, you say?"

Charlie exhaled. "Yeah, when there's a special assignment like this, he briefs us personally."

"And he told you these people you were instructed to follow were blackmailers?"

"That's what he told us."

"Okay, relax. I'll be back in a few minutes," Phil said.

When he joined Bishop and the rest, he was smiling. "Edward Koner is Stewart Anderson's contact. Stewart gave up that piece of information to me an hour before you guys arrived."

Bishop said, "And Inspector Edward Koner is the guy who escorted me through customs the day I arrived. He's with the RCMP."

Gillian stared at the email on her phone. She frowned. "Guess who escorted the visiting FBI Agents to Picard Island to interview Stewart Anderson?" She looked up at them. "Koner."

"Sounds like Inspector Koner's been a busy fellow," Nigel remarked.

Gillian said, "Phil, you work on the bunch we just brought in. See if their stories all match. I have to contact the director's office. We know there's at least one dirty RCMP in the mix—could be more."

TWENTY-EIGHT

Bishop stood beside his bed and poured scotch into a glass. Nigel already had one while reading Dr. Phil's report on the interrogation of Stewart Anderson. Gillian ended her call and dropped the cell back into her bag.

"That wasn't what they wanted to hear," she said.

Bishop passed her the glass, and she took a sip. "What did your headquarters say?"

"Not much—I think I stunned them a little." She stood in front of the sliding glass door and stared into the night. "They want Foster and his guys to check out the island again."

Bishop shrugged. "If we're ever going to get to the bottom of this, that's where the answers are."

Nigel dropped the report on his lap and rubbed his eyes with his thumb and index finger. "Think I've figured it out." He sat up in the large chair and took a swallow. "When this all started, Anderson must have already had some sort of working relationship with Inspector Koner. Somehow Koner finagled or got assigned to the RCMP part of the virus investigation. When he discovered Picard Island was under suspicion, he tipped off Anderson. And when the visiting FBI agents went to the island, Koner made sure he went along to keep them away from anything incriminating."

Bishop and Gillian stared at each other a moment before they both nodded.

"That's as good a working theory as any," Bishop said.

"But what does Anderson or Koner know about the virus?" Gillian asked.

Nigel held up the report. "According to this, nothing. Anderson thinks Mercier is involved in some kind of shady business deal with this Colonel Hong character but hasn't the foggiest about the nature of it. A dullard, if you ask me."

"If Anderson knows nothing, then it's a good bet Koner knows even less," Gillian added.

"What did your HQ say about picking him up for questioning?" Bishop asked.

Gillian walked back and sat beside him. "They don't want to tip him off—hoping he'll lead them to others in the conspiracy."

Bishop set his empty glass on the desk and stretched. It was late—past two o'clock. "We've been playing a rigged game for the last week. We need to go back over everything we've done and recheck our facts now that we know about Koner's involvement. There is one place we might find some answers about the virus—Belousov's."

Gillian's weary eyes narrowed. "What do you expect to find there?"

"I don't know, but we never gave the place the once-over because the constable was there. Since we discovered he was murdered, I think we should take a closer look. After our interview, I had the feeling he'd held something back. Remember?"

Gillian pursed her lips before saying, "Yeah. I'll talk to Foster about doing a recon on the island and we'll pay another visit to Belousov's tomorrow. I'll have to call the constable to get the key first."

"Don't think I'd do that if I were you," Nigel said.

She stared at him for a second before apparently realizing her error. "You're right. I'm too tired to think straight." She stood. "If we can't trust the RCMP, who else can't we trust?"

———

Mercier stood alone in the dark bedroom and stared out the window. She sipped the gin, and emotion welled up inside. Why had God cursed her? Was this payment for her one and only great sin? It *had* been a sin—murder always is.

Memories of her early years as a young researcher flooded back. Those were the happiest of her life. Twelve years ago, when she was thirty-one, they'd called her a rising star. Her brains and looks would take her to the top, she'd been told—and they had. The day she had briefed the board on the new vaccine brought her to the attention of the company's owner and CEO.

————

After the meeting, he requested she remain and answer a few additional questions. His last one surprised her: "Will you have dinner with me tonight?"

She grinned. "Is this a business dinner—or strictly social?"

He confidently sat on the edge of the conference table. "Can't it be both?"

He had a reputation. Twice her age, once married and divorced, he traveled in all the right circles. And why shouldn't he? His ex-sister-in-law is now royalty—part of The Firm. His net worth fluctuated between seventy and eighty million pounds sterling, depending on the stock value of his company, Alo Vita Labs.

A demure smile cracked the corners of her mouth. "I'll be ready at seven. I'm staying at the Bristol."

————

She turned from the window at the thought and took a swallow of gin. Why had she married the man? What could she have seen in him? She shook her head and stumbled toward the chair. As she flopped down, some of her drink sloshed on her hand. Yes, she'd sinned, but the penalty was too severe. No one deserved her punishment.

She'd tried making a go of the marriage. What else could she do? The social events, dinners, theater, and parties seemed to never end.

The first time she'd caught him cheating, she issued a warning—never again. But it was his game, like polo and clay shooting. Conquering younger, more attractive women was as natural as breathing. When the whispers and stares became intolerable, she'd given him an ultimatum.

———

"Your women, or me?"

He laughed in her face. "Or you'll do what? Divorce me? Ha, I think not." He strutted around like a peacock. "You've seen my will—divorce me, and you'll get a pittance. Stay married, and you'll inherit it all."

Claudine made her decision at that moment. She still puttered around in the company lab outside London once a week, so her presence there a week later caused no suspicion. At five o'clock, when the techs departed, she went to work. She knew where all the reagents were. She'd checked them out earlier. Before entering the lab, she disabled the CCTV cameras. Even though the place was mostly deserted, she feared discovery when she used her coded ID badge and entered the stock room. Three years earlier, the lab had worked with little success on a treatment for killing cancer cells. They'd ordered a large consignment of rosary peas from Costa Rica. They had not been disposed of after the failed experiment. She scanned the computer file in the stock room. They were listed as being stored in bin 42-C. She located it and took a peek. In the stainless steel drawer, she found eight one-pound plastic bags of rosary peas. She donned a pair of latex gloves before removing exactly one ounce of peas from each bag. To all appearances, nothing had been tampered with.

Back at the work area, she put on a second pair of latex gloves, a respirator, and safety glasses. She poured the tiny red peas into a grinder. They weren't really peas, but red seeds with a black spot covering one end. She'd seen them used many times in necklaces worn by locals and tourists alike in the tropics. She placed the cover back on top of the grinder and gave it a firm twist. When the seeds were ground, the suspended powder could cause severe illness if inhaled. She set the machine to fine-grind, and—taking no chances—held the lid with one hand as she hit the switch. The peas turned to a soft, red powder in seconds.

Claudine carried the container to the bio-safety cabinet. She pressed the power button, which activated the air circulation fan. Sliding the container under the Plexiglas hood, she opened it. The red cloud of powder that floated from inside the container whirled up toward the top of the cabinet, where the fan passed it through a HEPA filter. She screwed the lid back in place, pulled the mask off, and headed to the work area.

The lab door opened behind her and one of the uniformed security staff walked in. She knew him—Roger.

His look of surprise soon faded. "I didn't realize there was anyone still here."

She forced a smile even as her stomach flipped. Could her wobbly legs support her? "Good evening, Roger—long time no see."

"Just doing the first walk-through. You going to be much longer?"

Her dry mouth made it difficult to answer. Roger studied the container in her hand. Finally, she mustered enough courage. "Just finishing up an experiment. Probably should have waited 'til tomor-row." His confused expression scared her. *What if he hangs around to talk? The rapid pulse in my neck must be obvious.*

Roger's ringing cell phone broke the silence. He answered it and listened for a moment. "I'll check it out," he said and disconnected. "Suspicious vehicle in the parking lot—gotta go."

She relaxed a little. "Don't worry—I'll lock up when I leave."

"Thanks." He opened the lab door to exit but stopped.

Just as Claudine believed she might pull it off, Roger turned back. "Wait a minute." His suspicious tone sent a chill through her. "You know you're doing something wrong."

She skipped a breath and shook—her pulse felt like it would tear through her neck. "Excuse me?"

Roger winked and flipped on the wall switch. "You forgot to turn on the 'experiment in progress' light in the hall. No one should bother you now. See you later." He let the door close behind him.

Staggering to a lab stool, she collapsed. Her heart pounded and breath came in pants. God, that was close. She kept a death grip on the container until her nerves steadied. All the suspended particles had settled. Claudine poured the light red powder through a large funnel into a big, open-mouthed flask and immediately corked it. Then, opening the top, she poured enough distilled water into the flask to cover the powder, eliminating the inhalation danger. Claudine whirled the slurry round and round, adding additional water every few seconds. After the powder dissolved, she lit a Bunsen burner and set the flask on top. She then switched out corks to one with a hole in the center and inserted a glass tube. She attached the other end of the tube to a smaller flask sitting on the lab bench.

Then she waited. The condensation vapors rose from the flask on the burner and into the glass tube, ending as a slow drip into the second flask. *Kinda like making moonshine*, she'd mused. After twenty minutes, a pale red-yellowish liquid settled into the second flask. Claudine poured the liquid through a filter sitting atop a small beaker. She removed the filter and studied the yellow and red impurities. The liquid in the beaker now resembled water—crystal clear. At this stage she could have stopped but didn't want to take any chances. One last step would ensure the absolute lethality of the brew.

Claudine poured the fluid into an oversized test tube and affixed a stopper. She slid it into the centrifuge and closed the lid. When it powered up, it hummed like a small box fan. She let it run for fifteen seconds. The bottom of the test tube was coated with minute, clear crystals. She again poured this through a filter, and marveled that the substance flowing into the small vial was much more deadly than ricin. Abrin—pure, synthesized abrin. And the most amazing thing: once administered, the chance of discovery would be almost nil. No English pathologist would ever dream of testing for it. After all, who would poison an English gentleman with such a nasty tropical toxin?

Cleaning the lab proved a bigger challenge than she realized. Washing all areas had been the easy part; disposal of the residual abrin the toughest. Nothing could remain which indicated the procedure had taken place. She finished a little before eight. Driving past the guard shack, Claudine threw a wave. She was carrying exactly one half milliliter of the deadliest liquid on earth.

As usual, her husband wasn't home. The maid reported that he'd called from his club and requested a hot bath be drawn. Claudine marveled at how a man's habits could be his downfall. Always a hot bath, then a glass of Chateau Lafite sherry before bed. They hadn't slept in the same room for some time, but that night would be different. She bathed and dressed in a sheer, nude-colored robe. The slamming of his bedroom door was the signal. She tiptoed across the hall and cracked the door. As Claudine listened, the sound of the toilet flushing was soon followed by splashing water. She eased into the bedroom and sneaked to the credenza. Then, she removed the small vial from her robe and emptied the watery liquid into a glass. She filled the glass with sherry and smelled it—no trace of an odor. The sound of singing drifted from the bathroom. He liked singing in the tub. Claudine set the glass on his nightstand.

She filled a second glass with sherry and sipped it—not bad. While he had lounged in the steamy tub, she eased into the bathroom. His eyes were closed, and the soft singing continued. She leaned over so one of her firm breasts hung slightly out of the robe and let it touch his nose. His eyes flew open, and he jumped. His lips showed the hint of a smile, and without a word, he leaned up and licked her nipple. She grinned and took a sip of sherry.

"I hope you don't mind—I stole some." *I've baited the trap.*

His smile widened as his hand slid under the robe and between her legs. He glided it to her crotch and massaged her. "You've been a very naughty girl. Stealing must be punished." He pushed hard inside her, and she winced. She hated him—as always, his touch felt like sandpaper.

"I am bad," she giggled. "If you'll get out of the tub, I'll show you just how bad." She stood and let the robe drop to the floor. His eyes drifted over her perfect body. She stepped back. "No, not yet—I want to finish my drink first. It'll relax me."

"Mind pouring me one, old girl?"

"With pleasure." Claudine retrieved the poisoned glass from his nightstand and set it on the bathroom sink. "I'm waiting." She swished back into the bedroom. Lying in bed, she watched him dry off through the open bathroom door as he sipped the sherry. He kept a teasing eye on her while applying that wretched aftershave she hated so much—it smelled like manure. She had a horrid thought: what if he attempted to kiss her with the poison on his lips? She'd have to maneuver him into his favorite position, fast. He swallowed the last of the drink and strolled naked into the bedroom. She was past the point of no return. There wasn't an antidote for the poison—she had fully committed herself. She rolled to her stomach and lifted her rear to him.

A little after six the next morning, Claudine awakened to the sound of pounding on her chamber door. She'd sneaked back to her bedroom after the insatiable man dropped off into a sexually fulfilled sleep. Being found in bed with a sick man after not sleeping with him regularly might be too suspicious. She slipped on a long, quilted robe before answering the door.

Hobbs, the butler, waited with a grave expression. "Madam, your husband is ill. He's requested we summon a physician."

"What's wrong?" Claudine pulled the robe tighter.

"It appears to be food poisoning, or possibly stomach flu," Hobbs speculated. "He's vomiting."

She followed Hobbs to her husband's room and found him collapsed at the toilet. "Help me get him up," she commanded.

They moved the old letch into a seated position, and she wiped his face with a wet cloth. He rested against the tub, his eyes cracking open. "The oysters—the damn raw oysters at the club," he mumbled.

This couldn't be better! Claudine almost laughed. She wanted to scream, *No, you old fool—it's not the oysters. You won't get off that easy.* "Hobbs, go wait for the doctor downstairs. I'll stay with him."

"Yes, madam."

"And Hobbs—bring him up straight away."

"Yes, madam."

Claudine counted to ten after the butler left, then snatched up the abandoned sherry glass from the sink and fled to her bathroom. Pumping liquid soap from the dispenser, she thoroughly washed and dried it. She ran back across the hall and replaced it on the credenza next to the decanter with the other clean glasses. She then took her empty sherry glass from the previous night and placed it where his had been in the bathroom.

The rancid smell in the bath made her gag—bloody diarrhea. He stared at her through squinted eyes and mumbled something. His eyes closed, and he slumped down into the pool of excrement. Moments later, the sound of footsteps echoed from the hall as Hobbs and the doctor approached.

Seeing the man toppled over into the bloody mess, the doctor exclaimed, "Good god—call an ambulance, now!"

Hobbs retreated from the bath, and Claudine cried, "What can I do, doctor?"

"Help me lay him down—anything else can wait until an ambulance arrives."

Hobbs ran back into the bath. "They're en route, sir."

This had to be her best performance, so Claudine didn't hold back. She staggered toward Hobbs and allowed her knees to buckle, "I think I'm going to—"

Hobbs caught her in mid-fall.

"Get her out of here, man," the doctor screamed.

She allowed herself to be dragged to the bedroom before apparently coming around. "What happened?" she whispered.

"You just fainted, madam," Hobbs said. "Come, sit down."

Claudine lowered herself into the chair beside the credenza and pointed at the sherry decanter. "Please, a small glass, Hobbs."

"Yes, madam." He grabbed the glass she'd just washed. Hobbs poured it half full and raised it to her lips. She took a few sips and waved it away.

"Go, help the doctor—I'm fine." *Now the stage is set. The coroner will never think to check for abrin with the oyster story circulating.* She knew that, if anyone asked about the glasses, Hobbs would honestly say he'd used a clean glass to pour her sherry, and they'd find only a small residue in a glass from the night before. Everyone would assume it had been used by her husband the previous evening. Claudine had second thoughts after the ambulance left. She grabbed Hobbs. "I'll get dressed and go to the hospital. Have the maids give this chamber and bath a thorough scrubbing."

"I'll see to it, madam."

Her philandering husband died seventeen hours later. It was not a peaceful departure. The wild screams, horrible hallucinations, and seizures seriously distressed all in the intensive care ward. The first signs of trouble came before the funeral. Stories of his mysterious death made the rounds in the press. A full autopsy revealed nothing. Tested samples of body fluids, tissue, hair, and organs left the pathologist with no reasonable explanation. Hobbs' testimony at the inquest shed no light on the circumstances surrounding his master's death. As expected, he'd told the story about the sherry, but efforts to examine the glasses had been useless. The maids did a thorough job of cleaning. The decanter was tested with no trace of poison found. Hobbs' testimony about pouring Claudine a drink from the same decanter seemed to exonerate her, but the English tongue-wagging continued.

The final coroner's report listed the cause of death as from source or sources unknown. This did nothing to quiet the rumor mill. Invitations to parties dried up. When she meet people she knew, the friendly rapport disappeared, replaced by suspicious stares. His friends' wives were the worst. Each seemed to think this young, beautiful widow had eyes for *her* husband. In a mad effort for acceptance, she even hosted several large dinners, but almost everyone declined. Claudine's reputation was permanently destroyed in England. Even in her native Canada, she wasn't able to escape the stares and whispers.

In a desperate attempt at resurrection, she fled to the United States. She left the corporate business to a chairman and board while she retained ownership. Supervising experiments in the California lab was what she really enjoyed. The next few years were heaven, until the accident. That changed everything. Her curse—her punishment from God.

TWENTY-NINE

Bishop called General Cook the next morning and briefed him on the previous night's activities.

"That's not good," Cook said.

Bishop shifted the encrypted phone to his other ear and watched a large sailboat drifting out of the marina toward open ocean. The morning sun washed over the sail, making it look like an enormous angel wing. "Yes, sir, it complicates matters on our end."

"Fuller's been stalling the White House, hoping you'd turn up something—he won't be happy."

"Nothing from the satellite, General?"

Cook grunted. "No, Picard Island's quiet as a mouse. If they're expecting a shipment of something, it hasn't arrived yet."

Bishop glanced at his watch. "I have to meet someone. Is there anything else?"

"No—stay in touch," Cook said.

Bishop finished dressing and met Nigel and Gillian in the hotel's restaurant. "Sorry I'm late. Miss anything?"

From Gillian's expression, something was wrong. "Good news, bad news," she whispered. "Got a call from Foster earlier. They're being withdrawn."

"Why?"

"Ottawa threat," she said. "Prime minister ordered all anti-terrorist units back to the capital."

"Serious?"

"Very. Apparently uncovered a bomb factory and new terrorist cell. They're taking them down tomorrow."

Nigel downed the last of his tea. "Well, that delays our look-see of the island."

Gillian shrugged. "Can't be helped. I'll get them back as soon as they finish. Until then, we're on our own. They did do us one last favor."

"What?"

"They quietly picked up the day shift of our park followers and delivered them to Dr. Phil."

"Was that the good news?"

"Yeah, that and the fact Phil completed his interrogations on the ones from last night. All their stories check out. Just a bunch of old, retired cops trying to supplement their retirement income with some off the books work. They're not involved and have no idea why they're being held."

"Rather leaves us with little to do," Nigel mumbled.

Bishop picked at the remains of a croissant on Gillian's saucer. "I'm for checking Belousov's place before lunch."

Nigel dropped his napkin on the plate. "I'm ready."

Twenty minutes later, Bishop rolled the window down and the fresh smell of forest drifted into the car. He checked the clouds: a warm morning usually meant a cloudy or rainy afternoon. The winding, shaded road on the way to Sooke reminded him of his and Nigel's first meeting. He thanked god he'd shown up when he did. Gillian, though bright, still had much to learn about covert operations. Having Nigel to bounce ideas off and give advice meant a lot. Bishop's mind still boggled at the thought the Canadians weren't taking this pathogen business more seriously. Of course, they couldn't ignore a bomb factory and active terrorist cell, but leaving Gillian without support wasn't a good compromise. Just then, a snore drifted from the back seat. Nigel's head tilted back, rocking from side to side.

"Never knew anyone who could fall asleep so fast," Gillian whispered. "Must have a clear conscience."

Bishop peeked again at him. "I used to envy guys like that when we were awake for days at a time in Afghanistan—the ones who could drop off for those ten- or fifteen-minute naps always seemed more rested."

Gillian glanced at Nigel from the rear-view mirror. "I'm happy he's retiring and going back home, but I'll miss him."

Just then, the 17-Mile House Pub came into view. Bishop shook Nigel's knee. "Rise and shine—we're almost there."

Nigel's left eye crept open, and he yawned. "Getting too old to stay up with you young people all night. Where are we?"

"Belousov's place is just around the next curve." Bishop took a small, black leather case from his pocket. Gillian turned left down the gravel road and pulled into the half-circle drive in front of the cabin.

Bishop strolled to the door and dropped to one knee. He opened the black leather case and removed two lock picks.

Nigel got out, stretched, and eyed the old-growth forest and water beyond. "Beautiful."

"You should see the view from the back," Gillian said, ambling toward Bishop.

Nigel followed. "How long will it take to—"

Bishop twisted the knob and swung it open.

"—unlock the door."

Walking inside, Gillian squinted at Bishop and stuck her tongue out. "Show-off."

The stale cigarette odor had been supplemented by another—a wet, musty smell. The living area remained a disaster. Stacks of books, magazines, and folders spilled their paper contents over the floor. Bishop opened the blinds, and filtered sunlight wormed its way into the cluttered room. A chill hung in the air—the chill of tragic death. Bishop hated that chill.

"Not one for a good housekeeping award," Nigel muttered. He peered out the back window at the dark blue waters of Sooke Basin. "But I see what you mean about the view."

Gillian turned around several times. "Where do we even start?"

Bishop peeked into the bedroom. "Take your choice. I'll start here."

Nigel sat at an old roll-top desk in the corner. The thing was layered with dust and piles of papers. "I'll work on this."

Gillian shrugged, slipped on a pair of gloves, and started rummaging through the loose papers on the floor near Belousov's shabby recliner.

For the next few hours, they searched in almost total silence, except for an occasional *yuck* or *jeez* when Gillian discovered something disgusting. At last, she stood and shook her hands. "I think I just unearthed an old cockroach cemetery."

Bishop sauntered back into the living area from the kitchen. "Bedroom and kitchen are done." He grabbed a stack of folders from a cardboard box and sat in Belousov's recliner.

"What are we looking for again?" she asked.

He glanced her way. "You'll know it when you see it."

"Half the stuff I've seen is in Russian," Nigel grumbled. "It could be the bloody Rosetta Stone, and I wouldn't know the difference—hello, what's this?" He held up a folder. "Who's Avery?"

Bishop kept thumbing through the stack of papers in his lap. "No idea."

"That was Belousov's cat—remember the one that ran under my legs?" Gillian answered.

"Oh, yeah."

"Well, here's his vaccination record file," Nigel laughed, tossing the folder to Gillian. It landed on the floor between her and Bishop. She didn't bother to examine it but kept sifting through papers.

Bishop twisted his neck and closed his eyes for a second to relieve the strain. When he opened them, they came to rest on the folder Nigel just tossed. A piece of paper had come loose and lay halfway out on the floor. He studied it as he picked it up. It had nothing to do with cat vaccinations. It was a hand-drawn sketch of a boat... a small motor launch from the looks of it. Someone had taken great care to illustrate the rear section. On each side of the outboard motor was the outline of a cylinder. Below it, a notation: *3000 PSI*. On the cylinders, the symbol of a biohazard trefoil sent a chill through him. His mind flashed back to his run along the trail the other day. Those landscape people… the old man and the Asian kid. The scuba-tank-looking thing hooked up to the hose spraying the snake tree—*compressed insecticide.*

Bishop snatched up his phone and dialed Dr. Fletcher at USAM-RIID. He needed an expert's advice. There was surprise in her voice when she answered. "Mr. Bishop, I wasn't expecting to hear from you."

"Sorry if I interrupted anything, Colonel, but I have a question."

"Certainly, how can I help?"

Nigel and Gillian stared at Bishop holding the drawing while he spoke into the phone. "Colonel, please check and ensure you're switched to secure voice."

"Confirm, secure voice," Fletcher repeated.

"Could this pathogen be pressurized?"

"Pressurized?"

"Yeah, could it be put into a cylinder of some kind and brought up to three thousand pounds per square inch without rendering it inef-fective?"

There was a moment of silence before she answered. "Pressurizing would do no harm—in fact, it may help stabilize it."

Bishop had her on speaker, so Nigel and Gillian were following every word. "Okay, try

out this scenario. If someone loaded this virus into a pressurized tank, could it be successfully dispersed from the rear of a boat?"

Colonel Fletcher's voice took on a forbidding tone. "Yes. In the fifties and sixties, when we were engaged in chemical and biological research, that very method was extensively tested. It proved highly effective."

"If they wanted to do it, how would it work?"

"I'm not an expert on biological warfare, but it basically boils down to maneuvering the boat upwind and traveling parallel to the target area before the pathogen is released."

Nigel's expression deepened, and Gillian whispered, "Good god."

"Anything else?" Bishop asked.

"Contamination would be the only drawback to that type of plan,"

Fletcher said. "The people driving the boat would have serious risk of exposure unless precautions were taken. Some sort of hazmat protection—the more the better—and also, a full decon of the boat and passengers with a strong chemical solution afterwards might work."

Bishop's throat went dry. "Thanks, Colonel. That's what I needed to know."

"Mr. Bishop, may I ask you a question?"

"Sure."

"I probably shouldn't be asking, and if you can't tell me, I'll understand—have you found such a biological dispersement device?"

Bishop glanced at Nigel and Gillian, then back to the drawing in his hand. Since he'd not informed General Cook, his next words were very measured. "Naw, just a hunch. Thanks, doc."

———

Cook and Maxwell sat in Cook's office and listened to the encrypted phone while Bishop described what he'd found and what Colonel Fletcher had just told him. Cook rubbed his temples in a useless effort to relieve the latest headache. He glanced at Maxwell after Bishop finished.

Maxwell asked, "What other documents were found relating to this?"

"Nothing—that's it," Bishop said.

Cook ran his hand down his face and leaned over the phone. "That's pretty slim evidence."

"Yes, sir, it is."

A long silence followed as everyone considered the options. Finally, Cook broke the spell. "There needs to be another recon of that island—specifically that yacht—to see if its motor launch has such a modification."

"Does the satellite show the thing uncovered?" Bishop asked.

Maxwell spoke up. "Negative, all photos show it covered."

Bishop exhaled. "Okay, we can check the island again, but we'll have to do it ourselves. Our Canadian commando support has been pulled back to the capital for a threat."

"Yeah, we heard," Cook said. "Wait until I get clearance from the national security advisor before you do anything—I'll get back to you."

"Could we get a SEAL team up here to do a night recon on the yacht? They could finish the operation in a couple of hours."

"That's not looking likely," Cook said in a whisper. "There are political sovereignty issues working beneath the surface. I won't bore you with details, but State Department doesn't want us touching it officially. If I can get the authorization, could you and your team handle it?"

"I'll need all the satellite images you've got on that yacht."

"We'll send them, and I'll work on the authorization."

Bishop hit the disconnect button and sat back in Belousov's old recliner. Gillian and Nigel had heard every word.

"We're probably going back to Picard Island," Bishop said. He could read their expressions. They didn't want to go any more than he did. The last trip had been a close call—he'd been lucky. This time would be harder. The island's security force would be ready, and the odds stunk.

"When?" Gillian asked.

A sharp clap of thunder rocked the cabin. Rain poured off the roof and down the window. Bishop paused in thought. "Let's look the place over one more time before we go. We can do that tomorrow after this storm passes and go tomorrow night if we get authorization."

Nigel stood and dusted his trousers. "I hate politicians," he grumbled.

When Bishop and Gillian stared at him, he explained. "The only reason they're playing soft with Mercier is her loose connection to the royal family. Anyone else, they would have plowed right through the door and done a complete search."

Gillian peeled off the gloves and dropped them into a trash can. "I think you're right. Every time I talk to headquarters, I sense a reluctance to go too fast on this. We have enough information to send in a full SIS team and crash the place. I don't understand why they're waiting. This kid glove treatment is driving me crazy."

Everyone walked down the dark hall to the front door. Bishop opened it and glanced outside. Strong wind and rain whipped the tall trees in the yard. Nigel pulled his collar tighter and turned to Gillian. "I hope to god those pencil necks make up their minds to act soon." He stared at Bishop. "Before one of us gets killed." With that, he rushed for the shelter of the car.

THIRTY

Wu Chen waited for the general secretary of the Politburo to finish reading the report. He studied Chen across the desk and removed his glasses. "A most unfortunate turn of events, comrade Minister."

The minister of state security met his hard gaze. "That is why I requested this private meeting."

The general secretary dropped his glasses to the desk and leaned forward. "So, what do you propose?"

"Since the final shipment of pathogen cannot be safely delivered, it would be unwise to wait. We can still knock out ninety percent of their West Coast ports with what has already been delivered. Our analysis determined that is sufficient to cripple their shipping and economy."

The general secretary settled back into his chair, slipped his glasses back on, and reviewed the last page again. "Why does Colonel Hong believe Western intelligence may be involved?"

"A number of unexplained incidents."

"Such as?"

Chen crossed his legs and interlaced his fingers in his lap. "The intrusion onto the island several nights ago, the unfortunate disappearance of Mr. Anderson, and the sudden increase in Coast Guard patrol activity, which has prevented the last shipment from arriving. Taken as individual occurrences, each could be explained—together they are troubling."

"What does Hong recommend?"

"Colonel Hong recommended we continue without delay," Chen said. "He would not suggest proceeding unless he believed he could succeed."

"I can approve this proposal, but with conditions. May I assume a disengagement plan is in place?"

"Yes, I've approved it. Colonel Hong will begin its execution immediately."

"Does it erase all evidence of our involvement, Chen?"

"Yes, comrade General Secretary. Our country's participation will remain secret."

Chen felt the man's icy stare. "And that includes everyone with any knowledge about our participation?"

Chen squirmed in the chair. "I can assure you, when Hong leaves, all trace of our involvement will leave with him. I have instructed him: everyone on Picard Island must die."

———

Bishop recalled Yogi Berra's old saying: *This is like déjà vu all over again.* Sitting in the 17-Mile House Pub, at what Nigel now referred to as "his table," they sipped their drinks. It had been less than a week since he'd met Nigel there on a similar stormy afternoon. A crash of thunder echoed through the pub, and several patrons jumped. The smell of burgers cooking made Bishop's stomach rumble. Gillian and Nigel were quiet. The jovial atmosphere they'd enjoyed last time was gone—replaced by dread and doubt. He couldn't blame them. The withdrawal of Foster's team and General Cook's insistence on doing another recon left them in a funk.

Bad attitude and lack of confidence couldn't be ignored. Bishop had seen enough go wrong when confidence was high. He didn't want to ponder the implications of starting a life-or-death task without a strong team behind him. He took a swallow of dark ale before speaking.

"If Washington decides it's a go, I want to do the insertion a little differently this time."

Nigel looked up from his scotch. "Differently?"

"Yeah. The last attempt failed because they knew we were coming. The way I'm going in this time, they'll never suspect it."

"But we've eliminated all the surveillance teams watching us," Gillian said.

"Have we?"

Nigel grinned. "What he's trying to say, old girl, is we've eliminated all the known surveillance. He's not willing to bet his life we got them all."

She eyed him. "What are you going to do?"

Even though they sat at the back table, away from the rest, Bishop still leaned forward and whispered. "I'm coming at them from the Vancouver Island side—not the ocean side—this time."

Nigel's expression changed. "Good Lord, that's got to be at least a half-mile swim, and through open ocean to boot."

"Closer to a mile, the route I intend to take."

Gillian said, "Then you'll use the sea sled?"

"Nope."

"Nope?"

"Won't need one—I'm riding the current this time."

"What?" Nigel and Gillian asked in unison.

"Look, I studied the tidal charts. All I have to do is time the outgoing tide just right, and it'll shoot me to the island."

The two shared a stare which basically said, *You're crazy.*

"Think about it," Bishop said. "No one would expect an attack from the beach side—it's just too improbable."

Gillian spoke up. "It's too improbable because it's crazy. That's a risk you don't have to take."

"Yes, I do."

"Why not take the sea sled? It'll be much easier," Nigel said.

"And what if they've figured out I used one last time? They could drop sonar in the water and possibly hear my approach."

She leaned back with a frown. "What will you need?"

"Updated current and tidal charts depicting Picard Island."

"Anything else?"

"Yes." He turned to Nigel. "Can you get us another boat—less conspicuous?"

"I suppose, but I really love the cigarette boat."

Bishop continued to stare, saying nothing.

Nigel sighed. "But I suppose that might be a bit obvious—wouldn't it?"

"Yes, a bit," Bishop said.

Nigel declared he was hungry. No one objected to pub grub for lunch.

Gillian turned the bottom up on her ale and slammed the glass to the table. "Now all we have to do is wait on the politicians."

———

The president tugged at his collar. He hated black-tie functions—especially on nights a game was on. The mix and mingle that precedes each official state dinner gave folks an opportunity to work their agendas while drinking on the government's tab. Senator Hughes had just bent his ear about Iowa corn subsidies, and Congresswoman King led the president of South Korea around the room, whispering god-knew-what in his ear. At least his wife and the Korean First Lady were getting along—dresses and fashion be damned. Across the room, his national security advisor weaved through the mob toward him. "Evening, Jeff."

Fuller eased to his side. "Mr. President." As they studied the room, Fuller touched his arm. "May I have a word?"

The president nodded. "Sure."

They turned and slipped out into the corridor. A startled Secret Service agent moved aside, walking a few steps down the hall while talking into his sleeve mic.

"So, what's going on?" the president asked.

"I just hung up with the Canadian minister of public safety. He oversees the Security Intelligence Service up there. Seems he's getting some pushback on this pathogen inquiry."

The president shoved both hands in his pockets. "What kind of pushback?"

"Parliament—several members appear to be in Claudine Mercier's pocket, and they're causing a stink about it."

"How did they find out?"

"They're on the intelligence committee—SIS reports to them in Canada."

The president pursed his lips and hung his head. He looked up. "How do you read it?"

"Our man in Victoria just informed General Cook that he has a new lead, but it involves another covert entry onto Mercier's private island. Last time they tried, there were fireworks, and she used her political muscle."

"Do we really believe she's involved?"

"She's involved in something nefarious—we can't be sure if it's the pathogen business."

"What do you think?" The president leaned back against the wall and crossed his arms.

"General Cook's man discovered a plan to mount a biological dispersement device mounted on a motor launch. No way to confirm if it came to fruition or is now mounted on her motor launch unless someone takes a look."

The president shook his head and grimaced. "And no one has the stomach for confronting her up there?"

Fuller shrugged. "She has so much political support that the prime minister doesn't want to antagonize her—bad politics for him in Victoria."

"What's your call, Jeff? If we do this without Canadian approval, we're all balancing on a razor-thin wire. It could fall either way."

Fuller nodded. "I say check it out. However, if it goes south, we shouldn't expect the SIS or Canadian government to provide any political cover—they'll be busy trying to cover themselves."

Just then a round of laughter drifted from the ballroom. The president turned in its direction and took a deep, cleansing breath. Just above a whisper he said, "I have to get back inside—tell Cook it's a go, and good luck."

THIRTY-ONE

After leaving the 17-Mile House Pub, Nigel turned in early. Bishop sat in his room and studied his laptop, flipping through dozens of Colonel Maxwell's satellite photos of Picard Island. Cook told him he'd received authorization from Fuller to proceed. He assured them the White House had been apprised of the situation and given its full backing. Maxwell had been right—not one photo showed the yacht's motor launch uncovered.

Bishop leaned closer to the screen. A fifty-gallon drum at the rear of the yacht sat suspended on a metal stand. It was only feet away from the covered motor launch. A coiled red hose hung from the stand and was attached to the clear plastic drum. The thing appeared to have some green-tinted colored liquid inside, but he couldn't be sure—maybe just the way the light struck it.

Bishop closed that file and opened the email sent from Gillian's contact at MARPAC. Several PDF coastal maps popped up. A second look didn't improve them.

"Hell," he whispered.

"Hell what?" Gillian asked, stepping from the bathroom.

"Oh, nothing—just looking over the approach to Picard Island."

She strolled over and wrapped her arms around his neck from behind. "What's wrong?"

"It'll be trickier than I thought, that's all."

"Like how?"

Pointing to the screen and current chart, he ran his finger along the shoreline. "This shows a rip current where I need to enter the water—that could pose a problem."

She dropped on the bed beside him and leaned toward the computer. "So just enter from a different location."

"Can't do it. If I don't enter the water here—" He ran his finger along the PDF photo. "I can't guarantee I'll hit the island at the right point. Anyway, a rip current might not be all bad. At least it'll propel me away from the beach."

They both studied the computer screen in silence.

"But the rip current might push me too far west." He swirled his finger on the screen. "If I don't time the outgoing tide just right, I could miss the island. The current's too strong for a swimmer to fight."

"So if that happens, Nigel and I will just pick you up in the boat he's renting tomorrow—right?"

A sudden apprehension washed over Bishop, but he maintained a relaxed demeanor. No need exciting his team unnecessarily. He turned to her and grinned. "Sure. You'll just pick me up."

———

Colonel Hong sat in his cabin aboard Mercier's yacht and outlined the timetable for disengaging from Picard Island. Mercier had made it easy by giving most of her staff a mandatory two-week summer vacation. Only a cook and a couple of security men would remain on the island. Since Mercier's personal assistant, housekeeping staff, grounds crew, and the bulk of her security personnel wouldn't return to the island for a couple of weeks, this gave Hong time to complete the West Coast pathogen cruise and disappear. Mercier hadn't informed the yacht's captain or crew she'd be sailing, so Hong's men would crew the ship down the West Coast. He and his men would eliminate the loose ends, as he referred to the witnesses, before departure.

They would leave no trace of the murders and take the bodies with them on the yacht. Once offshore, they would be weighted down before dumping them overboard into the depths of the Pacific. Then Hong and his men would sail the yacht as they traversed down the West Coast, distributing the virus from port to port. Once finished, he would point the yacht out to open sea. After dark, a Chinese submarine would meet them in the middle of the ocean. They would scuttle the yacht and sail home underwater. The entire trip down the US West Coast should take less than a week.

This was something he had experience with. Distributing death and disease had made his career. That was how he first became noticed. Pitching the idea to his superiors in 1997 had taken guts, and Hong had plenty of those.

———

"Do you think it could work?" Captain Fu had asked.

Young Lieutenant Hong had snapped to attention. "I'll guarantee it, sir." He must have been insane to say such a thing, but he was much younger and full of confidence.

Fu shifted uncomfortably. "Sit and explain further."

After taking a seat, Hong handed his superior the paper he'd just completed. While Fu thumbed through it, Hong summarized its content: "Sir, foot-and-mouth disease is the most highly infectious, viral animal disease known. It affects cloven-hoofed animals. The incubation period is roughly six days. It can be transmitted in a number of ways—I recommend use of a fomite."

Fu looked up from the papers. "A what?"

"Sorry, sir. It's an inanimate object, like clothing, capable of transmitting infectious organisms."

Fu grunted and frowned.

"As I was saying, someone could easily infect one animal, and the disease would quickly spread to the entire herd. Scientists at the US Foreign Animal Disease Diagnostic Laboratory at Plum Island fear it above all others."

"So how is it you know so much about this kind of thing?"

Hong's back stiffened with pride. "Both my undergraduate and graduate degrees are in biology."

Fu glanced at him but ventured no comment.

"I could have continued at the university and received my doctoral, but—"

"Hong!" Fu snapped. "I have no interest in your personal problems —you should feel honored to serve the state in whatever capacity we see fit."

Hong bowed his head. "Of course, sir. My apologies."

"Could this ever be traced back to us?" Fu asked.

"No, sir—never. We could use a common serotype like Asia 1. There are several genotypes—it's an RNA virus found across all of Asia."

Fu attached a paperclip to the report and casually dropped it into his out-tray. "Very well, I'll send it up. That will be all."

Hong sat frozen, looking at his report lying in the green metal tray. He hadn't been able to speak—the barbarian had treated it just like any other office correspondence.

Captain Fu's voice rose. "I said that will be all, Hong."

But that wasn't all. In less than a week, his plan had not only been approved—it had been cheered as a way for China to attack a competing neighbor's economy. Agroterrorism wasn't just a word—it was a real weapon, and Hong knew how to use it.

A few days later, Hong had directed a cow to be infected with the virus and placed in isolation. Seven days later, it became symptomatic. A government vet clothed in protective gear entered the chamber as Hong watched through the glass from outside. The vet removed a man's handkerchief from a sterile zip-lock bag and wiped the animal's mouth and nose. The string of foamy saliva attached to the cloth, and the vet retreated to a nearby table inside the chamber. He reinserted the handkerchief inside the bag, sealed it, and then sprayed his gloves and the bag with a strong disinfectant. He dried it, slipped it inside a second bag, removed his gloves, and brought it out for Hong.

Hong gazed at his new bioweapon. Needing to deploy it as soon as possible, he selected the Hsinchu Prefecture in Taiwan as the trial site. If he met with success there, he could spread it in other locations.

Hsinchu had a large pig population—the ideal place for an agricultural bioweapon.

Hong traveled there the next day under false identification and located the target farm. He rented a hotel room, had dinner, and watched TV until almost one the next morning. He drove his rented car fourteen miles to the farm and approached one of the dozens of swine pens. After donning plastic gloves, he withdrew the handkerchief from the bags and dropped it into the pen. A few curious pigs stirred as he removed the gloves and walked back to his vehicle. Later that morning, one or more of the pigs would sniff the handkerchief and infect themselves—so simple, so easy.

———

The plan had worked much better than anyone could have dreamed: the mortality rate was almost 100 percent. At the height of the epidemic, 300 new farms had been infected daily. Swine depopulation had to be handled by the military, as over 200,000 per day had needed disposal. In the end, 3.8 million swine had been destroyed, with almost seven billion in US dollars lost. The Taiwanese pig industry never fully recovered.

That little bit of work had earned him a promotion and brought him to the attention of people in high places. Like Taiwan, his 2010 foot-and-mouth attack on Japan and 2011 attack on South Korea also earned him promotions and further advanced his career. With a successful conclusion to this affair, he would undoubtedly make general. While Hong reveled in his successes, he was saddened by the fact he'd never been given the opportunity to advance his studies in Biology at university. If he had, he'd be in charge of this operation like Dr. Tee and not it's security coordinator. But advancing his standing as a general would ease the pain of the past.

THIRTY-TWO

Friday could not have been more beautiful. Victoria could dish out glorious sunny mornings just as easily as it washes the world with pop-up evening storms. Bishop sat on his balcony as the sun grew brighter and warmer. The crisp air made him appreciate his Washington Redskins sweatshirt while he finished his first cup of coffee. He stood, stretched, and slipped back into the room for a refill. Gillian leaned toward the mirror, applying lipstick.

"Want a cup of java?" he asked.

"I'll wait 'til breakfast."

The sound of a boat mooring at the hotel marina filtered through the open sliding glass door. Bishop glanced out. The hum of the motor died, and a voice boomed from the marina.

"Will this do?"

Bishop did a double take and spotted Nigel looking up at him, still holding the mooring line of the twenty-foot Glastron Bowrider.

Gillian asked, "What's going on?"

"You'll never believe this."

"What?" She strolled to the balcony. "Is that Nigel?"

"Who else?"

"When do we meet for breakfast?" Nigel shouted.

"Fifteen minutes," Bishop yelled back. This was *not* the way to conduct covert operations in a foreign country. Nigel felt comfortable because he was in Canada. Bishop never felt comfortable anywhere during an ongoing operation. If there were any watchers still around, they now had a front row seat to the team's plans.

But that's just the way Bishop wanted it.

Just as Bishop and Gillian walked into the hotel restaurant, Nigel disconnected from his cell call.

"You're up early," Bishop said.

"Slept marvelously."

"Where did you get the boat?" Gillian asked.

Nigel wiped his mouth with the napkin. "Same place I got the cigarette boat. I just traded down. Was that show a moment ago sufficient to gain attention?"

"Perfect," Bishop said. "If we still have unseen watchers, they couldn't help but notice."

"I'm not clear on why we're going back to Picard Island this morning," Gillian said. "If someone is still watching us, won't that give away our plans?"

"It doesn't matter," Bishop answered. Her confused look caused him to explain further. "If we're still being watched, I want them to concentrate on the new boat. It can be a distraction tonight while I'm coming at them from the beach. I want them watching the boat's movements and not mine. Besides, I need an up close and personal look at the yacht today. All the satellite photos in the world aren't worth one good look in person. My approach will be critical—screw that up, and it's game over."

"Then let's finish breakfast and get on with it," Nigel said.

An hour later, Bishop had much less trepidation about this boating excursion than he did the last time Nigel took them out for a day on the water. For one thing, Nigel was sober, and the boat wasn't built for racing. Bishop took some solace in the fact he didn't have to wonder if all his personal affairs were in order.

Nigel slowly coasted out of the Inner Harbor at such a leisurely pace that Bishop actually enjoyed the ride. The orcas and seagulls were especially active this morning, and the fresh, cool sea air invigorated him. Gillian's sweater and his windbreaker soon gave way to short sleeves as the temperature shot up with the sun. When Nigel entered Ross Bay, he turned the wheel over to Bishop, retreated to the stern, and proceeded to mix drinks from a cooler. Just before they approached Douglas Park, Bishop asked Nigel to take back the helm and Gillian for her mini-telescope.

Nigel settled into the driver's seat. "So, what do you want me to do?"

Bishop pointed at the park. "Head toward that big tree on shore, then turn hard to starboard and slowly coast toward the island. I'll tell you when to break hard to starboard again and head home."

Gillian handed him the telescope. "Is that the course you're swimming tonight?"

"Yup—I'd like you to be up front, next to Nigel. We want to appear as non-threatening as possible. I'll be on the deck behind you, getting a visual on the approach route."

Gillian dropped into the front seat. Bishop crouched behind her with a tarp draped over his head and shoulders, training the scope on the island and yacht. Nigel propped his arm on the edge of the boat and looked like an older man on holiday with his much younger wife. Bishop studied the yacht, and especially the lower portion of the wooden dock beside it. If he could get to the pilings underneath, he would be able to work himself around to the yacht.

They were about three hundred yards from the island before Bishop ordered Nigel to turn for home. Bishop waited until they were almost a mile away before emerging from cover.

"Learn everything you wanted?" Nigel asked.

"Yeah, that picture was worth a thousand words."

"Better buckle up, then."

"What?" Bishop asked—just before Nigel slammed the throttle all the way forward. Bishop was thrown back into the seat while the boat jetted across the water at speeds he didn't want to imagine. *Is my will at my attorney's office or still in my safe deposit box*?

When they arrived at the inner harbor, Gillian insisted on fish tacos at a little walk-up place on the downtown dock. After Nigel coasted into a slip, Bishop jumped out and tied them off. Gillian and Nigel made a beeline to the taco shack. Bishop slid his cell from his pocket and dialed Hal while following them.

Hal answered with the words he'd hoped to hear. "You're clear. My guys and I were all around the hotel when you shoved off. We would have seen anyone surveilling you. The only ones paying any attention were two seagulls swimming by the rocks."

Bishop relaxed. "Thanks, Hal. You'll be on my tail tonight when I drive to the park?"

"Still leaving at eleven-fifteen?"

"Plan to."

"We'll be your shadow all the way."

"Thanks." Bishop disconnected just as it was his turn to order.

————

Foster stuffed the last of his equipment into the black bag and zipped it just as his phone rang. "Commander Foster," he answered.

The voice of Vice-Admiral Davis Collins caused him to perk up. "Foster—thought I'd let you know I just received a call from the minister of public safety. He's very pleased with you and your men's performance in Ottawa—very pleased."

"Thank you, sir."

"The nervous ninny still wants support for his little intelligence operation in Victoria," Collins grumbled. "When can you be back there?"

Foster released an exhaustive breath. "Sir, my men and I have been up for over twenty-four hours and have a long flight ahead of us—we're pretty well spent."

A moment of silence followed. "Very well—stand down and get some rest. When's the earliest you can get back to Victoria?"

Foster checked his watch and did a mental calculation. "We should be able to leave any time after midnight, sir."

Collins said, "There's a military flight departing Ottawa at 0030 hours. That will get you to Victoria by 0530—be on it. Contact that Hathaway woman when you have wheels down."

———

Bishop spent the rest of the afternoon in his room reviewing satellite photos, tide and current charts, and checking his equipment for the night swim. He would use the drysuit because the water temperature demanded it. He'd also have the rebreather available in case the need arose, but he planned to do the approach on the surface. There would be no room for error riding the outgoing rip tide. He needed to see the island to hit the island.

He wished Foster and his men were back. Under normal circumstances, Delta or the SEALs would utilize at least a six-man team for this type of transport, incursion, recon, and exfiltration mission. Doing it with only three dramatically increased the risk. But there was nothing he could do about that. Due to the sensitive nature of the operation, the Canadians insisted Foster and his men were the only ones they wanted to use. On the other hand, Washington was scared to death and wanted answers yesterday. This put him squarely in the middle—a place he hated.

"So, do we do Italian again tonight?" Gillian asked.

The last time he made a night swim, he'd demanded pasta to carb up. "Yes, if that's okay with you and Nigel."

"You're the one doing the heavy lifting, cowboy—what you say goes," she said.

She had a nervous, tense look and tried hiding it with humor. He met her eyes and saw through the façade. Her expression changed and she swallowed hard before squaring her shoulders. He walked to the bed and sat beside her. He took her in his arms, and she rested her head on his shoulder. No one said a word.

———

Colonel Hong knocked on the study door before entering.

Claudine Mercier's voice answered, "Come in."

Hong bowed. "I've just been informed we are to sail at 0600 tomorrow."

"Tomorrow? I expected more notice," she said.

"My apologies, but I was just now notified myself," Hong lied.

Mercier let out an exasperated breath. "Oh, very well, it's about time. We've stalled too long already. How long before we should be back to Picard Island?"

The question caught him by surprise. He quickly calculated the distances. "I believe we can return in ten to fourteen days, depending on weather."

"Good. I want to be back as soon as possible, before all hell breaks loose."

Hong nodded. "That should be no problem."

"Very well, I'll be ready. Make sure my stateroom refrigerator is stocked with my wine."

Hong's jaw tightened, and the facial twitch started again as he bowed. "Of course, ma'am."

"That will be all."

He marched out, cursing under his breath. He wanted to kill her now, but she might be needed on the ship in case they met any challenges sailing down the US coast. Who better to ensure a problem-free cruise than the ship's owner? He'd never calculated the days necessary to return to the island since this would be a one-way trip. As for Mercier—she would be dead in the yacht's freezer when it went down. That last thought caused a smile to crack the corners of his mouth.

THIRTY-THREE

Bishop loaded the diving equipment in Gillian's car. Because he'd not heard from Nigel since lunch, he knocked on his door before going back to the room.

Nigel swung the door open. "Come in."

"No thanks—just letting you know we're doing Italian take-out in my room about seven o'clock."

"Splendid; I'll be there."

Bishop turned to leave but stopped. "Watch out for Gillian tonight. I think she's a little concerned for me, and skittish about the plan."

Nigel's expression softened. "She'll be fine—you'll see."

"Yeah, I know."

When they met in the room a couple of hours later, Gillian wasn't much better. Her morose stare and dark mood caused Bishop more concern. Nigel also wasn't his old self. He told no funny stories and had little to say. It was clear he wasn't comfortable with the plan either. They finished their meal in silence. Bishop was the only one who cleaned his plate. He checked his watch.

"You guys need to shove off. I won't leave until a quarter after eleven. That'll give you plenty of time to get into position before I enter the water at midnight."

Nigel stood and slipped on his jacket. "We'll be on station and waiting."

Gillian rummaged through her large bag and pulled out three plastic cases. She dumped them onto the bed. "Foster left these for us —in case we needed them."

Bishop popped the top on one and examined the radio and tactical headset. It looked like a good one. They switched on the units and did a quick voice check. Satisfied, Bishop packed his back into its case. "We'll make good use of these but take your cell phones as a backup." He walked them to the door, and they all stopped. No one wanted to be the first to open it. That meant there was no turning back, and no one wanted to make that call. Bishop figured he had a little better than average chance of making the thing work. Only, he knew all the dangers in such a venture. He'd downplayed the risk to Nigel and Gillian but couldn't convince himself. At last, he opened the door.

"Keep your eyes peeled for the red flare, and don't run over me as you pick me up," he joked.

Nigel's expression turned serious and somber. "Good luck." They shook hands and he headed down the hall.

Gillian had a twisted grin and sad eyes. She hugged Bishop, squeezing him tight. He felt her heart racing, and she shivered just before she released the embrace. She gave him a kiss. "I'll see you later," she croaked, her voice filled with emotion. She turned and followed Nigel.

"Later," Bishop whispered. He closed the door and dialed Hal's number.

"Hello, Bishop."

"They're coming down—get ready."

Fifteen minutes later, he walked out his door just as Hal called back. "They're all clear, no surveillance on them."

"Good. I'm heading to the park—stay with me."

"Giddy-up—we're ready," Hal assured him.

The drive to Douglas Park seemed surreal. Bishop maneuvered through almost-deserted streets out to the dark stretch of road near the park and stopped at the large tree he'd pointed out earlier to Nigel. There wasn't a designated parking area along this section of beach, so he needed to make a few adjustments to Gillian's car to keep the police from towing it. He unloaded his diving equipment and slammed the trunk. Then he popped the hood and removed the small bulb illuminating the engine. He left the hood open and locked the doors, indicating a driver with car trouble.

The lights of Picard Island shone dimly in the distance. He dialed the first number and Hal answered.

"You're all clear."

"Thanks, Hal, see you later."

"Good luck."

Bishop dialed the second number, and the voice answered immediately. "Cook, here."

"I'm about to enter the water, sir."

There was a pause before Cooked answered. "Good luck."

"Thank you, sir."

Bishop dialed the last number, and Gillian answered. "How's it going?" he asked.

"We're en route." Her voice fought the engine's noise.

"I'm about to start—just letting you know."

She didn't answer, and he wondered if she'd heard him. Just before he repeated it, she said, "Okay, be safe."

"You, too." He dropped the phone in his bag. Staying under the cover of the tree, he changed into the dry suit. He slid on the rebreather, adjusted his buoyancy compensator and weight belt, and then stowed the rest of his equipment in the waterproof gear bag. The smell of salt water invigorated him as he walked to the water's edge.

He dropped to the sand and slipped on the fins, mask, and snorkel before standing. He turned his back to the ocean and shuffled to the rear until waist deep in the surf. He took a couple of test breaths from the rebreather, fell backward, rolled over, and kicked. The force of the current took over, sweeping him toward the distant island.

———

"I see no reason to delay—we'll start with the housekeeper and then the security personnel." Hong rose from his desk on the yacht.

Captain Yin stood at attention. "Yes, sir."

Hong checked the magazine of his 9mm and returned it to the pistol. "Your weapon is silenced?"

Yin drew back his jacket to reveal the silencer screwed into place.

"Good—let's go."

They walked the length of the dock to the house. Hong pressed the button on the back patio wall and looked up at the camera. He waved as the electronic lock released with a click.

He and Yin strolled down the back hall and stopped at the housekeeper's bedroom. Hong cracked opened the door. The woman snored as they slipped to each side of her bed. Hong had put on leather gloves prior to entering. He knew from firsthand experience how people reacted when being suffocated. The scratches he'd received last time took forever to heal.

Yin bumped something in the dark and it fell over. They both froze, eyeing each other as the housekeeper moaned and rolled on her back. Hong lifted a large pillow from the settee and nodded. Yin immediately fell onto the woman, pinning her arms to the bed just before Hong pushed the pillow on her face. She tried screaming, only a muffled whimper escaping the room.

Yin had a lot of trouble keeping her on the bed. She kicked and tried pushing herself off. Just as Hong had feared, she broke loose with one hand and scratched viciously against his gloved hand holding the pillow. He held her until the kicking stopped. Hong silently counted to ten before lifting the pillow. Her eyes and mouth were open, and her expression showed the terror she must have experienced.

They strolled toward the security office, also on the ground floor. Both the guards were rocked back in swivel chairs in the cramped room. The twelve small monitors and bank of alarm lights provided the only illumination as Hong and Yin entered the half-open door. The security officers turned just as the two men drew their weapons.

———

At the Pentagon, neither Cook nor Maxwell had left their offices. They'd agreed the situation warranted monitoring until Bishop was safe. Maxwell stared at his computer screen, totally bored. When he saw the images, it took him a second to realize what was happening.

"General, you should see this!" Maxwell leaned closer, staring at the live satellite feed of Picard Island, courtesy of the National Reconnaissance Office. Cook rushed in just as the infrared camera picked up the four white figures rounding the corner of the house near the long wooden dock. Only the heat signature of the figures reflected back to the satellite.

"What's happening?" Cook demanded.

Maxwell pointed to the images. "Don't know. They just walked out of the house."

Cook squinted and drew nearer to the monitor. "The two in front—do they have their hands raised?"

"Looks that way," Maxwell said.

"Who are they? Can't be Bishop." Cook checked his watch. "He's still in the water... isn't he?"

"He should be." Maxwell picked up the phone. "I'm sending him a text to let him know."

Cook continued staring at the screen. "What the—"

The two leading figures stopped and knelt in front of the two shapes to their rear. Maxwell looked back just in time to see the bright flashes from the hand of one of the standing forms. Both kneeling figures collapsed onto the ground.

"Son-of-a-bitch," Cook whispered. "They executed them."

"That's not all." Maxwell pointed to the lower left corner of the monitor.

The rear of the yacht emitted a red glow as the heat signature of the engine registered.

"They've started the engines—she's getting ready to sail."

THIRTY-FOUR

On the boat, Gillian pulled the parka tighter. The temperature had dropped, and skimming across the cold water in an open craft only made it worse. A chilling mist raked her face. "How much further," she yelled into Nigel's ear.

"That should be it off to the right—only island around this beach." He cut the engine back to half speed and checked the time. "Bishop should be about halfway there by now."

She didn't answer, but gazed through the night at the speck of light growing closer each minute as they drifted on the current toward the island.

Nigel said, "I'll circle around the place at a distance so they won't hear us, and hang out until it's almost time to pick him up." He switched off the boat's running lights.

She tugged his sleeve. "Stay close to the beach. If the coastal patrol catches us out here in open water without lights, they'll stop us and give away the whole plan." She drew a breath and stared at the island. Somewhere in those dark waters was the man she loved. She cursed the reasons she'd never told him how she felt.

Ten minutes later, Nigel asked, "How does this look?" before cutting the engine.

He floated about fifty meters from the beach. The headlights of a lone vehicle drove down the coastal road. She glanced in his direction. "Good as any. Throw out the anchor."

He untangled the line and tossed the weight overboard. He pulled it taut. "We're shallow—very shallow."

She didn't answer. Her concentration focused on the dark water.

"Gillian."

She turned.

"He'll be fine. He's Delta, you know—they're the best."

She nodded. "Yeah, he'll be okay." Then she turned back toward the water.

They bobbed around for the next twenty minutes. Nigel lost his chattiness and finally neither spoke. At last, he said, "We should be going."

She pressed the button on her sports watch and the time flashed. "I think you're right."

Nigel started the engine and it sputtered to life. "Pull up the anchor."

She tugged at the line, but it wouldn't budge. "It's hung up—give me a hand."

They put everything they had into freeing it, but it had become locked tight on some underwater obstruction. After several unsuccessful minutes, Nigel gave up. He sat back and caught his breath.

"Okay, have it your way, you bloody twine," he swore. With that, he drew his pocketknife and cut the line. He saluted as the boat drifted toward Picard Island on the outgoing tide. "Prepare to get underway." He dropped the gear from neutral to run. The engine sputtered again and died. He turned the key, and nothing happened—only a long, grinding sound. "Blast this damn machine. The cigarette boat wouldn't have let us down this way."

Gillian checked the fuel line and wiggled some wires. "What do we do now?"

He tried the key once more and got the same result. He stood and walked back to her. "Looks like we have a decision to make—actually, you have to make it."

She glanced up. "What?"

He pointed toward the open bay. "We're adrift. If we can't get this thing started, we'll end up god knows where. Of course, Bishop is expecting us to pick him up. We can either drift out to sea, or it might be possible to maneuver close enough to the island for us to land. It's your country, your choice."

Gillian made her decision. "Let's try for the island. We'll try and contact Bishop."

"I'll do the best I can with this dead rudder, but I can't guarantee anything," he replied. "We're in a strong current with little wind to help us maneuver."

When Gillian's cell rang, she jumped.

"Hathaway?" the familiar voice asked.

"This is Hathaway—who's this?"

"Deputy Director Collier."

Gillian knew him—he was the SIS director's righthand man. "Mr. Collier, I'm glad you called."

A moment of confused silence followed before Collier said, "We were just notified by the Americans that their infrared satellite indicated at least two people shot on Picard Island. Wanted to make sure you were still safe."

Gillian's stomach flipped, and she steadied herself against the windshield with one hand. She answered, but her mind was on Bishop. "Sir, we're fine, except for a little boat trouble."

"What kind of boat trouble?"

"It stopped running. We're attempting to land on the island but need help."

"My lord. I'll call you back."

The lights from Victoria faded a little more each minute as they drifted further away from shore.

Nigel put all his weight on the steering wheel. "Who was that?"

"My headquarters—they're sending help. I'll try and call Bishop." After several attempts, she gave up. "It's no good—I can't get through."

Nigel said, "Try the headset thing Foster left."

She fished around in her bag and pulled out the two headset boxes. She handed Nigel his and opened hers. She slipped on the device and punched the power button. "Bishop, can you read me?" She tried several more times and turned to Nigel. "Nothing."

They'd drifted so far from the beach it was only a faded memory. Nigel struggled to turn the boat to the island, but the strong current fought him every inch of the way. Gillian braced herself—*we're going to get wet tonight*.

———

The frigid water stung Bishop's face—*I hate cold water*. He let the tide do most of the work and only used his legs as rudders to correct his course, but there was a problem. Just as he'd feared, the rip current near the shore had swung him a little too far out. The lights of Picard Island grew dimmer the farther the current carried him.

He wasn't going to land where he needed to unless something changed in a hurry. There was only one thing to do, but he hated the thought—this was going to hurt. He tapped the self-inflate button to add more air to his buoyancy-compensator and slid his hand to his waist and found the weight belt clasp. As he released the belt and it dropped to the depths, he passed a point of no return. Without the thirty pounds of weights, he could never dive and stay under again. He'd be on the surface from now on, no matter what happened.

He lowered his head and swam hard toward the island, fighting the strong current every second. The dry suit acted like a drag, forcing twice as much effort for half the results. Fifteen minutes later, his chest felt like it would burst. The burn in his shoulders and legs was unbearable. His breaths came in more labored gasps—exhaustion soon set in. The dock was less than thirty yards away, but the current kept pushing him away from it. With one last burst of energy, he dug into the water and swam for his life.

A minute later, his hand slapped something, and he grabbed for whatever it was. A slimy piling—he'd made it. He swung himself under the dock and held on. He tied himself off and lay back in the water. Bishop spit out the rebreather mouthpiece and breathed deeply, trying to draw in as much air as possible. He'd done a lot of hard swims, but nothing like this. The strong current, cold water, and fatigue of fighting to get to the island left him completely drained. He needed rest before trying to climb the underside of the dock and board the yacht. He'd been out of communication with Nigel and Gillian for over an hour but dared not try until later.

The ship's engine was running. The soft hum echoed under the dock, and the vibration in the water confirmed it was at idle. When large yachts docked, there was always a power cord attached from the dock to run the electrical devices on the boat without switching on the engines. *If the engines aren't on to produce power, then why start them?* Ships' captains fired them up every day or so in port to conduct a systems check, or a few hours before getting under way. It was the middle of the night.

Ten minutes later, Bishop climbed the support beams underneath the dock. He was about to climb on top when voices sounded above. He froze as they became louder—two men speaking Chinese. From the tone, it sounded like they were arguing, or one was complaining about something. Bishop looked up through the space between the boards just as they walked up the gangplank. The source of their irritation appeared to be the long, white body bag they struggled with. The dock light wasn't on, so after the voices faded, Bishop scrambled to the top and slipped aboard unnoticed.

Who was in the body bag? *Perhaps one of the guys killed in the fire fight the night Bishop tried scouting the island?* His curiosity must remain unanswered. Bishop had one mission tonight: check the rear of the motor launch for the modification and get back into the water unnoticed. He would barely have enough time to make it to the pickup location where Gillian and Nigel were waiting. He squatted behind a dark corner and opened his gear bag. The rumble of the engines vibrated the deck, and a whiff of diesel floated through the air.

Bishop again heard voices, and he stuck his head around the corner in time to see the two men leave the boat and walk back toward the house. When he reached into his bag, his hand sloshed inside, and his spirits sank. The watertight container had a leak. He tried powering up the phone, but that was too much to hope for. It lay dead in its own watery grave. He examined the pistol—it looked fine.

Bishop popped the top of the tactical headset box. The interior felt dry. *Well, at least one thing was watertight.* He fitted it onto his head and switched on the power button just as he again heard voices from the dock. The same two guys toted another body bag. *What is going on?*

He whispered into the mic, "Gillian, do you copy?" He tried again. "Gillian… Gillian. Do you copy?"

"Thank God," she answered. "Are you all right?"

He remained in the shadows on the main deck. "I'm fine, but there's a problem."

"What?"

"Something's going on here. They've carried two body bags onto the yacht, and the engines are running."

"I know, the satellite picked up two people being shot. My headquarters are sending help. But we have another issue."

He paused before asking, "What?"

"Our motor's gone out—we're drifting."

"Where are you?"

"We're about a hundred meters from the island, on the opposite side of the house."

"Don't land—it's too dangerous. Just drift on past. I'll hide somewhere until help arrives."

"No, you won't have a chance if they decide to look for you."

Nigel's voice interrupted. "We're going to make it. Get ready to jump."

"I have to go," she said. "Make your way to our side of the island— help's on the way."

Before Bishop could offer any objection, she disconnected.

———

Nigel's efforts paid off. They were only a few yards from the island. In another minute, they would drift past and be pulled out to sea. Now was their chance. Gillian scrambled to the bow. A scraping noise rose from the boat's bottom as it came into contact with submerged rocks.

Nigel crawled beside her. "Now," he said, and leaped toward shore.

She jumped as the current caused the boat's stern to swing around. Her foot slipped on the slick bow and landed far short—she went completely under. The water was god-awful freezing. When she touched bottom, she pushed hard and broke the surface. Nigel grabbed her wrist and pulled her toward shore. She coughed out a mouthful of seawater.

"Not exactly a perfect dive, but it'll do." He helped her over the slippery rocks and onto dry land.

She lay back and breathed hard. "I thought we were closer in." While Nigel was totally dry from the waist up, she was completely wet. Her teeth chattered and her wet clothes weighed a ton. The current carried their disabled boat out to sea. She raked hair from her eyes and stared at him. They lay there for five minutes, listening. Nigel pulled a pistol and eased further up the bank. Only the sound of waves lapping at the rocks and crickets disturbed the night.

She shivered and searched for her cell phone. She always kept it in her handbag and couldn't recall where she stuck it before abandoning ship. It suddenly dawned on her.

"Oh, no," she groaned, sliding it from her pocket.

Her attempts at powering up the soggy phone were unsuccessful, and the soaked headset wasn't working either. Nigel tried powering up his wet cell, but with no luck. Neither had prepared to get wet that night.

"We're out of communication with Bishop," she lamented.

"Not so fast." He snatched his tactical headset box from his parka.

Gillian perked up and leaned on an elbow. "Does it work?"

He fiddled with it for a moment and switched it on. "We'll soon find out. Hello, Bishop. Do you copy me?"

THIRTY-FIVE

Bishop's headset came to life with Nigel's voice.

"I hear you, Nigel. Are you safe?"

"Yes, we're on the island."

"They've loaded two bodies on the yacht. See if you can figure out what's going on, but don't take any chances," Bishop said. "Probably best to sit back and wait for the cavalry."

"Will do."

Bishop finished drying off the pistol with a rag he found, then crawled to the stern and located the motor launch. He worked his way to its rear and found the propeller. Lifting the tarp, he squinted in the darkness and felt on each side of the for any kind of device or ramp to mount a compressed air tank.

He found two ramps complete with straps, hoses, and nozzles, waiting to be connected to a compressed air tank. There could be little doubt: the thing was rigged to deliver a biological aerosol to a target. He pulled the tarp back into place and squatted in the shadows. Just then, voices drifted from the dock. He peeked over the top of the launch, and the same two guys carried another body bag. He couldn't figure it out. *Where are all the bodies coming from?*

Bishop squatted back down and caught a whiff of chlorine. He sniffed, turning his head from side to side. Just behind him sat the fifty-gallon plastic container he'd seen in the satellite photos. He leaned over and sniffed again—yup, some kind of strong disinfectant. What had Dr. Fletcher said? *"There would have to be a full decon after disbursing the pathogen."*

Bishop crawled to the edge of the rail and eyed the two guys hauling the third body bag up the gangplank. When they went below, Bishop sneaked to the door they just entered and, staying out of sight, followed them through the hatch. They turned left and he hung back, waiting for them to stop. From the sound and vibration, he suspected the engine room was right below him. As the voices faded, he swung around the corner and caught sight of them opening a large metal door —a walk-in freezer. They dropped the bag inside, slammed the door, and left. Bishop stayed hiding in the shadows between an industrial-sized washing machine and dryer and let the pair pass before venturing toward the freezer. He opened it, and the light came on. Three body bags lay side-by-side on the floor. He checked each bag. Two guys and an older woman—he didn't recognize any of them.

Bishop calculated his options. Make his way off the yacht, find Nigel and Gillian and wait for reinforcements, or attempt to disable the boat to delay its departure. *But is it even necessary to delay it?* It presented an immediate threat in its current condition. He still had the explosives Gillian got from the base. He could set off a small charge in the engine room—that would do it. Or he might find something to tamper with down there to delay the departure. Delaying the thing from leaving carried as much risk as reward. *When in doubt, attack.* Bishop eased around the corner and down a flight of stairs. As he slipped into the engine room, the clatter of twin diesels vibrated off the walls and a lubricant smell hung thick in the air.

In the far corner, a large metal cabinet with a clear acrylic front was mounted against the bulkhead. Several green LED lights blinking at the top of the cabinet caught his attention. It resembled a refrigeration unit. He could just make out the tops of SCUBA tanks laying side-by-side on racks. As he examined the box, a door-mounted thermometer read 1.6667 Celsius—about 35 degrees Fahrenheit. *Why keep compressed air tanks cold?* Opening the door, he counted tanks rested in twenty-five of the twenty-nine slots. He recognized the stenciled abbreviations below each slot. SFO, for San Francisco, SEA for Seattle, SD, for San Diego, and twenty-six more. *The targets for the pathogen release—the US Western seaboard.*

Bishop studied the map of the West Coast taped above the case. Twenty-nine port cities with large populations were highlighted. But there were only twenty-five tanks in the case. Those missing tanks worried him. The death toll would be staggering, the contamination beyond belief, and the clean-up cost in the billions. All thoughts of meeting Gillian and Nigel disappeared. His only concern now: stop the ship from sailing.

If he set off charges in the engine area the concussion might cause the tanks to rupture and leak their deadly contents. He needed to let Nigel know about this.

"Nigel, do you copy—over?" Bishop checked the radio and tried again. "Nigel… Nigel, do you copy?"

Nothing but a low static noise answered him. If the headset had been configured for international use, it would be bouncing off a communications satellite about now. This one was probably set for local use only. With its range, and him being below deck, he'd be lucky to hit the far side of the island.

Bishop forgot about the engine room. If the bridge blew up, the ship couldn't sail. He had a new target.

———

Nigel understood that staying where they were wasn't going to work. His eyes searched the area and only found tall trees and large, slippery rocks. Getting Gillian to a warmer place had to be the first priority. Their luck had held as far as not being spotted, so that gave them time to maneuver.

"Come on—let's have a look around," he said.

She brushed her soaked hair back and reached under the wet parka. When her hand reemerged, it held a black automatic pistol.

Nigel did a double take and grinned. "Glad you came prepared. We'll meet Bishop as soon as he can manage." They scrambled up the steep bank and crouched at the wood line. Before leaving the cover of the trees, they studied the huge house. The ground floor lights were off, and only a dim light showed from a second-floor window. They sprinted across the lawn toward a gardener's shed. As they pulled the wooden door open, the musty smell of compost, plants, and dirt greeted them. Nigel silently closed the door and switched on his pocket Maglite. Wire baskets, a wheelbarrow, hoses, and a dozen other tools were scattered about. A pair of dirty, insulated men's coveralls hung on a nail. Wadded up on a planting table was an old wool sweater—filthy, with dozens of holes—looked like a cat bed.

"Here we are—just what every girl needs to complete her wardrobe." He grabbed the clothes. "Get those wet things off and slip into these. I'll keep watch outside." He left his Maglite for her as she began stripping off her soggy clothes.

Nigel cracked the door and peered out. Only the sound of crickets and frogs drifted through the night. He ran back to the wood line and worked his way around to the side of the house, staying in the shadows of the trees. He knelt and listened. The diesel rumbling from the yacht drifted across the lawn. Just then, a ground floor light switched on. He caught the movement of something to his left. A man with a flashlight walked toward the garden shed.

———

Gillian finished zipping the coveralls just before the shed door jerked open. She was blinded by the flashlight, but she knew one thing for sure—*that wasn't Nigel.* Whoever it was said something in Chinese and stepped toward her. She didn't stop to think. Didn't stop to be frightened and didn't say a word. She skipped forward to close the distance between them, planted her left foot, and with her right foot delivered a swift kick to the man's groin.

Only a muffled grunt escaped his lips before he dropped to his knees and released the flashlight. Another person appeared behind him in the doorway. Panic gripped her. *There are two of them!* The new figure stood silhouetted by the dim yard lights. He wound up like a major league pitcher and slammed the pistol he held in his hand into the right side of the kneeling man's head. The man on his knees rocked once and collapsed onto the concrete floor. Gillian's heart raced—until Nigel's voice broke the tension. "Looks like it wasn't this bloke's night. What the hell did you do to him?"

She gasped for air. The adrenaline rush had just caught up to her, and her hands shook. "Front snap kick. Took karate as an elective in university."

Nigel stepped over the man and closed the door. "Good work." He wiped blood from his pistol. "Hope I didn't break it on that guy's head —" He stopped in mid-sentence and listened to the headset. "Yes, I read you, Bishop. Go ahead with your transmission."

With all the excitement, Gillian had forgotten about Bishop. When the expression on Nigel's face changed, she figured the news must be bad.

"Good god," he exclaimed. "Okay we'll check the house, and you wire the boat. Right, we'll meet you at the beach."

When Nigel's eyes met hers, she knew. "He found the ramps on the motor launch, huh?"

"Afraid it's much worse. He found evidence they're about to attack the US West Coast with the virus."

"You mean it's on the yacht?"

Nigel frowned. "Let's get this one trussed up. Bishop wants us to check the house and find out how soon they might leave."

A sick feeling crept into her stomach. She hadn't prepared herself for such a thing. This was all going too fast. When they finished gagging the guy, Nigel found a black 9mm pistol in the fellow's waistband.

"Well, well—a QS-92." He inspected the weapon before slipping it inside his parka. He looked at his watch. "It'll be light soon. Let's see what's up in the house, and then make our way to the beach. Bishop will meet us there when he finishes with the yacht."

Gillian rolled up the sleeves of the baggy coveralls. She was still cold but starting to warm up. She had a bad feeling about checking the house. She believed it was a better idea to lay low and wait for Foster and his men. But with an imminent threat against his country, Bishop was on the offense. She wouldn't sit on the sidelines and let him do it alone.

They raced across the lawn to the rear of the house. When they reached the back patio, Nigel knelt, extended his arm for her to stop, and stared at the door. "We need a long-handled rake or hoe."

She hadn't a clue why but didn't bother asking. She returned to the garden shed and grabbed a hoe. When she got back, he had plastered himself against the wall and was edging his way to the patio door. He motioned and she handed it to him as he kept his eye on the camera pointed straight at the entrance. Anyone entering would be seen for sure. He slid the hoe against the wall and gently pushed the camera up toward the porch ceiling.

"That should do it," he said.

"What about alarms?"

"If the alarm was set, the chap would have tripped it when he went out to the garden shed."

She tightened her grip on the pistol and her stomach knotted—still a little unsure.

"Right, let's go." He edged toward the door.

The kitchen light was on, but no one stirred. Nigel kept his pistol pointing down the dark hall to the right as they entered. They crept deeper into the blackness. A faint light from an open door caught their attention. They tiptoed and looked inside. A small, windowless room with television monitors lined the upper wall. An alarm panel glowed in the darkness.

"Security office," Nigel whispered, "but where are they?"

They stepped inside the room, and Nigel sifted through some papers on the desk. "Nothing of any value here."

"Except this." Gillian lifted a Glock pistol from its shoulder holster hanging behind the door.

"Let me have it," Nigel said. He slid the gun under the desk, out of sight. "We won't leave a weapon behind for our enemies to use against us later."

She glanced at the stairwell. "Where to now?"

"Let's see what's upstairs. Keep your gun at the ready."

THIRTY-SIX

Bishop eased back onto the open deck and waited in the shadows. The voices he'd heard earlier were gone, but a trace of cigarette smoke told him someone was near. He listened for voices. After two minutes of complete silence, he crept forward. When he'd first boarded the yacht, his only mission had been to check for ramps on the motor launch. What he found in the engine room changed the rules of engagement. Whereas before he only wanted to get off without being seen, he now had to do as much damage as possible before leaving. He didn't know exactly how many people it took to sail a large yacht, but he planned to eliminate everyone he encountered, do anything to delay their departure. This was war.

Bishop bent down and unsnapped the dive knife from his lower leg. Drawing it, he silently eased across the deck and knelt. He peeked around the corner at the short man leaning on the rail with a cigarette glowing between his fingers. Bishop stood, took a deep breath, and rushed him.

The guy's head turned, and even in the dark, the terror in his eyes told Bishop he realized he was looking at his killer. Bishop slapped his left hand over the guy's mouth while plunging the dive knife into his chest all the way to the hilt. He must have hit the heart, because all the fight drained from him immediately. The fellow fell back against the railing and collapsed in a heap. Bishop slid his hand from the mouth and a last breath escaped the lips. It smelled sour, like rotten fish and tobacco.

No one reacted to the short commotion. Bishop wiped the blade on the man's pants and dropped it back into its sheath. He lifted the body over the rail and slowly lowered it toward the water. He hung onto the guy's legs and eased him closer to the dark, wet grave. When he released him, he prayed the splash wouldn't be too loud.

He sneaked up the external stairway to the main deck. Looking both ways, it appeared all clear from the foredeck to the aft. He stopped and listened. There were at least two men—he'd seen them. The other guy had either gone back to the house or still lurked some-where on the yacht. Bishop craned his neck over the rail and listened for sounds from the deck above—nothing. Only soft waves splashing against the hull and the engines humming.

Bishop hadn't spent much time on yachts but had studied them from an operational sense. Last year, before he blew up one off the coast of Lebanon, he'd memorized its layout. The bridge deck held the wheelhouse, radio room, and captain's cabin. He grabbed the handrail and tiptoed up the metal stairs.

From the outside, the bridge deck looked all clear, but he hesitated. The door to what he hoped led to the bridge hung open—not secured. Bishop turned toward the east. The first traces of light shone on the horizon—almost dawn. He had to hurry. He took off the diving equip-ment and bulky dry suit. As he slid off the last of it, he made his deci-sion. He wouldn't attempt a water escape. He'd walk off the yacht victorious or be carried off dead. He scurried toward the open door, and an alarm sounded from inside—a sharp, high-pitched beep.

———

Hong stretched and yawned before making his way to the head. The short nap refreshed him. He would collect Mercier just before time to sail. He slipped into his pants and picked up the radio. "Captain Yin, are you there?"

Yin answered, "Yes, sir."

"Come to my cabin, now."

"Yes, sir."

Hong made a mental note to complain about him upon their return to China. He was totally unsuited for covert work. The only reason he had been assigned to the operation was because of his naval knowledge and experience.

Hong finished buttoning his shirt and put on his boots. He checked himself in the mirror just before hearing the knock at the door. "Come."

Yin entered and bowed. "Sir."

"Is everything ready?"

"Yes, sir."

"Then assemble the men. I wish to have a word with them."

"Yes, sir." Yin gave another quick bow before leaving.

Five minutes later, Hong had just reached the end of the dock and started walking up the path to the house when Yin rushed out the door. His troubled expression caused Hong to stop cold.

"Sir, two of the men are missing."

———

Bishop dropped to a knee on the outside steps of the yacht just as the alarm stopped and a light switched on inside the cabin above his head. He lay on the deck and froze. It took him a few seconds to settle down —nothing to get excited about. Someone just woke up, turned off their alarm clock, and switched on the cabin light.

Bishop rose off the deck outside Hong's cabin. He'd overheard two guys speaking Chinese but had no idea what they said. One thing was clear: things were about to happen. You didn't start a boat's engine and set an alarm clock unless you intended to leave. He needed to quickly get into the wheelhouse and set the charge.

Bishop crawled to the door—no sound. He stood and silently eased into the hall. The first door was the captain's cabin, where he'd heard the voices. Further down the hall, the control panel lights of the wheelhouse glowed in the dark. Bishop slinked into the wheelhouse and stopped. No sounds—no one else there. He unsealed the waterproof bag: four blocks of C-4 and two timers. He only needed one of each. Any more and the whole ship would be blown out of the water. He found the ship's navigational console, crawled beneath, and attached the explosive. Time to get out of here. As he stepped outside on the steps, he tried contacting Nigel again.

"Nigel… Nigel, do you copy?"

———

Yin caught his breath. "The two men aren't answering their radios, and we can't find them."

"Which two?"

"Zan and Bo."

Hong had handpicked all the men for this assignment. Those were two of the best. Good service records, complete obedience to the Party. "When did you last see them?"

"I sent Bo to locate a garden hose to wash the blood off the grass, and Zan was on deck watch at the yacht."

Hong didn't like this. The likelihood of both having radio problems seemed remote. If that wasn't a consideration, there could be only one other answer.

"Send one man to search for Bo and post the second to guard the gangplank. Tell them to be careful. Someone else is on the island."

"What about me?"

"Go to the bridge and make ready to sail. I'll get Mercier. We'll leave immediately. Is Dr. Tee still on board?"

"No, sir. He's in the house. Just saw him enter a moment ago."

"Okay, I'll get him and Mercier. Make ready to sail." If someone else was on the island, that changed everything. Loading Mercier and Tee and getting underway was the only priority.

———

Nigel and Gillian stared down the long, dark hall on the second floor of the house.

"Stay behind me," he whispered, leading the way. The light that shined from the door to their right was his focus. They crept to it, and he tried catching a look inside, but the crack was too small. Using one finger, he pushed it open a few inches.

Claudine Mercier sat at her desk. She looked straight ahead, as if thinking about something. The only illumination was the tiny desk lamp. She didn't move—had to be in total concentration mode. He motioned to Gillian and pointed inside the room.

She leaned in for a look, squinted and whispered, "Something's wrong."

"What do you mean?"

"She's dressed in a business suit, hair and make-up perfect, and there's no scarring on her face."

Nigel took another look. "Hasn't moved an inch since we got here." He stood and swung the door open. Mercier took no notice—didn't move a muscle. They strolled to the desk and stood in front of her.

"A mannequin—a wax mannequin," Gillian said.

"Don't move," a man's voice boomed from the shadows, "or I'll kill you both where you stand. Put the guns on the floor, raise your hands, and take three steps backward."

The earpiece in Nigel's headset came alive. It was Bishop.

"Nigel... Nigel, do you copy?"

Nigel lowered his gun to the floor, and Gillian did the same. They both raised their hands and backed away.

"That's better," the voice said.

A floor lamp switched on in the corner. The man waved a semi-automatic pistol at them. "Step a little further from the pistols—don't make me nervous."

They both moved a couple of feet to their right. "Inspector Koner, I presume?" Nigel declared.

The man walked to their front and grinned. "I see you know me—did Bishop tell you?"

"Yes, he described you perfectly—said you looked like a weasel."

Koner's grin morphed into a frown. He recovered and laughed—false bravado.

"You set a good trap with that mannequin," Nigel said. "You were expecting us?"

Koner raised his eyebrows. "Actually, I expected Bishop. Where is he?"

Nigel didn't answer.

Koner smirked. "Your silence speaks volumes. He's close then, right?"

A worried expression lined Gillian's face, but Nigel's remained unchanged.

Koner motioned. "Turn around and kneel, facing the wall—hands on the back of your head."

They turned at the same time and knelt.

Koner collected the pistols and keyed his radio. "Hong, we have two guests in Mercier's office."

"I'll be right up," came the reply.

"So you're in league with that bunch," Nigel said.

Koner sat on the edge of the desk and kept the pistol leveled at the pair. "Hadn't planned to be. Stewart Anderson and I had a deal, until he disappeared. Guess you probably had something to do with that."

Nigel turned his head to face him. "Anderson's in a safer place than you are right now. If you're smart, you'll release us. You don't want any part of what they're planning. Did Hong tell you what they were up to?"

"I don't know or care. He paid me well and promised to get me out of Canada. It's the best deal I've been offered."

"Then you have no idea what he's involving you in."

A brief look of concern crossed Koner's face. "Okay, so why don't you tell me?"

Gillian blurted out, "They're planning to attack the US West Coast with a pathogen. It's already on the yacht. You've been briefed on the virus—you know what that means."

Koner rocked back on the desk and his expression clouded. "I'm not involved in anything like that—I'm just hitching a ride."

"No, you're not—you're in it up to your neck the second you step on that yacht," Nigel hissed. "Don't kid yourself. Let us go and we'll speak up for you."

Just then Hong walked through the door. "Who are they?"

Koner snapped out of his trance. "MI6 and Canadian SIS working with the American."

Hong stood beside Koner. "We'll take them with us. I'm not leaving any evidence or loose ends. I'll get Mercier and we'll go to the boat together. Where is the American?"

Koner motioned at the pair with the pistol. "They won't say, but he's not far behind. Probably outside somewhere, I expect."

Hong studied them for a moment. "We'll use them as cover to get to the boat. Any move by the American—kill them."

Koner shook his head. "Now hold on. I didn't sign on to kill anyone, just—"

Hong looked his way before lifting his gun in Koner's direction. "You signed on to do what you're told… unless you want me to terminate our contract now."

Koner's eyes shifted back and forth between Hong's gun and Nigel and Gillian as he considered his new dilemma.

"Well?" Hong asked.

Kroner's eyes lowered and he nodded.

Nigel shook his head. "Using us as hostages won't work."

Hong pushed off the desk and kicked Nigel in the stomach. As he folded to the carpet, Gillian caught him. She glared at Hong. "Leave him alone, you bastard!"

Hong laughed, then hurried from the room as Koner walked behind Gillian and Nigel. "You heard him. If Bishop tries to stop us, I'll kill you," Koner said in a hesitant voice.

Nigel hugged his stomach and struggled to one knee.

Koner reached down and snatched the tactical headset off Nigel's head, throwing it on the desk. "You won't need this anymore."

Nigel didn't want to think about that just now. He still had a weapon—the pistol they'd taken off the man in the shed—unless Koner decided to search them. He wasn't sure where Bishop was, but he was certain he realized their predicament.

THIRTY-SEVEN

There are many types of tactical radios and headsets. The type Commander Foster left was the standard belt radio that attached to an ear listening plug and tiny mic. It fit neatly behind the head and allowed the wearer lots of freedom of movement. But the best thing was the voice-activated transmit feature. You could talk without pushing any buttons. Bishop thanked god for that. He had heard everything Nigel and the rest just said.

His plans now changed, again. If he let them leave with Nigel and Gillian, they were as good as dead. He wasn't sure how many men Hong had left. Thinking logically, he'd need enough to operate the boat, deploy and recover the motor launch, and disperse the virus. Probably four to six guys—bad odds. His only consolation: he knew their plans, and they didn't know his. Bishop waited on the outside starboard stairs as he considered all his options.

More voices and footsteps from the dock. Bishop peeked around a bulkhead as two men walked up the gangplank. They stopped on deck and the tall, older one spoke rapidly to the other in Chinese. He gestured toward the house and finished by issuing an order. Bishop didn't have to speak every language in the world to understand an officer giving a direct order to a subordinate. The younger one snapped to, babbled a brief reply, and posted himself where the gang-plank rested against the yacht's deck. With that, the older one sprinted up to the outside port stairs.

From the verbal exchange, it was clear who the officer was. Bishop figured it was better to go for the high value target first. He could take care of the guard at the gangplank later. Bishop flattened himself against the bulkhead and waited. The footsteps continued pounding up to the bridge deck. Just then, the tip of the sun crested above the Eastern horizon and brilliant laser-light streaks of light rushed to fill the dark void. Bishop felt like a spotlight had been turned toward him —no shadows to hide in. He listened, but only silence came from inside the ship's bridge.

Bishop moved back through the unsecured door he'd used before and down the short hall toward the wheelhouse. The glowing control panel still signaled all clear as the sun's rays illuminated the area. Sneaking inside, Bishop scanned every inch—nothing. *Where did the guy go?* Just then, a toilet flushed in a cabin behind him, and Bishop backed away from the door deeper into the wheelhouse. He peeked around the corner as the man exited the head and walked toward him. Bishop readied himself. One way in, one way out—time to fight.

————

Hong knocked on Claudine Mercier's door, then opened it. She walked from her bath into the bedroom, buttoning her jacket.

"How dare you enter my chambers without being invited?"

"Something's come up—we must leave immediately."

"I'll be ready once I've had my tea. Mary isn't answering the kitchen phone—I don't know what's wrong."

"We already have tea on the yacht," he lied. "You can enjoy it from your cabin as we sail."

Her eyes narrowed as she studied him. "What's wrong? Has something happened?"

"We found some people snooping around last night."

"What people?"

"There're from the government. We have them in your study."

"But how—?"

"No more questions," he snapped. "We must leave, now."

Mercier nodded, and her expression showed she understood. "I see —just give me one minute." She retreated back into the bath.

Hong stepped into the hall just before his radio crackled. "Sir, I've found Bo. He was in the garden shed. He's been attacked—he's hurt."

Hong answered. "Take him to the dock. We'll meet you there and go to the yacht together." Hong now needed to locate Dr. Tee.

Two minutes later, Hong and Mercier walked into her study. Koner waited behind the kneeling Gillian and Nigel.

"On your feet," Hong yelled. "We're leaving."

Gillian and Nigel stood as Hong sauntered over to them. "Which of you attacked my man?"

When neither spoke, he punched Nigel in the face. Nigel staggered back but did not fall, showing a contemptable sneer.

Gillian screamed, "You son-of-a-bitch!" and drew back her foot to deliver another front snap kick.

She wasn't fast enough—Hong slapped her with the back of his hand, and she toppled to the floor. A line of blood dripped from her lip.

Nigel advanced toward Hong, but Kroner placed his pistol to his head. "Don't do it."

Nigel helped Gillian to her feet.

Hong glared at them. "You won't die easily—I'll make sure of that."

"If you're finished, I'm ready to go," Mercier said, standing by the open door. She wore brown pants, a gold wool sweater, and brown jacket. A white wide-brimmed hat cocked to one side hid most of the facial scarring. She eyed Gillian and Nigel as one might a strange bird —an expression of mixed curiosity and detached interest.

Dr. Tee entered the room and appraised the situation. "I see we're about to depart."

Hong drew his pistol and motioned Nigel and Gillian toward the door. "Let's go."

———

The wheelhouse was shaped like a crescent—the base probably fifteen feet across. Bishop flattened himself against an interior bulkhead behind a tall locker and prayed the guy turned left when he walked through the door. If he turned right, he would spot him.

Bishop slid the pistol into his dive belt. He couldn't afford to shoot with a non-silenced weapon. He drew the knife from its sheath and breathed evenly, willing himself to relax. The tall officer entered the wheelhouse and turned left. He leaned over the navigational console and studied a monitor. The distance between them was farther than Bishop liked, but he had no other choice. He eased from behind the locker, knife in hand, and carefully advanced. He measured each step, making sure he didn't bump anything. His eyes never left the figure hunched over the console. The guy shuffled a stack of papers and stared at the monitor again. Bishop lowered himself into a crouch and continued easing across the deck. The approach was perfect—not a sound.

Bishop had long been a proponent of the lizard-brain theory. Some scientists like to use it to explain sixth sense. It finally hit the guy leaning over the console when Bishop was about halfway across the open space. The man turned his head, and they locked eyes. His jaw dropped, and for a second, he froze. Bishop didn't—he had too much space between them to be effective with only a knife. He rushed the man. He got within four feet and already had the knife drawn back to strike when the guy delivered a lightning-fast side kick that caught Bishop square in the middle of the chest.

It was a fast kick, but not a good one. It felt more like a hard push that only stopped his advance for a moment. The guy used that moment to his advantage. He drew the silenced pistol from its holster and swung it toward Bishop. Bishop lunged for the gun and his hand made contact with it as a shot rang out. With the silencer, it only sounded like a large book being slammed shut, but when the subsonic bullet passed an inch from Bishop's ear, he swore it made a loud cracking sound.

Bishop wrapped both hands around the wrist holding the gun. He pushed it toward the deck as two more rounds launched into the polished wood floor. The man's face contorted with fear and determination to live, he pounded Bishop's head with his free fist, then kneed Bishop's thigh. Bolts of sharp pain, like electricity, caused Bishop's leg to collapse—but he never let go of the pistol, pulling the man to the deck with him.

They rolled back and forth while another shot slammed into something metallic and ricocheted. Bishop rolled on top of the guy. This would be his best chance to end the fight. Bishop kept his left hand clasped on his opponent's pistol hand, pinning it to the floor. With one swift motion, Bishop formed the fingers on his free hand into a tight wedge before jamming them straight down into the man's Adam's apple.

The effect was immediate. He coughed, gagged, released the pistol, and reached for his neck. Bishop had crumpled the man's windpipe.

Bishop grabbed the pistol with the silencer and slid off the dying man. The fellow kicked and rolled for a moment, trying to breathe. When he finally came to rest, his hands still grasped his throat. His eyes stared straight ahead. Bishop slid across the deck and leaned back against the console. He took a moment and caught his own breath. When he stood, his left leg still ached from the kneeing. He glanced out the window toward Claudine Mercier's house. The back door opened, and a line of people walked out.

Bishop limped down the starboard stairs. He still had the guy at the gangplank to deal with. He looked around the corner and spotted him. Bishop had his pistol and the silenced pistol—plenty of firepower. The guard leaned back against a ladder and watched the group as they stepped onto the 150-meter dock leading to the yacht. Bishop rested the silenced pistol against a bulkhead as he took aim. He knocked three times with his spare hand. When the guard spun around, Bishop shot him between the eyes with the pistol. The guy dropped without a sound. Bishop stared at the approaching group—no one reacted. The guard had been far enough under the upper deck to still be in the shadows. Bishop crawled to the man and dragged him from the gangplank area.

The group was less than seventy-five meters from the yacht when Bishop chanced another peek. A short Asian man, dressed in dark colors and carrying a pistol, led the way. Walking beside him, a small, middle-aged woman wearing a large hat—*Mercier?* Behind them, another Asian man assisted a third, who appeared injured. Still another Asian man followed them. He was tall, had a goatee, and carried a black briefcase. Last in line were Gillian and Nigel, hands on heads, being escorted by Inspector Koner. Five targets with two friendlies and an unknown. Years ago, Bishop had played this scenario a hundred times in the Delta training kill house. *Shoot the bad guys and don't hit the good ones.* But there was one problem. During his Delta years, he'd never been in a situation to utilize that particular technique. He'd only done it in training—a long time ago.

Before leaving the wheelhouse, he'd set the timer on the block of C-4 to blow in one minute. Bishop checked his watch as the group got closer—that timing might just have been perfect for the distraction Bishop needed.

As the party reached the gangplank, the high-pitched roar of at least two speeding boats approaching the island caused several heads to turn to the right. A second later, the whole side of the port bridge deck blew outward, showering the group with flying glass, metal, and other debris. Everyone either fell to their knees or ducked as the shock wave rolled over them and a black smoke plume rose from the top of the yacht. The explosion rocked the ship so much Bishop had to reacquire his pistol's sight picture, which was dead on Koner's nose. Before he could do that, Nigel's right hand dropped from his head, and he jammed it into his coat pocket. His sudden shift put him in Bishop's line of fire—no clear shot. Bishop changed his aim to the man helping the injured guy.

He shot both of them twice with the silenced pistol, and they fell back onto the dock. Bishop refocused his aim at Koner in time to see the gun in Nigel's hand. Nigel spun and swatted Koner's pistol away while pushing his gun into the guy's midsection. Several rapid shots followed, and Koner staggered back, raising his gun toward Nigel. Bishop, Nigel, and Koner all fired at almost the same time. The top of Koner's head exploded from Bishop's shot, his upper chest sprouted a red bloom from Nigel's—and Nigel rocked back and fell. Gillian leaped on top of him, shielding him from further harm.

The Asian man escorting the woman wearing the hat snapped his head toward the yacht and pointed his pistol in Bishop's direction, looking for a target. He spotted Bishop and sent three wild shots, barely missing him. Bishop ducked below the deck as bullets ricocheted around him. He figured he had at least half a dozen bullets left in the silenced pistol but wanted his own gun—thirteen rounds of .357, locked and loaded. Pulling it from his belt, he came right back up, ready to fire, but his sight picture had changed. Everyone was down but three people. The tall guy with the briefcase had no weapon and presented no threat. He stood frozen with his mouth gaped, staring at Bishop.

The short Asian man dressed in black had assumed a new position. He stood directly behind the small woman, his gun at the side of her throat. Her hat had fallen to the dock and rolled into the cold blue water below. Bishop kept his aim on the man's head, partially hidden behind the woman's. With the hat gone, he now recognized the face of Claudine Mercier. The ugly scarring took away all doubt. The sound of the approaching boats grew louder, but Bishop never looked, never blinked—he kept his sights on the Asian guy's right eye.

"I'll kill her—I'll kill her right now," he screamed. Fear and anger raged in his face. "Drop your gun or I'll kill her!" He must have realized where Bishop was aiming because he jerked his head behind hers.

This could only be the Colonel Hong that Stewart Anderson had described. From his description, Bishop didn't figure this guy would just roll over. He had that look—the one that said *I have nothing to lose and everything to gain.* It was a crazy, dangerous look. Bishop took up all the slack on the trigger. Seconds ticking by seemed like minutes. His full concentration stayed on the front sight, waiting for Hong to show a small part of his face. Bishop breathed with a slow, even rhythm. This probably wasn't going to end well.

He studied Mercier. She had a relaxed look he'd seen before. That look that people got when they knew their time was up. They'd played their best hand and lost. She'd been a decent person at some point in her life. When did she decide to turn? She fixed eyes with him, and her body stiffened as she took in a deep breath. She stared—a stare that seemed to say, *I know this is it.* She took another deep breath, and a resolved smirk crossed her lips before she nodded. Bishop didn't understand at first, but it dawned on him just about the time Gillian looked up and realized what was happening.

She screamed, "Kill the bitch, Bishop!"

When Hong flinched and turned his gun toward Gillian, Bishop shot. He fired ten rounds into a saucer-sized hole in Mercier's petite chest. The force of the high-velocity bullets carried half of them into Hong. The pair fell where they stood. Hong's left arm still embraced her in a death grip. A splash sounded, and Bishop turned his head in its direction. The guy with the black briefcase had disappeared. The two tactical assault boats coasted to the dock. Foster jumped out and directed half his men to secure the house and the rest to check the boat.

Bishop dropped the gun and walked down the gangplank as four of Foster's commandos rushed past him and deployed to different areas of the smoldering yacht. Gillian rolled Nigel over as Bishop knelt beside her. Foster also took a knee and tried to get a pulse from Nigel. After a few seconds he withdrew his hand and shook his head. A strange sense of calm seemed to fall over Gillian.

She shifted Nigel's head to her lap and brushed his hair back. She looked at Bishop through teary eyes. Her lip quivered. "He saved me, you know? Kept me going by his defiance—he just wouldn't give up." She dropped her head to Nigel's and began slowly rocking back and forth as she wept, like a mother soothing a sick child.

Bishop took Foster below to the engine room. When they walked through the door, he pointed at the refrigeration unit in the corner. Foster marched to the cabinet and opened the door. It took him all of five seconds to figure it out. His eyes widened and he backed away from the tanks filled with the deadly pathogen. He had his cell out and was dialing before they made it top side. After a brief conversation, he disconnected.

"We've got this. A recovery team's en route from the base."

After officially handing it off to Canadian authorities, fatigue swept over Bishop. He scanned the area for Gillian, but she and Nigel's body had disappeared. One of Foster's boats was missing.

Foster touched his arm. "My orders are to get all foreign intelligence personnel off this island immediately. That includes you."

Two of Foster's men rushed Bishop into the second boat, and they raced for the naval base. When they docked, there was a caller on hold for him. He lifted the encrypted phone to his ear. "Hello."

"Are you okay?" Maxwell asked.

"As well as can be expected."

"Cook wants you out of there, now! The Canadians already have a plane on the flight line to take you to Andrews."

Bishop figured he knew the reason, but he asked anyway. "What's going on?"

Maxwell lowered his tone. "For political purposes, the Canadians have to try and smear lipstick on this pig. Having foreign intelligence types in country makes it more difficult."

Bishop had been right. When an intel op went sideways, the politicians scrambled for cover. It hadn't exactly gone sideways, but it ended messy. "Yes, sir. I'm en route."

THIRTY-EIGHT

Six days later, Bishop stood outside the ancient stone chapel in the village of Middlesbrough, England. He'd called Gillian several times, but never talked to her—his voice-messages had gone unanswered. Nigel's relatives filed past and glanced at the tall stranger by the door, leaving Bishop feeling a bit self-conscious. Soft organ music floated out of the church, and a white tent was erected in the old English cemetery, covering the gravesite. Majestic oaks lined the graveyard's ivy-covered stone wall.

A dark sedan pulled up, and Gillian got out. She seemed different somehow—smaller—more awkward than he'd known her before. When she noticed him standing on the steps, her pace quickened. He assumed she'd pause, but she fell into his arms. "God, I missed you," she whispered.

"I called," he said.

"They wouldn't allow me to talk with you until the preliminary inquiry was complete. They finished yesterday and released me to attend the funeral."

He stroked her back, and her muscles relaxed.

Gillian looked into his eyes. "I suppose you heard the news reports.

Pharmaceutical mogul killed in kidnapping attempt by Chinese criminal gang—pretty original, huh?"

Her sarcastic voice echoed Bishop's thoughts.

Her nostrils flared, and in an angry voice she said, "They made that asshole Koner the hero. Veteran RCMP inspector killed trying to prevent the crime. What a bunch of crap." She pushed back to arm's length. "Is that how it'll stand? Is that what Nigel died for—a lie?"

Bishop didn't mince words. "If you want glory, you're in the wrong profession."

A tear rolled down her cheek. "I don't want glory, just a little justice. If I hadn't decided to land on the island that night, he'd still be alive." A look of self-awareness streaked across her face. "But then you might be dead."

He pulled her to him again, giving her a long embrace before saying, "Stop it—if you start playing that damn what-if game, you'll be useless as an agent. We're paid to make decisions and take chances. Nigel knew that."

She dabbed her cheeks with a tissue, straightened her back, and took his hand. "Okay, let's get this over with."

THIRTY-NINE

Two days after the funeral, Bishop and Gillian arrived at Cesky Krumlov. The restored thirteenth-century medieval town was a World Heritage Site in South Bohemia near the Austrian border.

That was the subject of his last voice message. "Bring extra clothes and request additional leave. We're going somewhere to relax." He had reserved an attic apartment with a large, canopied bed, exposed wood beams, and a high cathedral ceiling. Gillian rushed in and flung open the French doors leading to the balcony. The Vitava River below, with the huge castle rising out of its ford and homes with red-tiled roofs on the opposite hill, made for a magnificent view. On the last evening of August, they wandered through the maze of cobblestone streets and explored all the shops.

They spent the next three days sunning, swimming, and kayaking on the river. The water was cold, which Gillian described as "brisk" and Bishop said was "freezing." The early-season cold front arriving surprised them. The sudden temperature drop shocked their systems enough that they bought wool sweaters to supplement their light jackets.

The day before they were to leave, Gillian lay on the sofa checking emails, and Bishop had just finished lighting the small fireplace when someone knocked on their door. He answered it. The tall, young man greeted him with an embarrassed grin. He read from a card attached to the basket of fruit. "Mr. Bishop?"

"Yes, I'm Bishop."

The fellow pushed the basket forward. "We apologize for the error."

"What error?"

"This welcome gift should have been delivered when you first arrived—a mix-up of some kind." He shrugged and smiled.

Bishop handed him a five and closed the door. He walked the basket to the sofa and slid beside Gillian, eying the fruit.

"I love grapes—want some?" he asked. He began untying the bow that held the clear plastic cover.

She glanced his way. "No, thanks. Strange they took so long to deliver it." Gillian's phone chimed—she had a new email. She opened it and read for a moment before sitting up. "Oh, my god."

Bishop stopped unwrapping. "What?"

"Stewart Anderson's dead."

Neither had mentioned the operation since leaving England. Anderson was the last guy they'd discussed. Of all the people involved in Biowatch, they and Anderson were the sole survivors—now he was dead.

"What happened?" Bishop asked, going back to untying the basket's stubborn red bow.

Gillian's eyes widened as she scrolled through the email. "He'd been transferred to a maximum security facility the day before, awaiting trial. They found him dead the next morning in his cell." She kept scrolling. "Suicide's not suspected, no marks or trauma of any kind. Still awaiting autopsy results." She continued scrolling.

"Got it," Bishop declared, reaching in and pulling out the bundle of grapes.

"Oh, no!" Gillian whispered. She turned Bishop's way before saying, "The body they recovered that they believed was the tall man with the briefcase—you know, the Dr. Tee guy Anderson told us about?"

"You talking about the one that jumped off the dock?" Bishop asked.

She nodded. "Yes." She bit her lip and rubbed the back of her neck. "It wasn't him."

"Huh?"

Gillian repeated, "The body recovered wasn't Dr. Tee. He's still at large."

Gillian's phone chimed again, and she opened the final email as Bishop plucked a fat juicy grape from its stem. "Another email about Stewart Anderson," she mumbled.

Bishop had the grape halfway to his mouth when Gillian's hand clasped his wrist in a vice grip. Their eyes met, and her gaze shifted to the grape.

Her shoulders tightened. "The email says they believe Anderson's food was poisoned."

ACKNOWLEDGMENTS

Time is precious. Once lost, it is impossible to recover. I am incredibly grateful to my beta readers, proofers, and editors who took the time to read and make valuable suggestions to the original manuscript. As always, it was a team effort, and I could not have a better team.

Thank you, Daryle McGinnis, Ann Barnhart, Ron Knotts, Fred Wulf, and Kelli Grant, for your keen attention to detail. Your efforts are much appreciated.

Thanks to my editor, Twyla Beth Lambert, for her meticulous work and keeping me between the lines. I'd be lost without you.

Thank you, DFW Writers' Workshop members, for your time spent listening and critiquing the work.

Last but not least, Jodi Thompson and Fawkes Press, thank you for your valuable help and for believing in the project enough to see it completed.

If you enjoyed this story and would like to read more:

- Leave a review on your favorite book site
- Tell a friend about Larry Enmon's work
- Ask your local library to put Larry Enmon's books on the shelf
- Recommend Fawkes Press books to your local bookstore

CONNECT WITH US ONLINE

WWW.LARRY-ENMON.COM

WWW.FAWKESPRESS.COM

FAWKES PRESS

ALSO BY LARRY ENMON

Class III Threat

Worst Case Scenario

Rob Soliz and Frank Pierce Mysteries

Wormwood (UK)

The Burial Place

City of Fear

Murder So Foul